HERE COMES THE RAINNE AGAIN

INVERTARY BOOK 6

JANET ELIZABETH HENDERSON

ISBN: 978-0-473-46134-8

Cover design by Janet Elizabeth Henderson

Editing by Liz Dempsey

❀ Created with Vellum

CHAPTER 1

* RAINNE AND ALASTAIR *

"I have nothing to say to you."

Alastair's words sliced through the fragile courage Rainne had wrapped around herself. She looked down at her purple moon boots as she fought back the tears that prickled. The boots, which she'd thought were fun when she'd bought them, now looked stupid against the pristine white snow.

"I'd like the opportunity to explain." Rainne looked back up at him.

He'd bulked out in the past three years, matured into his size by adding muscle. He was bigger, harder, colder. Yet there were still touches of the man she'd known—hair that flopped onto his forehead, sinfully lush lips that begged to be nibbled and sharp, intelligent eyes that missed nothing.

"I don't need explanations, Rainne." He folded his arms over his wide chest, blocking the doorway to the old abandoned church. "It was a long time ago. We both got on with our lives." He glanced behind him into the brightly lit interior. "I need to get back to work."

There was scaffolding around the building and a sign saying it was being renovated. Invertary was going to get its first ever spa. It wasn't where she'd expected to find Alastair. She'd gone to his workplace first, the fishing tackle shop Alastair owned with his father, but there had been a sign on the door saying they were closed due to bad fishing weather. It said in case of an emergency, go to the old church. She wasn't sure what constituted a fishing emergency, but the sign led her to Alastair.

"You're doing building work now?" Rainne said, trying to buy a minute more of his time with inane small talk. It was pathetic. *She* was pathetic.

"Helping out a friend."

They stood in awkward, heavy silence.

"Can we talk, Alastair, please?" Yeah, she had no problem begging. Pride wasn't something she deserved. "I'm really sorry about what happened and want to explain."

He shook his head. "You've had three years to explain. You could have taken the chance when I found you in Glasgow the week after you ran away. As I remember it, you wouldn't even open your door to me." He let out a heavy sigh. "Look, we both know you're only here because Lake's getting married in the morning. It's best for everyone if you just enjoy your brother's wedding and forget about the past. I have. It's over. It's done. You want absolution, you've got it. You can carry on with your life guilt free. You were right; I was too young. I jumped in too fast and too hard. Don't worry, I'm all grown up now and I won't make the same mistake again."

His golden brown eyes stared right through her. His face was blank. He was utterly closed off to her.

"We done here?" he said.

She flinched at his words. Were they done? Yes, it seemed so. Rainne wanted to curl in on herself, but she didn't. She wasn't that person anymore. Sure, she'd never be massively courageous, but she'd worked hard to stop cowering and hiding at the first sign of conflict. Alastair wasn't the only one who'd grown up.

"Yes. Yes, it seems like we're well and truly done." She wrapped her arms around her padded, down-filled coat and hugged herself. She took a deep, shaky breath and looked up at the only man she'd ever loved. "I understand. I won't bother you again. But I want to let you know I'm sorry for how I behaved. I was lost, inside myself." She fought the tremble in her bottom lip and raised her chin. "I waited too long to come back to you, to see if it was possible for us to try again. I thought about it every day but I was afraid. It took Kirsty and Lake's wedding to force my hand." She took a deep, shaky breath. "I want you to know that I still love you. I've only ever loved you."

She gave him a tremulous smile. "That's it, I guess." She fought tears to put on a brave front, while Alastair stared at her, stony-faced and silent. "Okay, well, I'd better get over to the castle. It's the hen party tonight." She was rambling. She bit her tongue to stop herself and nodded. "Okay," she said again. "I should go. Have a good life, Alastair."

She turned on her heels and walked back to her tiny, ancient Ford Fiesta. The light from the church's open doorway made the snow glow around her. She picked her way carefully, her vision blurred from tears that hadn't yet managed to fall. Slowly, the glow around her disappeared and she heard the door click shut behind her.

One tiny sob escaped as she unlocked her car. She climbed inside, rested her forehead on the steering wheel and wept silently. She'd gotten exactly what she deserved, and yet, even knowing that, it still shredded her heart.

"THAT WAS HARSH." Jodie Miller leaned against the hall wall, completely unashamed of eavesdropping.

Alastair had met Jodie through her brother Deke, who was a keen fisherman. It was an acquaintance he deeply regretted. The woman loved to poke her nose in where it didn't belong.

"It's none of your business, Jodie." Alastair walked past her and into the kitchen, where he was clearing up the mess he'd made fitting cabinets all afternoon.

Of course, Jodie didn't listen. "That girl laid her heart at your feet and you stomped all over it. I didn't think you were that callous."

Alastair frowned at her. "You know nothing about what went on between us. You don't get an opinion."

She feigned injury, clasped a hand to her chest and swayed backwards. "I'm wounded. Now you're being harsh with me too. Touchy, touchy Alastair. Did she catch you at the wrong time of the month? Are you man-struating?"

"You know it's at times like these that I totally get why you're divorced."

The brunette narrowed her eyes and gave him what he'd come to think of as her Wolverine glare. "We don't talk about that."

"But it's okay to talk about my past relationships?"

"You're a baby. How many relationships are we talking about? One? Two? And I'm not counting the one with your mummy. You broke that girl's heart on my doorstep, which makes it my business. Don't you think you should man up and let her talk to you? I mean, what harm will it do? Will it hurt your poor, delicate feelings?" She batted her eyelashes and faked a sympathetic pout.

"One of these days," Alastair said as he packed up his tool-box, "that mouth of yours is going to get you into trouble."

"I've been telling her that for years." Deke, Jodie's younger brother, sauntered into the kitchen. "Those cabinets look great. Thanks for helping out."

Alastair just nodded. It was no big deal. Helping out was what people in Invertary did. Some day he would need a hand from a neighbour, or friend, and Deke would step up. It was the way things worked in the Highlands.

Deke ran his hand over the surface of the central island. It was a very specific type of marble, one the spa's chef had insisted on. Alastair had expected him to install a standard stainless steel professional kitchen, but Deke wanted marble, wood and brushed steel. It looked good, warm, welcoming. Which was a big plus, as the kitchen was open to the dining area and the guests would be able to watch the guy work. Alastair hoped he didn't go all Gordon Ramsay on them. That would *not* make for a pleasant dining experience.

"Alastair just rejected a girl who poured her heart out to him on our doorstep. She declared her love and he sent her out into the snow, probably in tears. Most likely to her doom. It was nasty. Totally heartless." Jodie obviously wasn't going to let the topic go.

"And I care why?" Deke looked every bit as thrilled with the conversation as Alastair felt.

"Because," Jodie said slowly, like they were both on the simple side, "he shouldn't have let her go."

"Please tell me you're not matchmaking." Deke groaned. "You're crap at it, Jo. You know that; your track record speaks for itself. Leave the guy alone."

"It's Leap Day tomorrow. The day traditionally set aside for women to pour out their hearts without being trodden on. The day they can propose without being mocked. That opportunity only comes once every four years, boys. It's sacred to women. And he"—she pointed a talon at Alastair —"was mean to a girl. I'm pretty sure there's a law against that."

Deke barked out a laugh. "Like you care about Leap Year.

You don't have a romantic bone in your body. Give it up; you only want to mess with him."

Alastair found himself nodding. He'd only known Jodie a couple of months, but that sounded spot-on.

"Whatever, Leap Year, sheep year. Who cares? The point is, he was mean. Are you telling me you feel nothing for that girl?" Jodie pointed towards the front door.

Alastair ignored her. It was none of her business what he did or didn't feel for Rainne.

She threw up her hands in disgust. "Fine, I'll leave it alone. But I'm seriously disappointed in you." She stuck her nose in the air and stomped out of the room.

Alastair looked at Deke. "Am I supposed to feel bad now?"

"Yep. She's losing her touch. I've seen her bring grown men to their knees with that move." Deke eyed the doorway thoughtfully. "I wonder if she's sick?"

The doorbell rang, and Jodie shouted that she'd answer it.

"I need to get going or the truck's going to get snowed in." Alastair watched the thick snowfall outside the kitchen window.

"Haven't seen a storm like this in years," Deke said.

"Aye, it's a bad one."

"Deke," Jodie called in a singsong voice that made Alastair's hair stand on end.

He flashed a look at Deke, who seemed equally suspicious.

"What?" Deke called.

They watched as Jodie appeared in the doorway, a gleeful smile on her face. She stepped to the side to reveal the person standing behind her. Rainne. Of course it was Rainne.

"This is Rainne. She came to talk to Alastair, but now her car won't start. Can you take her to the castle?"

Rainne's eyes were red and swollen as she looked every-where but at him. *Hell.* He'd made her cry.

"Sure thing, gorgeous." Deke pushed off from the counter where he'd been leaning. "Let me get my coat and keys."

"Thanks." Rainne tucked a strand of hair behind her ear and smiled at Deke.

Three years ago she'd had long rainbow-coloured hair; now it was light brown and skimmed her shoulders. Grown-up hair. Serious hair. Like changing her dye job would change the woman inside. Yeah, right.

"No problem." Deke stopped in front of Rainne and held out his hand. "I'm Deke, Jodie's brother."

Rainne blushed, and Alastair went rigid as Deke held on longer than necessary.

"I haven't seen you about town," Deke said.

Rainne's eyes flicked to the floor before she looked back up at the traitorous bastard. "I'm Lake's sister. Here for the wedding."

"Staying long?"

What the hell? He was flirting with her? Couldn't he see her red eyes? Her distress? She wasn't in any fit state to deal with his sloppy come-on. Alastair frowned at his soon-to-be ex-friend. It slid off him.

"No, I don't think so." Rainne's eyes flickered to Alastair for a beat.

And bloody Deke still hadn't let go of her hand.

"Now that's a shame," Deke said. "I would have liked to show you around. This is a cute little town."

"Rainne has already seen the town." Alastair folded his arms and took a step towards them. "She used to live here."

"Is that right?" Deke looked amused. *Dickhead.* He smiled at Rainne. "Well, maybe you can show *me* around after the wedding?"

Rainne blushed again. Why wasn't she telling the guy to get lost? Where was her common sense?

"Let's get you to the castle before we get stuck in the

snow together." Deke pressed his hand to Rainne's lower back as he turned her towards the door. "Although you don't need to worry. If we get stuck in my truck, I have a survival kit and we can cuddle up for warmth."

Alastair had heard enough. "I'll take her." The words were out of his mouth before he could stop them.

Three sets of eyes turned on him. Jodie was smug, Deke amused and Rainne shocked.

"Don't worry." Deke put his hand on Rainne's shoulder in a possessive gesture. "I've got this."

Alastair waited a beat, but Rainne didn't shrug off Deke's touch—as she should have done. She didn't even know the guy, yet here she was letting him touch her. She didn't have the sense God gave a snail. No normal woman let a strange guy paw her like that. It was a wonder she'd survived in Glasgow these past years. On top of that, she didn't know Deke from Adam and she was planning to get into a car with him. Okay, so Alastair knew he was a good guy, but that wasn't the point. It wasn't like she'd asked his opinion. Which would have been the sensible thing to do.

Alastair glared pointedly at Deke's hand. "I'm leaving right now anyway. No point in you going out. I'm passing the castle."

"Alastair, I don't think…" Rainne still stood too close to Deke.

Alastair strode towards her. "Come on, Rainne. We're going." He walked between her and Deke, making the man step back and drop his hold on her.

Rainne looked bewildered but didn't follow him. Instead she sent a pleading look towards Deke, asking for help. This was exactly what Alastair meant. She trusted far too easily.

"It's only a lift, Rainne. Get in the car." Alastair threw open the front door, ensuring the heat flooded out into the icy night. It was the least that interfering Jodie deserved.

Maybe while she was freezing her backside off she'd think about why she shouldn't meddle in people's lives.

"I, I…" Rainne still didn't move. Her pale blue eyes looked slightly panicked.

Deke's amusement faded, and he eyed Rainne with concern. "I'll get my keys."

"Rainne." Alastair softened his voice. A little. Not too much. "I can take you. It's no big deal. Do you want Deke to go out in the snow just for you?"

Okay, so it was a low blow to make her feel guilty, but this was pathetic. He could take her to the castle. It wasn't a big deal.

Her cheeks went red again. "Yes, you're right. I'm sorry." She turned to Deke and smiled. "Of course you should stay here. No point in getting cold when Alastair is going that way anyway. Thanks for the offer, though."

"Anytime, gorgeous." He smiled at Rainne before frowning at Alastair. "I'm sure Alastair will take good care of you and make sure your trip is totally uneventful."

In other words, don't make her cry. Again.

"Let's go," Alastair said to Rainne, and watched as she dragged herself towards him.

Like a woman to the gallows.

CHAPTER 2

"Why did you pick Betty for your best man?" Matt Donaldson grumbled over his beer.

The stag party had taken over the only pub in Invertary and the entertainment had fallen to the best man—eighty-nine-year-old Betty. Or as the locals called her—Satan.

"He picked me because I have bigger balls than the lot of you," Satan said, followed by her trademark cackle. "Look at you. Bunch of wee boys whining and complaining. There isn't a proper man amongst you."

There was a grunt. Betty's head spun towards the behemoth known as Grunt. "Okay," she conceded. "Maybe you can pass for a man. Or a mountain. Whatever."

The huge, taciturn American grinned at Betty.

"Seriously." Matt leaned across the table towards Lake. "Why?"

The town's only cop had known Betty his whole life. He spent most of his time trying to avoid the woman, or jail her, whichever was easiest.

Lake snorted. "Like I had a choice. It was this or she wanted to be father of the bride. Seeing as I actually want to marry Kirsty and she would kill me if I suggested Betty step in for her dead father, that narrowed the choice down."

"You made the right decision, son." Betty patted him on the head, like he was her dog, and then she waddled off towards the buffet table the pub's owner Dougal had laid out.

Lake grinned after her. It'd been three years since he'd inherited her along with the shop he'd bought, and he still got a kick out her. It was like having his own gremlin. Entertaining but kind of scary.

"Your relationship with that woman is sick and twisted," Josh McInnes said from the other side of the booth.

Lake couldn't argue with the American singer, so he said nothing. He was well aware that he was possibly the only person on the planet who appreciated Betty. He'd long thought her talents were wasted in the Scottish Highlands. If she'd been born elsewhere, or in a different era, she'd have been ruler of her own regime—or have given Mata Hari a run for her money. Under her tartan tent and hairnet was the mind of a criminal genius.

"Are we just going to sit around here and eat all night?" Mitch asked.

Josh's manager and best friend was one of the few unattached men in attendance. His idea of a party was living it up in Las Vegas, not eating chips at the Scottie Dog.

"Betty has entertainment planned," Lake said.

There was a unanimous groan.

"No," Harry, the resident boy genius, protested. "It will be fun. You'll enjoy it."

"What did you do?" Harry's brother, Flynn, said with a sigh. "What did Betty con you into this time?"

"Hey, I resent that." Harry glared at his brother. "I didn't do anything, and Betty isn't capable of conning me."

They all stared at him.

"Fine." Harry's shoulders slumped. "But I'm older and

wiser now. I know to be suspicious of everything she says." His eyes went wide with sudden panic and the men groaned. He had totally fallen for another con. "No," Harry said. "I checked out everything she said this time."

"And?" Flynn prompted. Like the rest of the men, no one was appeased by Harry's conviction.

"All she wanted was to use my credit card to book strippers. See, now the surprise is ruined." He threw up his hands in disgust. "They're coming up from Glasgow." He checked his watch. "Should be here any minute. They're probably delayed because of the weather."

Everyone looked out of the window at the snow. It was coming down thick and fast, almost obliterating the view of the streetlights glinting off the black loch.

"Wind's picked up," Matt said.

"Blizzard," Flynn said. "Weather forecast said it was coming. Said it was the worst to hit Scotland in decades. They advised we all stay indoors."

Mitch's head hit the table in front of him. "Just when I think this can't get any more lame, we start talking about the weather."

Lake's lip twitched at Mitch's pain. The guy was right. This was the worst bachelor party Lake had ever attended. The fact it was his own was kind of amusing. Apart from his friends, the pub was empty, as people had stayed home because of the snow. In all honesty, Lake would be home too, wrapped up with Kirsty, if he could. He'd been hassled into having a stag party, and only the fact Kirsty was holed up at the castle with the women kept him from staying home.

"Caroline will kill me if I watch strippers," Josh said.

"If Jena was here, she'd join in. She'd get up on one of the tables and dance for us." Matt obviously missed his wife as much as Lake missed Kirsty. "She's a great dancer."

"Yeah," Harry said. "But maybe not on the tables. Dougal's still upset about the last time."

"It wasn't her fault she fell off and people got injured. She can't help that she's accident prone."

"Maybe if she stopped wearing stilts for shoes, she wouldn't fall over so much," Harry said.

Mitch hit his head on the table again. "Now we're talking about shoes. Why don't we braid each other's hair and get this over with? Betty is right. She has more testosterone than the lot of us."

"Interesting group of friends you've got here," Callum McKay, Lake's buddy from when he was in the SAS, commented drolly.

"He collects us," Josh said. "We're his hobby. Lake would be lost without us."

Lake's lip twitched at Josh. Mitch sat back up and rolled his eyes at his best friend.

"He doesn't collect us. He makes no effort to be friendly. It's as though his lack of response acts like Velcro to all the needy people around him. *We* attach ourselves to Lake."

"Who you calling needy?" Flynn said.

"I don't need anyone," Matt said. "Well, maybe Jena." He leered. "But that's a good kind of need."

"I need people." Harry's fingers tapped on the table as though they couldn't function without a keyboard under them. "No man is an island."

Flynn grinned. "I'm an island. I'm bloody Ibiza!"

"*About a Boy*." His brother high-fived him. "Classic movie. Even with Hugh Grant."

Lake shook his head at the brothers as Callum watched in bewilderment. "Are you sure this guy is cut out for business?" He nodded at Harry.

Lake had spent the afternoon in a meeting with Callum and Harry, hammering out a business proposal that would make the three men partners. He knew Callum was still undecided, and part of that was due to working with Harry. At twenty-six, Harry had nowhere near the life experience of Lake and Callum. But they had nowhere near his genius. No one wrote security code like Harry. The guy was a programming genius and an asset they couldn't afford to exclude.

"This guy," Harry said without taking offence, "hacked into the Ministry of Defence when he was eleven and they never caught him. I confessed after I rewrote their security program for them. This guy heads a billion-dollar company. And this guy"—he pointed at himself with pride—"knows how to keep a secret. Anyone want to know who really killed Diana? Well, tough. These lips are sealed." He folded his arms and grinned at the men.

Flynn groaned. "Way to prove you're mature, bro."

"Was that what I was supposed to do? I thought I was proving I was skilled." Harry turned to Callum. "If you're looking for serious and mature, you're better off with Grunt."

Grunt grunted helpfully to prove Harry's point.

Callum shook his head. "What the hell am I doing here?"

"Having fun?" Mitch said. "No. Me neither."

Callum stared at Mitch, but Lake knew he was amused—his way of showing it was to frown less. Lake watched as Callum's hand twitched on his thigh and his jaw tightened slightly. Lake knew his friend was fighting the urge to rub his leg. He'd recently been fitted with two new prosthetics and they were giving him some trouble. Not that Callum would admit it.

"This is mind-numbing," Josh complained. "I would have arranged a much better party. Bet the women are having more fun at the castle. Who did you leave to guard them?"

"Ryan and Joe." Lake sipped his beer.

Josh shot up out of his chair. "No! You left two womanisers with the women. What the hell were you thinking? If those guys seduce my Caroline, I'm going to have a hit put out on you." He pointed at Lake.

There was a moment of silence before everyone burst out laughing.

"What the hell?" Josh demanded. "What's so funny?"

"Caroline," Mitch sputtered.

Josh looked ready to thump his best friend. "You think Caroline isn't attractive enough to seduce?"

"Get a grip." Flynn wiped his eyes. "What he's saying. What we're all thinking. Is that Caroline is unseducable. She would never cheat on you. Her head would explode even thinking about it. Not only that, she'd lecture the ears off any man who tried to seduce her."

"Damn straight." Josh slumped back, mollified.

"That's if she even noticed she was being hit on," Matt said.

Josh grinned. "There is that."

"You're not wrong about the party, though," Flynn said. "This is mind-numbing."

"Don't worry," Harry said with a grin. "It'll pick up soon. Strippers. Remember?"

"Let's get this party started," Betty shouted. "The entertainment is here."

"See?" Harry said.

They all turned towards the door and collectively groaned.

"She booked *male* strippers?" Harry wailed.

Four buff guys, dressed in fake fatigues with Velcro seams, swaggered into the middle of the room.

"She ordered soldiers?" Grunt spoke for the first time that evening.

"Lake's ex-forces. What else was I supposed to order?" Betty demanded.

"Well, duh, women," Flynn pointed out.

Betty cackled as she dragged a wooden chair into the middle of the room and positioned herself between the strippers. "Ready when you are, boys."

"I'm going to vomit," Matt said.

The music kicked in and the men started gyrating. Their packages inches from Betty's grinning face.

"Make it stop," Josh wailed.

"I need to call a therapist." Mitch turned his back in disgust. "I can never unsee this."

"I can't believe she conned me into paying for male strippers," Harry said.

Callum looked from the strippers to Harry's stunned expression, then to Lake. "Are you *sure* he'd make a good business partner?"

Lake tipped back his head and laughed loud and long.

CHAPTER 3

* KIRSTY *

"I'm telling you," Kirsty said to her best friend. "Lake doesn't love me anymore." She nibbled at her bottom lip as her eyes welled up. "I have to call off the wedding."

"What? No!" Caroline almost fell off her stool at the breakfast bar. "You're being silly, which makes me look silly for having such a silly woman for a best friend."

"Did you say 'silly' often enough in that sentence, do you think?"

The castle kitchen seemed to wobble. It was possible they'd all had a little too much champagne. Well, except for Caroline, who was pregnant with baby number two, and Abby, who was carrying twins and looked only slightly smaller than a house. The rest of the women were laughing raucously as they played a drunken version of pin the tail on the donkey. Only there was no donkey, just a life-sized cardboard cutout of Lake dressed in a tux. A blindfolded Heather Donaldson clutched a pair of men's thong underwear and tried to stick them to the right place on his body.

"That is a stupid game." Kirsty pointed at the women.

"Lake would never wear his underwear on the outside of his trousers."

"I don't know," Caroline said. "He does have a Superman complex."

"Yes, he does." Kirsty pointed at Caroline to prove she was serious. "That's part of the problem. He's always running off to help someone else. I know it's his business—protect people, rescue people, help people." She waved a dismissive hand. "But it's *all the time.* I've hardly seen him in the past six months. I think he's avoiding me." She hated that her bottom lip began to tremble. "I don't think he wants me anymore."

Caroline came off her stool instantly to wrap her arms around Kirsty. She squeezed her tight. "Of course he still wants you and loves you. That man adores you. He's been busy, that's all."

"Too busy to have sex?" Kirsty wiped her nose on Caroline's shoulder and felt her stiffen.

"Really? We're going to talk about your private affairs?"

Kirsty pushed back to look at Caroline. "You're a married woman. You have a daughter." She pointed at Caroline's belly. "And another one on the way. Please tell me you can say the word 'sex' now."

Caroline blushed and patted her slightly curved belly, which was covered by her classically chic dress. "Of course I can say the word. I just choose not to. I've learned you don't have to say it to do it." Her cheeks turned even redder. "It doesn't mean I can't lend you a sympathetic ear if you want to talk about…you know."

"I know." Kirsty patted her hand, thinking it was a miracle Caroline had loosened up enough to make children. She took a deep breath and confessed. "We haven't had sex in three months. Not at all. Not once. And before you start raking your memory to see if he was out of town and make excuses for him, the answer is, he wasn't. Apart from one weekend in

London talking to this Callum guy, he's been here the whole time. Here. In Invertary. *Not* making love to me."

Caroline's sympathetic look make Kirsty want to sob. "Oh, honey."

"There's only one explanation. He doesn't love me." She looked around the room at all the smiling women and ached. They were going to be so disappointed if the wedding didn't happen. "I thought pushing for the wedding would be a wakeup call for him. That he'd remember why we're together. Instead I feel further away from him. He's always in his office or on the phone. He's trying to avoid me. He hasn't even been involved in any of the planning for tomorrow. I don't think he wants to get married. I don't think he wants to be with me."

Caroline patted Kirsty's back as they watched one of the older women from Knit Or Die pretend to make out with cardboard Lake.

"You're embarrassing me, Mum," Megan Donaldson shouted at her mother as she walked back into the vast open-plan kitchen/dining room.

Heather didn't look ashamed. "I'm a woman. I have needs."

"Do those needs involve getting it on with a slab of cardboard?" Megan tossed her long, straight blonde hair over her shoulder and plonked down on the armchair beside her twin sister. "Why didn't you stop her?" Megan said.

Claire held up her phone. "I thought pictures were better."

They grinned widely and high-fived each other. Although the twins made no effort to dress the same, they'd still managed to turn up wearing matching boat-necked silver sweaters teamed with sleek black jeans.

"We need to dance." Jena Morgan jumped to her feet. The American was wearing a skintight golden dress that barely covered her backside. Her long, wavy hair swung to her waist and her eyes glittered with mischief. "Change the music, Caroline. We need something with a beat. Oh, wait. I have my iPod with me. You can plug it in."

She spun on her four-inch heels, tripped over her best friend Abby's feet and landed headfirst in the other armchair that flanked the fireplace. The rest of the women thought she was hilarious.

"I'll get it before you kill yourself." Abby rooted around in Jena's bag.

Jena struggled out of the armchair, pulled down her dress and ran her fingers through her hair, totally unfazed by her face plant.

Caroline took the iPod from Abby. "No dancing on the furniture. We're hosting a wedding here tomorrow and I'd like everything to remain in pristine condition."

"Jeez, you break one itty-bitty table and people expect you to trash their place." Jena rolled her eyes.

"Why didn't we have this party with the men?" Kirsty's mother said. "It would have been more fun with some hunks hanging around."

There was a disgusted snort from the hallway where Joe was keeping an eye the front door. "What am I? Chopped liver?"

Kirsty smiled at that. There was no way anyone could think the tall Italian-American was anything but gorgeous.

"Get in here and dance, then we'll decide if you rate being called a hunk," Margaret shouted back.

"I'm working here." He sounded amused. "Kirsty, keep your mother under control."

"Yeah, like that's possible." Kirsty smiled fondly at her mother.

"You aren't working," Margaret shouted back. "You're here to spy on us."

There was laughter from the hallway. As far as Kirsty

knew, the men had drawn straws to attend the hen party. As in, they wanted to be there. Joe and Ryan had won. They were supposed to hang around outside the castle, but it was freezing out there and about four feet deep with snow. Now they were guarding the women from inside, which pleased them immensely.

The music came out of the stereo at full volume. There were whoops of delight, and the coffee table was cleared to the side to make more space for dancing. Kirsty watched Jena dance. The former go-go girl was seriously talented.

As the women whooped and danced, Kirsty slowly backed out of the room. She wandered down the long hallway, past the ornately carved banister and regal staircase to the grand room—the venue of her wedding. As she stepped into the cavernous room, Kirsty's heart sped up at the sight before her. Even though the weather meant the ceremony couldn't be held in a marquee as she'd planned, the grand room was stunning.

Caroline had emptied the room of its usual furniture, leaving Kirsty to do as she liked with the space. She'd chosen to use the purple and green Campbell tartan as her theme. Rows of high-backed chairs dressed in white silk with dark purple bows, flanked a central aisle. The cream walls were hung with reams of purple silk, broken up with garlands of green laced with purple irises and white roses. Tomorrow morning, five-year-old Katy, Abby's daughter, would walk down that aisle scattering purple petals made of silk for Kirsty to walk on. The silk flowers were a last-minute addition to save Caroline's cream carpet from being stained by fresh petals.

"I love the windows," Caroline said as she came into the room. "I may keep them like that when this is over."

"It is pretty." Kirsty smiled at her friend.

They'd draped the vast bay windows with purple chiffon,

making a perfect backdrop for the lectern, which was decorated with yet more white roses and irises. The room was exactly as Kirsty had imagined it would be—elegant, simple and beautiful.

"I had another word with the caterer today," Caroline said. "Just to make sure everything will go smoothly."

Kirsty made a mental note to give the caterer a hefty bonus for dealing with Caroline.

"And will it?" She knew the answer before she asked—Caroline wouldn't tolerate anything short of perfection. It made Kirsty smile.

"I told her we wanted to set up tables in the conservatory for the meal. They'll do that first thing in the morning."

The conservatory was a new addition to the castle, and Caroline was eager to see how it worked for entertaining. The new room sat off the dining room and looked out over the garden. The floor-to-ceiling windows meant the view would be stunning—especially with the snow.

"I made Josh plan some music in case the band can't get here. He says he's happy to sing if he's needed. It's all going to be great."

Kirsty hadn't even thought about the possibility of the band she'd booked being snowed in. She knew she should be grateful that Josh was willing to sing at her wedding—the guy usually sang to crowds in Wembley or Madison Square Garden—yet she couldn't work up the enthusiasm.

She looked around the elegant room and wondered if Lake would even notice the surroundings. He'd been absent for most of the planning. She really couldn't imagine that he'd care what the place looked like. A low throb started in her stomach as she wondered again if she was forcing them to make a huge mistake.

"Don't worry." Caroline read her mind. "You're just getting cold feet. It happens to all of us."

"You're probably right." Although Kirsty knew it was something else. She didn't have second thoughts about marrying Lake; instead she was terrified he had them over marrying her. "We'd better get back in case Jena is wrecking the place."

Caroline rubbed her hand across Kirsty's back. "It will all look better in the morning. You and Lake need to have a chat, that's all. Once you clear the air, you'll feel much better."

They walked, arm in arm, back into the dining room, where the women of Knit Or Die were showing off their twerking skills—something they'd learned for Caroline's wedding—and Jena was giving them tips to smooth out their technique.

"I really don't need to see my mother shake her booty," Kirsty said.

"I need to bleach my eyes after this," Megan shouted past the loud music.

"I'll give you—" Kirsty's words were cut off when the lights went out.

The music stopped dead and there was a loud shout of protest. The women wanted to dance.

"Power cut," Joe said as he came into the room. It was easy to make out his huge frame in the glow from the fire. "Nothing to worry about. Do you have a generator, Caroline?"

"No, we don't. I should have thought of that."

Kirsty knew Caroline was mentally adding "buy a generator" to the list she kept going in her head.

"At least the heating isn't electrical." Heather pointed to the raging fire and the gas central heating. Not exactly fixtures that were accurate for the castle's time period, but as Caroline had pointed out to Kirsty, restoration only went so far when you had to live in a place.

"Is the whole town out, or only us, do you think?" Caroline said.

"Whole town, I'd say," Kirsty said.

"Don't worry." Abby came up beside Caroline and put an arm around her. "Our place has a generator. We needed it when we were mushroom farming. The kids will still be able to watch the Disney Channel until their eyes turn square."

Caroline was visibly relieved. "Jessica's scared of the dark."

"Of course she is, honey, she's only twenty months old. But honestly, they're okay. Mum and Lawrence are there, there's central heating, a generator, plenty of food and candles in case all else fails. The kids are in a better position than we are."

"You're right. I just worry."

"Motherhood is fun like that," Abby said, rubbing her huge belly.

"It never stops," Kirsty's mum said as she wrapped an arm around her daughter's waist. "You always worry. Even when your kids are too old to listen to you."

"I listen to you," Kirsty protested, and her mother laughed.

"I found candles." Magenta had been rooting around in one of the kitchen cupboards. She stood up, her arms full. "You have a whole cupboard full of candles. Does a person need that many?"

Caroline stuck her nose in the air—a classic defensive move. "Josh thinks they're romantic."

There was a chorus of "aww"s, which made Caroline duck her head.

"Well, we have candles, a warm fire and champagne," Shona declared. "This is the most romantic hen night I've ever been to. Good job we're comfy. If this weather keeps up, we might be here for a wee while."

As one, the women's attention was drawn to the huge bay windows, where the snow could be seen falling thick and fast. Silence fell as they watched a beam from a flashlight scan the ground outside.

"Joe?" Kirsty said. "Is Ryan outside?"

"Nope, gorgeous, I'm here." Ryan walked into the room holding a box of matches.

"Then"—Kirsty pointed to the window where there were now beams from two flashlights—"who's that?"

Ryan dropped the matches and reached for his gun.

CHAPTER 4

* RAINNE AND ALASTAIR *

"You didn't need to take me to the castle," Rainne said into the silence.

The ten-minute drive had taken almost half an hour through the snow. They could barely see two feet in front of them, the flakes were coming down that thickly.

"You planned to what? Walk?" Alastair pointed through the windscreen.

"Jodie's brother could have taken me."

"No. He couldn't."

Rainne watched in bewildered fascination as Alastair clenched his jaw tight. Was he mad at her for inconveniencing Deke? Getting a lift to the castle wasn't her idea. She'd only asked for help to get her car started. She should never have gone back to the old church. She should have just walked to the castle. If she'd been lucky, she'd have made it there by midnight without dying of hypothermia.

"He could have helped me fix my car, then I could have driven myself." Why she was carrying on this ludicrous argument, she didn't know. No. That wasn't true. She did know—

she wanted Alastair to talk to her instead of freezing her out with his silence.

Alastair snorted. "Your car didn't even have snow tyres. There's no way you'd have made it through this. They cleared these roads this afternoon, and look at it now. This truck is barely managing."

Okay, so he had a point. His pickup truck came with four-wheel drive and snow chains. Her economy car came with fuzzy dice.

They turned into the castle's driveway only to find the normally closed metal gates wide open. A prickle of unease climbed up Rainne's spine. The guardhouse beside the gate was dark and no one came out to check their right to be there. She scanned the area ahead of her—no light was coming from the castle. She twisted in her seat to look behind at the rest of the town. No lights anywhere.

"I think there's a power cut. But why is the gate open?" Rainne said. "Josh never leaves it open. There's always paparazzi hanging out here trying to get in."

"Look around. See any cameras? How about people? Anybody with any sense is tucked up indoors. Josh probably left the gates open to make it easier for the partygoers to get in."

"Maybe." Rainne studied the snow-covered driveway in front of her. There were a lot of footprints. "Those prints are recent. If they weren't, the snow would have hidden them by now. Why are there so many people walking around out here? And where's the guy who mans the gate?"

Alastair's glance made it clear he questioned her sanity. "You notice footprints now?"

Rainne tucked her hair behind her ear. "When Lake talks, I listen. He doesn't talk often and I don't want to miss anything. Plus, he knows a lot of useful stuff from his time with the SAS."

"Useful stuff like when to worry about footprints in the snow?"

"And to be suspicious when a guardhouse shows no sign of life."

"The guard is probably at the castle. They can monitor things from there. Josh has a state-of-the-art security system."

"One that works in a power cut?"

Alastair was silent. The darkness felt oppressive. Maybe Rainne's imagination was working overtime, maybe it was residual anxiety from earlier in the evening—whatever it was, she had a bad feeling.

"This doesn't feel right," she said. In fact, if she still believed in having a sixth sense, she would say hers was screaming at her.

"You're just freaking out because the power has gone out. That tends to make people jumpy."

"No, there's definitely something wro—"

Her words cut off mid-sentence as a man appeared in their headlights. He was dressed top to toe in white snow gear, including a balaclava covering his face.

"What the hell?" Alastair shouted. When the man didn't move out of their way, he hit the brakes, making them skid.

As if in slow motion, the man raised his arm towards them. There was a gun in his hand.

"Gun!" Rainne screamed.

Alastair cursed. He thrust the gears into reverse. Tyres slid on the snow, kicking up clouds.

"Nonononononono..." Rainne grabbed the handle above the door and held on tight.

The man pointed the gun straight at them and fired. The truck jolted backwards, speeding out of the gate, sliding over the road. Alastair fought for control as they spun away from the castle. They were going too fast. Even with chains on their tyres, the truck lost its purchase and tilted on the uneven surface.

"No, damn it!" Alastair shouted.

He strained, muscles bulging as he fought to keep the truck on the road. The gears ground. The brakes squealed. The truck lurched, its weight pulling to the side. They hit the snowy verge at the side of the road. Time froze as Rainne waited in horror for the inevitable. The truck tilted.

And then it rolled.

Rainne thought she might be screaming.

There was a deafening crunch. They slid for some distance on the driver's side. Glass shattered. Metal ripped. There was a horrendous thud. And then there was silence.

Stark. Absolute. Silence.

Rainne's seatbelt cut into her chest. She could barely breathe. Without thinking, she un-clicked it and fell downwards into Alastair. He hung limply from his seatbelt, his head resting on the icy ground beneath the shattered window.

There was blood on his face.

Glass in his hair.

"Alastair." Rainne's hand trembled as she reached for his cheek. "Alastair. Talk to me."

He didn't move. He didn't speak.

"Alastair?" Rainne placed her hand on his chest. Was he breathing? She couldn't tell. "Please." She begged him to wake up. To be fine.

"Alastair." Terrified, she reached for his throat to feel for his pulse.

And her world stopped dead.

CHAPTER 5

"Was that gunfire?" one of the women said into the silence.

"Yeah. It was." Joe jerked into action, barking out orders. "Secure all windows and doors. Shut all curtains. Now!"

The women scurried, doing as they were told.

"Not you." Joe nabbed Caroline as she passed him. "Do you have a panic room?"

"No." Her voice trembled slightly as her hand flattened over her baby bump. "Should I?"

Joe had no doubt in his mind that after this night was over, Caroline would have a panic room installed. In the meantime, they would have to make do. "Where's the safest place in the castle?"

"I would normally say the basement, but it's full of furniture right now. We're storing everything in there until after the wedding. There's no space for people."

"What about the tower?" Kirsty came up beside her friend, looking completely, and suddenly, sober.

Adrenalin could do that to a person—or fear.

"The cellar sounds more secure," Joe said. "Can we move

the stuff out? Or to the side, or something, anything to make space?"

"No. It's packed. I've been using it for storage since the renovation. The furniture from the grand room filled every last bit of free space."

Ryan came up beside Joe. He held up his phone. "Dead."

From the storm or courtesy of the guys outside? Either option wasn't good.

"Someone needs to tell Lake what's happening." Kirsty's voice trembled. "We need him here."

"I can't get through to him." Ryan looked grim. "We're cut off."

Joe could physically feel the tension in the room as it rose.

"We need to get the women secured." Joe ran a hand over his jaw. "What about this tower room?"

Ryan had worked security at the castle before and was more familiar with the place.

"It could work," Ryan said. "It's the only room on the fourth floor."

Joe nodded. "It will have to do." He didn't like it, but they had to get away from the ground floor and all those damn windows as fast as possible. They were sitting ducks at the moment. "What weapons do you have?"

"Weapons?" Caroline stared at him.

"Guns."

"None. Josh is a singer, not a mercenary. You might find a tambourine lying around, but you won't find any guns."

This just kept getting better. Joe eyed Ryan. "What you got?"

Ryan held up his handgun. "That's it. It won't last long."

Joe cursed. "That's about what I've got too."

"Josh has a baseball bat," Caroline said.

They were up shit creek if a baseball bat was all they had

for backup. Still, he'd use anything he could get his hands on at this point.

"Grab it," Joe ordered, making Caroline frown. He'd forgotten she didn't like taking orders. In Caroline's world, she was boss. She'd have to get used to a different order of things, because this was a situation she couldn't control.

"There are knives in the kitchen," Shona said.

"Yeah, and how many of you know how to use a knife?" Joe asked her.

Every hand in the room went up.

"To stab someone," Joe amended, and all the hands went down again.

"Someone needs to go fetch Lake," Kirsty said again. "We need him."

Joe noticed the redhead had folded her arms in an attempt to hide her trembling hands.

"We'll go," the twins said at the same time.

"No. Absolutely not." Were they trying to get him killed? "If I let Grunt's wife go out into danger, he'll kill me."

"And I suppose it's fine to let me go on my own? What do you think I am? The disposable twin?" Megan put her fists on her hips and glared at him.

"There's a good chance we're all going to die while you lot stand around arguing," Margaret said.

"Thanks for that cheery thought, Mum," Kirsty said.

"Magenta can go with Megan," Joe said, pointing to the moody goth.

"No," Margaret said. "We need Magenta here. She has skills that might come in handy."

"Like what?" demanded the goth. "I'm a caving expert. Does it look like we're underground?"

"You could rappel off the side of the building. You know what to do with ropes. You have skills. Survival skills. We might need them. You stay." Margaret used her no-argument voice.

Magenta rolled her eyes.

"Look, the longer we stand around arguing, the less chance we have of anyone getting out of here to fetch help. I'm going with my sister." Claire gave Joe the same look she gave her husband when she was being stubborn. It had no effect on him. He was pretty sure you had to be having sex with her for it to work.

"No. You're not," Joe said.

"Yes. I am. Which puts you in a bad position, Joe, because if I go Grunt will kill you, and if Megan goes alone and anything happens to her, I will kill you."

"Or at least get Grunt to do it," Megan amended. "Either way, you're Grunt food."

"Fuck."

"Language!" Heather Donaldson shouted. She turned to her daughters. "I don't like the idea of you two going outside. We don't know what's out there. We don't know who's waiting. It's dangerous."

Joe pointed at Heather. "What she said."

"Suck up," Megan told him. "Mum, we're the best option. You lot are too old and will never be able to run in the snow." She motioned to the retired women of Knit Or Die.

"Thanks a lot!" Shona snapped.

"Caroline is pregnant. Kirsty is getting married tomorrow," Megan carried on, as though Shona's outburst was irrelevant. "Magenta is too conspicuous, as she's dressed in her usual black, and hello, we're surrounded by white. Jena is too accident prone; she'll knock herself out before she gets anywhere. Abby has a kid and two more on the way." She eyed the huge belly. "Possibly any day now," she added. "And Julia has been hiding behind the ficus for the duration of the party. We all know if she's confronted by a scary guy, she'll just pass out. No offence, Julia."

"None taken," squeaked the ficus.

"Oh, for goodness' sake," Margaret said to the huge plant in the corner. "I thought working for Lake these past months would give you some confidence." She turned to Kirsty. "She isn't any better now than she was when she worked for that television producer."

"She's doing great." Abby scowled at Margaret. "Don't mind them, Julia. You're doing great."

"Lake says you're the best assistant he's ever had," Kirsty added.

Joe pinched the bridge of his nose. They were giving him a migraine. "Ladies, there are men with guns out there. How about we focus on what's important here?"

There were grumbles, but they stopped discussing Julia's lack of a backbone, which was a step forward.

"Okay," he said. "Megan and Claire will go for help. Take the baseball bat. It's better than nothing." He handed it to Megan.

The twins nodded their agreement—with matching looks of determination.

"Everybody else will hunker down in the tower room while Ryan scopes out the situation. Got it?"

"No," Margaret said. "We're not going to hunker down. I don't even know what that means. If it means hide like a bunch of children, then no, we won't be doing that. There are people out there threatening the women of Invertary. People trying to ruin my daughter's wedding and assault Caroline's home. We're going to do what Scottish people do best. We're going to defend our castle."

The women cheered, completely ignoring Joe's protest. As far as they were concerned, he was invisible and the leader of Knit Or Die was running the show.

"To the tower," Margaret shouted. "Bring any weapons you can find."

The older women charged from the room.

"At least they're defending the castle from inside the tower room," said Caroline. "Maybe once they're in there you can convince them to hunker?"

Yeah, and now Joe's head was really throbbing. He asked himself, yet again, why he'd decided to stay in Scotland when his best friend, Grunt, fell for Claire. He could work anywhere. With anyone. He didn't need to work with Lake's security company. He didn't need to deal with the crazy women of Invertary.

He turned to see Jena helping the very pregnant Abby up the stairs. What were the chances stress would bring on early labour? Shit, he hoped not.

"I wish we had hot oil," one of those crazy grey-haired women shouted over her shoulder as she scurried from the room. "We could tip it on their heads like in the old days."

"I have olive oil," Caroline called as she hurried after them.

Jean stopped to talk to Caroline. "How much?"

"A couple of bottles."

Jean sighed. "Not enough." She brightened. "Bring the alcohol."

"We can't drink and fight," Heather scolded.

"Not to drink. To make Molotov cocktails."

"You're a genius. Women, the alcohol." They changed direction and hurried to the cabinet in the corner of the dining room that housed the bar.

"Wait," Rayan shouted after them. "You don't use alcohol in a Molotov cocktail."

It was pointless. They weren't listening.

"You're wasting your breath," Joe told him.

"Okay, we're ready," Megan said as she came back into the kitchen.

The twins were decked out in matching snow gear, all of it red. So much for their argument against sending Magenta. They weren't any better at blending with the snow.

"You stand out too much," Joe said.

"It's the best we can do," Megan said. "Don't worry. We'll keep to the shadows. No one will be expecting us to go for help. We're just a bunch of helpless women." She grinned, and it was kind of scary.

"Good luck keeping them in line," Claire told Joe while she pointed at her mother. "I'll make sure Grunt doesn't kill you."

Joe grabbed the hood of Claire's jacket as she headed for the door. The twins were acting like this was an adventure. It wasn't. And he was an idiot for letting them go. But they needed all the help they could get, and he was out of options.

"Stay low to the ground," he said. "Go out the door at the side of the house. Most people don't even know it's there, and it's shielded by those hedges we kept telling Josh to cut down. They'll help with cover. If anything comes at you, swing the bat. Otherwise, run like the wind."

"Got it." Megan saluted, and then the twins were gone.

"I am so freaking dead." Joe groaned.

The beams from flashlights scanned over the glass of the new conservatory. Time had run out.

"Upstairs," Joe shouted.

There was a thunder of footfalls as the women ran four flights of stairs to the tower.

CHAPTER 6

* RAINNE AND ALASTAIR *

There was a pulse.

Thank you, God. There was a pulse. Rainne brushed the hair from Alastair's forehead as tears streamed down her cheeks. He still hadn't opened his eyes. Why wouldn't he open his eyes?

She looked around them in dismay. The truck was resting on its side. Snow fell fast and thick in the black night. Only the dim lights that came on when the door was damaged illuminated the interior of the truck. Rainne was lying half on, half off Alastair, her back squeezed against the steering wheel.

"What now?" she asked the silence.

She couldn't leave him lying in the broken glass, but could she move him? What if he was injured? What if his neck was broken? What if moving him killed him?

She took a minute to slow her breathing. To force herself to calm down. It was time to be practical. She could do practical. She wasn't the same airy-fairy woman who'd left Invertary three years earlier. She could do this. She could be useful. She just had to think.

Help. They needed help.

She rooted around in her pocket until her hand hit her mobile phone. No signal. And very little battery left. She'd forgotten to charge it. As usual. She could still use it as a flashlight, but only if she was desperate.

She eyed the back of the truck. Alastair had put his tools in a locked box on the flatbed. She'd bet there was a better flashlight in there. Key. She needed the key.

"Sorry," she whispered as she rooted around in Alastair's pockets.

His jeans were snug. The heat from his body and the solid feel of his muscle under her touch made her cheeks flush. A totally inappropriate reaction to an unconscious man. But then, he was Alastair, and just being in the same town as him made her flush. His pockets were empty. No key. She let out a wail, cutting it off as fast as it erupted. She was an idiot. She wasn't thinking straight. The keys were in the ignition.

She leaned around Alastair and wiggled the key free. Alastair moaned as she jostled him. She froze. Was he waking? *Please please please...*

He didn't open his eyes.

Rainne took a deep breath, struggled up towards the passenger door and pushed it open. It was strange to exit the car the same way you'd come out of a submarine hatch. But then, nothing about this experience was normal.

Her climb out was awkward and graceless, ending in her landing on her backside in the snow. She didn't care. In a minute she was around the truck, staring into the back where the toolbox was secured to the flatbed. She used the flashlight app on her phone to find the locked box. It took several tries and lots of creative cursing to find the right key and get it into the lock. At last the box clicked open and the contents spilled out around her. She almost whooped with joy. There was a flashlight. A huge one with more bells and whistles than it probably needed.

She switched off her phone and used the space-age flashlight to examine the contents of the box—all the while terrified that the guy with the gun would see the light and come to investigate. She really didn't want to see that guy, or his gun, ever again. She stuffed her pockets with everything she thought might be useful, then scrambled out and back around to the cabin.

She leaned over the open door and shone the light inside. Alastair hadn't moved. There was blood on the snow beneath his head. Not good. Bandages. She needed bandages. She shone the light around the interior, hoping to find a first-aid kit, and spotted a small one strapped underneath the passenger seat. She let out a squeal of triumph as she reached for it. Alastair groaned in response. Adrenalin and hope shot through Rainne in equal measures. She dropped the kit and climbed awkwardly into the cab beside him, leaning on the side of his seat to stop herself from landing on top of him.

"Alastair, honey, you need to wake up." She reached over and brushed his hair off his forehead. "Alastair. Please. I need you."

He groaned again and moved his head. Rainne gasped. Should he be doing that? Should she have immobilised his neck? It made her furious with herself that she didn't know. All these years proving she was independent and it never once occurred to her to take a basic first-aid course. If they got out of this situation in one piece, she was so signing up for one. Along with a self-defence course. And a class on what to do if a crazy man shoots at your car in a blizzard.

Alastair grunted and turned towards her. His eyes flickered open, as though it took great effort to get his eyelids to work.

"Rainne?" His gaze was unfocused and the word was slurred.

That wasn't a good sign, was it? She needed to remember how you checked for a concussion. She'd seen it done on TV so many times. How did *House* do it?

He blinked at her as though she was coming into focus. "Rainne? Am I dreaming again? Why can't I get you out of my dreams? We both know you don't want to be there. You just want to run away. Why are women always running away from me? You can't be trusted. None of you. And why are you upside down?"

Huh? He was definitely out of it. Oh, she hoped there wasn't brain damage.

"It is me. I'm really here." She allowed herself a gentle caress of his strong jaw while he was too out of it to stop her, and shoved the fact she was taking advantage of an injured man to the back of her mind. "Someone shot at us. The truck went out of control. You hit your head. You've been unconscious." She hated how her voice trembled.

"Aye, now I remember." He groaned as he tried to move.

"No, not yet. I need to check for concussion and a broken neck."

"What?"

She did the only thing she could think of and flicked the beam from the flashlight into his eyes.

"What the hell?" Alastair scrunched them shut.

"I'm assessing you. Follow the light with your eyes."

"Get the light out of my face, Rainne."

"But I need to see if you have brain damage. How am I going to do it without the light?"

"I don't have brain damage, but I am being blinded. Turn the light off."

She flicked the flashlight off, leaving them with only the faint glow from the door lights. Alastair seemed relieved.

Rainne cast around for other ways to assess his injuries. She held up two fingers.

"How many fingers am I holding up?"

"It's dark in here, Rainbow. I can barely see your face."

"Oh, yeah. Okay, that won't work. You need to answer some questions. What's your full name and today's date?"

"My name is Alastair Stewart and it's the twenty-eighth of February. Want to give me a clue why we're playing twenty questions while I'm trapped in a broken truck with my face in the snow?"

"They always ask questions on TV when someone has a brain injury. Who's the current president?"

He opened one eye to stare at her. "Of which country?"

"I need to watch less American TV," she mumbled. "Who's the prime minister of Britain?"

"I really don't care."

That made her back snap straight. "How can you not care? Please tell me you voted in the last election. People fought and died for your right to have a say in how this country is run. To waste a vote is to spit in the face of their sacrifice. You shouldn't just care who's running the country, you should be interested in what they're doing. They're making decisions on your behalf. How can you not care about that?"

His lips twitched as though he was fighting a smile. "And there's the Rainbow I used to know. I wondered if you were still in there under your dull, generic clothes and plain brown hair."

"There's nothing wrong with my hair. You can't work in an office with multi-coloured hair. I like it brown. I don't think it's plain." She teased her bottom lip with her teeth. "Is it plain? Really?"

"Okay, are you sure you aren't the one with brain damage? Because if you think I'm going to lie here in an upturned truck, in the snow, and discuss your hair, you're seriously deluded."

He had a point. She was being inconsiderate. She should be thinking about him, not her hair. "I'm sorry, but there's a lot of blood on the snow under your head and I was worried."

"Head wounds bleed." He sounded as though he knew that for sure. Which was either really worrying or reassuring, depending on how you looked at it.

"Do you have pain anywhere?" she said.

For a minute she didn't think he would answer, and when he did his voice was tight. "Head. Neck. Right wrist. Ribs." He sounded like he was reciting a shopping list rather than injuries.

"Oh." Her hands began to shake. She wasn't cut out for this. She was the least capable person she knew. She was useless. No good to anyone...

No. Those were old thoughts. She wasn't that person anymore. Now she had skills. She was able. She could think for herself. She was useful.

Okay, so she didn't have the skills for *this* particular situation, but that didn't mean she didn't have options. She'd just do what she normally did when she was stuck and terrified—she asked herself what Lake would do. Suddenly things were clearer.

"We need to get out of the truck. We need to get out of the snow. Warm up. Patch you up. Get help." The words came out in a rush, tumbling over each other before Alastair could tell her the plan was stupid.

She frowned. He wouldn't do that. He wasn't her parents. Being back in Invertary was making it hard not to slip into old habits. Into old thinking.

He didn't move for a minute, and she thought he'd lost

consciousness again. At last his eyes opened and he stared up at her.

"You're right. Can you unlatch the seatbelt? And I'll try to make sure I don't fall when you do. Not sure the ribs will take it."

"I can do that." She put her thumb on the release button. "Ready?"

"Aye."

"Okay, releasing, now." She pushed. The seatbelt sprang free and Alastair toppled against his door with a thud and a grunt.

Rainne waited, itching to do something, anything to help him while he lay there breathing heavily.

"Alastair? What can I do?"

"I'm going to push myself up and out of here. You climb out to give me some space."

"I can pull you, help you."

He froze her in place with his stare. "Out, Rainne. I don't need help. I've got this."

"I can—"

"Rainne." His tone was icy cold. "I need space to move."

Rainne crumpled under his steely gaze. "Okay, but tell me if you need me."

She scrambled back out of the passenger door.

"I won't," she heard Alastair say behind her.

Of course he wouldn't. He'd made that clear earlier. He wanted nothing to do with her. Things between them really were unfixable. She should never have come back to Invertary. She should never have tried to come back to Alastair.

Rainne wrapped her arms around herself as she waited for him to climb out into the darkness. The snowflakes fell silently around her. Huge thumb-sized flakes. A thick sheet of them, reducing visibility to a couple of feet in all directions. Soft, fluffy snow built up fast around her feet. Making her think that if she stood still long enough it would cover her completely, wiping out all traces of Rainne Benson from the earth.

There was a time she would have thought that was a good thing.

Now she knew it wasn't.

"Okay," Alastair said tightly as he stood in front of her. "I have a plan."

Rainne lifted her chin as she looked him in the eye. "So do I."

"Aye, but I'm pretty sure I have a plan that will work. Just follow me and everything will be fine."

Three years ago she would have done as she was told. That was before she'd learned that her thoughts and opinions had value too. Guess Alastair really hadn't listened when she'd told him she'd changed. He was about to get a reminder.

Rainne stuck her hands in her pockets. "Let's hear it, then."

"We don't have time for that. Best if you just follow me. I know what I'm doing."

"Tell me your plan." She ground her teeth as she waited.

He heaved a sigh, which obviously hurt his ribs, as his lips tightened and went white.

"We'll walk into town and get help. The men are meeting at the pub for Lake's stag night." He looked around him and swayed on his feet. "It will take a wee while to get there in this weather, but it's the most sensible option."

Rainne stood up straight and pulled her limited courage around her once again. It was tattered and bruised, but it was still functioning.

"No," she said. "That isn't the best plan."

Alastair gaped at her. "What the hell, Rainne?"

"I have a better plan." She was grateful she sounded more confident than she felt.

"I seriously doubt it. We're walking to town."

"You haven't even heard my plan."

He actually rolled his eyes at her. Yeah, that wasn't offensive, at all. "I don't need to hear it to know I have the better plan. Knowing you, you'll want to march up to the castle and have a chat with the guy about how violence is a bad thing and we should sit down in a talking circle and communicate our feelings, peacefully and inoffensively. And while we're at it, we can all eat some tofu and braid each other's hair with ribbons."

Without thought, Rainne reacted. Her hand shot out and she slapped Alastair's cheek. Never in her life had she struck another person. But instead of feeling bad about it, she felt enraged. She glared up at the man she loved. The man who clearly had an extremely low opinion of her and asked the only question raging through her brain.

"How's that for inoffensive and passive?"

CHAPTER 7

"Tell me again why we volunteered," Claire said to Megan as they crawled on the snow alongside the bottom of the hedge.

"You heard my reasoning," Megan whispered back to her twin. "We're it. We're Charlie's freaking Angels."

"There were three of them. And they had guns. And hairspray. Lots of hairspray."

Megan stopped suddenly, making Claire bump into her rear end. She turned to her scowling sister and held a finger up to her lips to silence her. Megan tried to communicate by telepathy that there was a guy standing at the end of the hedge, but as usual it didn't work. So much for that fabled twin bond. Why they hadn't been blessed with any freaky twin skills—other than the same taste in clothes—she didn't know, but they would have come in handy right around now.

Left without the use of telepathy, she bugged her eyes out at her sister, pointed in the direction of the guy and mimed a gun. Claire's eyes went wide. Megan nodded. Yes, it was bad. Fortunately, she had a plan.

She put her mouth beside Claire's ear and whispered,

"You continue to crawl up behind him. I'll distract him. You hit him with the baseball bat."

"How are you going to distract him?" Claire whispered back.

Megan rolled her eyes. Now wasn't the time for long explanations. But Claire had her adamant face on, so Megan elaborated.

"I'm going to proposition him."

There was a pause before Claire exploded. Thankfully, she remembered to whisper while she did it. "Are you out of your mind? It's snowing. There's a power cut. He has a gun and you're going to offer him sex?"

Megan shrugged and stared at Claire. If she had a better idea, now was the time to share. She sat back on her heels, folded her arms and waited. No? That's what she thought. Megan pointed in the direction of the guy then made a shooing gesture at Claire. Telling her to get on with it. Before her sister could object again, she started to crawl to the other end of the hedge, back towards the castle. Claire's hand shot out to stop her. Megan squinted at her with a "what now?" gesture. Claire leaned in to whisper.

"What will we do with him when I knock him out?"

"Take him inside and interrogate him."

Claire gave her a look like she was nuts. Megan ignored it. She wasn't the one who wanted to hang around to whisper in the snow.

"What if I hit him too hard and kill him?" Claire worried her bottom lip.

Megan's heart filled at the sight. She gave Claire a quick hug and whispered the solution: "Grunt will help you hide the body."

Claire nodded, grinned, gave Megan a thumbs-up and resumed her crawl towards the guy with the gun—reassured by the knowledge that there was nothing her husband wouldn't do for her. Megan shook her head at her more cautious sister and resumed her crawl. She made it to the end of the hedge, beside the house, before standing. She dusted off the snow, pulled off her hat and fluffed her long blonde hair so it framed her face. She then checked to see if Claire was in position, which was bloody hard considering it was pitch black and the falling snow blocked her view. She thought she saw her twin standing, holding the bat, but it could have been wishful thinking on Megan's part. Either way, there was no going back now.

She plastered what she hoped was a seductive smile on her face and stepped around the hedge. The guy swung towards her. His gun pointed at her chest. Megan licked her lips and batted her lashes.

"Hey, big boy, fancy a good time?" she said.

The guy looked bewildered for a second before there was a dull crack and he fell face first into the snow.

Megan ran towards him as Claire dropped to her knees beside the guy. She pulled off her gloves and felt his neck.

"He's alive," she said on a sigh. "Yay for me."

"Get the gun," Megan ordered. "We need to take him inside before they notice he's missing."

"How are we going to do that?" Claire picked up the gun —it could have been a rifle, Megan wasn't sure, but she was damned well going to Google it when her phone was working. Claire used the attached strap and hung the gun over her shoulder like a handbag.

"We have experience with this. If we could haul your abnormally massive husband across a grassy verge when he was unconscious, we can move this guy into the castle." She eyed the man, noticed his face was still in the snow and turned his head so he didn't suffocate. "He's nowhere near as big as Grunt and we can slide him on the snow. Easy peasy. Grab an arm."

"Fine." Claire grabbed his arm. "But we need to stop knocking men out and moving them around. It isn't good for my back. I don't do enough yoga to deal with this crap."

"Whatever."

They slid the man over the snow and back towards the door they'd come through. It was surprisingly easy to get him where they wanted him. Between the snow outside and Caroline's polished wooden floor, they had him stored in the downstairs toilet in no time at all.

"Help me tie him to the toilet, and then you can go to the pub and get the guys while I interrogate him."

"He's out cold. I don't think he's up for answering questions."

They stared at the guy. He was kind of cute. Short brown hair, manly stubble and firm jaw.

"Do you think it's a gift that we only knock out good-looking guys?" Megan asked.

"Just don't marry this one," Claire said. "I don't think people would appreciate him after he attacked the castle."

"Grunt kidnapped Jena and people still like him," Megan pointed out.

"That wasn't a real kidnapping."

Megan assessed the guy. He was too big to get onto the toilet, so he'd have to stay on the floor.

"Take off your belt and scarf."

"I like this scarf," Claire whined as she unwrapped it. "Grunt bought it for me in Madrid."

Megan held her hand out until Claire handed it over. Together they made short work of tying his arms around the bottom of the toilet, under the u-bend to make sure he couldn't get away. Then they tied his ankles to the old iron radiator. There was no way that sucker was coming off the wall.

"Better gag him. You don't want him shouting for help."

"Smart." Megan stuffed the hand towel into his mouth and secured it to his head with her scarf, which, she had to admit, wasn't as pretty as Claire's.

They surveyed their work and it was good.

"Okay, you need to go get Grunt and Lake," Megan said. "I'll find Joe and tell him we have a hostage. Good luck."

She gave her sister a tight hug.

"I'll be back soon with the cavalry." Claire headed back out the side door.

"I know," Megan whispered after her. She didn't doubt her sister for a second.

When Claire had disappeared into the night, Megan shut the bathroom door on her captive and went in search of Joe.

"What the hell are you doing back here?" Joe snapped when Megan literally ran into his oversized chest as he came out of the kitchen.

He held his gun tight in his hand. His shoulders were tense and the happy-go-lucky smile was gone.

"Trouble?" Megan nodded to the kitchen.

"The guys are scouting the exterior, but they haven't made a move to come inside. Yet. I counted three, but there's probably more. Now, want to tell me why you're here instead of on your way into town? You're supposed to be getting help. And where's Claire? If anything happened to her, I may as well shoot myself right now. It'll save Grunt the trouble."

Megan stared at him for a second. "Has anyone ever told you you're really tense?" She held up a hand when he opened his mouth to answer her. "Claire's on her way to the pub. And there are definitely more than three guys. One of them is tied up in the downstairs loo waiting for us to interrogate him."

Joe gaped at her, which made Megan wonder if he was really cut out for life as a soldier for hire.

CHAPTER 8

Rainne's bout of anger disappeared as fast as it had flared. She covered her mouth with her hands as she gasped. She'd hit a man with a head injury. She started to hyperventilate. This was not good. Not good at all. Alastair had blood caked to the side of his head and his pallor was grey. He swayed on his feet, but was too damn stubborn to lean on the truck. And she'd hit him. On the head. His injured head.

"What the hell, Rainne?" He rubbed his cheek.

"Sorry?" She shook her head. No, she was *definitely* sorry. "I snapped. I hope I didn't damage your brain further. I've never hit anyone before, and I realise this is not the time to start. Are you okay?"

"I'm fine. You hit like a girl."

"I am a girl." Now she was a confused girl.

"Never mind that." Alastair waved a hand, dismissing her. "We need to start walking into town."

"No. We need to get out of the cold and tend to your injuries. The closest place is the guardhouse beside the castle gate."

Alastair shook his head, then flinched. Very carefully, as

though trying not to move, he looked at her. "Are you nuts? There's a guy with a gun at the castle. We don't know how many friends he has with him. We need to get away from the place, not move closer to it."

Rainne could feel herself wilting under his indomitable will. Every cell within her wanted to back off and avoid a confrontation. But she'd spent three years growing a backbone, and she was damn well going to use it.

"There hasn't been any sign of life at the guardhouse. I've been watching. No noise. No light. Nothing. If you want to walk to town, on you go, but you can barely stand, so I don't know how you'll make it through the snow. You'll probably pass out and die of hypothermia, but hey, you don't need help, so you'll be fine. Meanwhile, I plan to head to the guardhouse, where there's warmth, shelter and hopefully a landline so I can call the police."

When she finished her rant she stood before him, shaking but determined. She hoped desperately he wouldn't call her bluff, because there was no way she'd let Alastair walk to town alone, not when he was injured and needed her help. Even if he couldn't admit it.

"What happened to you?" He stared at her as though she was incomprehensible. "You were sweet and colourful. You worried about offending everyone."

"In other words, I always did what anyone told me to do."

He snorted. "Guess that's where I went wrong. I should have *told you* to stay instead of asking you nicely."

Rainne took the flashlight from where it was balanced on the wheel and thrust at it him—when what she really wanted to do was lob it at his head. Apparently the new Rainne had no problem with anger or violence. "You'll need this more than I will."

With that, she went for the big exit and turned towards the castle. She really, really hoped she wasn't shot when she got there. And she really, really hoped Alastair didn't die in the snow without her to protect him.

Alastair watched Rainne stride determinedly through the snow in the direction of the castle. Her purple moon boots were swallowed by each step she took, and she wobbled on her feet. But the stubborn mule kept on going. He could practically hear her thinking. She'd be grumbling about how unreasonable he was—while at the same time worrying about him. He shook his head and instantly regretted it when pain shot through his temple.

She didn't have an ounce of common sense. What was she thinking going back to the castle? What was she going to do if the guy with the gun was waiting? Lecture him on how to stage a peaceful protest? She was too soft-hearted. Ignorant of the evil people were capable of doing. He was pretty sure her head was filled with unicorns and rainbows.

The snow was falling so thickly now he could barely see her. He pinched the bridge of his nose. He couldn't let her go alone. It was like abandoning a kitten.

Damn it to hell.

With unsteady steps, he followed the woman who'd ripped out his heart and left him to rebuild a life without her. The woman he'd promised to never let near him again. Aye. That was the woman he was chasing through the bloody snow like an idiot.

"Wait," he said when he got close enough for her to hear.

She stopped dead in her tracks and seemed to take several steadying breathes before turning to him. Alastair ignored the hope in her eyes, the same way he ignored the pain in his side and wrist, and the thumping in his head.

"Stay low," he told her.

Her eyes went wide. "Crawl?" She looked down at the thick, fluffy snow. "I don't think that's a good idea."

"Crouch, not crawl."

"Oh, that makes sense."

She needed a keeper. His heart spasmed, adding another pain to the list. He'd wanted to be that for her. But she'd made it very clear he wasn't her choice for the job.

"Let's go." He nodded towards the darkness that swallowed the guard building. "I'll put the flashlight on low and keep it tilted to the ground. In this weather, they shouldn't see it."

"You can dim it?" She seemed fascinated.

Alastair grunted and switched the thing to the lowest setting. A faint beam illuminated Rainne's face.

She pulled her bottom lip between her teeth, clearly working up the courage to say something. "Do you want to lean on me?"

"No." The word came out sharp, like a bullet. He didn't want to touch her at all because part of him, deep inside, knew if he did he'd want to keep on touching her and never stop.

"Of course," she muttered. "Alastair Stewart doesn't need anyone for anything. He can do it all on his own. Okay, let's get inside."

They fought their way through the darkness, the cold biting at them, the thick snow swallowing their feet. Each step was agony. The snow was halfway up Alastair's calves and his jeans were soaked. He glanced over at Rainne. The snow was over the top of her moon boots, probably seeping into them. The padding on her boots wouldn't be much use if it was wet. At least her coat was doing its job. It was decently padded and came down to mid-thigh. He wondered if it was padded with proper down or some synthetic crap that wouldn't fend off moisture long enough to keep her properly warm. And what the hell was she wearing on her head? Her woollen hat had eyes. And possibly ears. He frowned. So much for her growing up—she'd obviously chosen the hat for the novelty factor rather than practicality. It was too thin for this weather. She'd have been better off with a waterproof hat with a fur lining.

"I don't see anyone," Rainne whispered.

Alastair looked around. She was right. Although the fact they could only see a couple of feet in front of them meant if someone was out there, they wouldn't know.

"The guardhouse looks empty," she said.

"That doesn't mean it *is* empty."

She nodded. "But it's got that feel about it, you know. The one where it seems hollow because the filling is missing."

Yeah, she had totally reinvented herself all right. Not.

Alastair motioned for her to crouch down behind the stone wall that flanked the open gate. She did as she was told, and he wondered why she couldn't have been that obedient earlier.

"I'll go check out the building," he whispered, each word making a cloud in front of his face.

"You're injured. I should go."

"No."

"You are unreasonably stubborn, Alastair Stewart. It's not an attractive quality in a man. But fine, if your poor, fragile male ego has to do this, then on you go. When you pass out in the snow, I'll drag you inside. I hope your manliness can cope with that." She folded her arms over her purple coat and frowned at him.

"I think I can live with that."

He uncurled from his crouched position. Too fast. The world tilted and his hand shot out to hold on to the snow-clad stones. He closed his eyes and waited for the feeling to settle. A minute. He just needed a minute. When he opened them, Rainne was gone.

What the hell?

He ignored the stab of panic that made his mouth dry, and scanned the darkness. There. A faint light. She was using her phone to illuminate her way to the guardhouse. And she called him stubborn? She wasn't even trying to be stealthy. She was just trudging forward, a huge purple target in the white snow. Heading towards a building she *felt* was empty.

Alastair was running after her before he even realised his feet were moving. He sucked in a lungful of icy air, tucked his aching wrist against his ribs and raced to get ahead of her. If there was someone in there, she wasn't equipped to deal with them. A niggle at the back of his mind reminded him he was injured and asked if he was in any better state to fight someone off. He squashed it down. At least *he* knew how to fight. Plus, he had at about a foot of height and at least eighty pounds of bulk on Rainne. At the very least, he could stand in front of her and form a wall between her and whatever came at her.

The frustrating woman had been back in town all of five minutes and already he was going insane from worry. And it didn't matter how many times he told himself she was someone else's problem. There wasn't anyone else around. He was it.

RAINNE TIPTOED, as much as was possible in knee-deep snow, to the door of the guardhouse. Really it was a one-room building built in a hexagonal shape that sat beside the huge ornate iron gates. The previous owners of the castle had put a small en suite in the old building and planned to rent the place out to tourists. The main problems with their plan were that the room was tiny, the location isolated and Invertary didn't get many tourists.

Rainne turned the door handle. Not locked. She pushed it open and stepped into the darkened room. It was so small, if someone had been in there, she'd have seen them straight away. Definitely empty.

Then a hand clasped over her mouth.

She sucked in air through her nose and screamed and screamed and screamed.

She kicked out against her assailant. Her muffled screams useless.

"Calm down. You're going to make yourself sick."

The voice penetrated. Alastair. The idiot. She sagged back against him as he slowly removed his hand from her mouth.

"Are you trying to kill me?" she asked, in what she thought was a completely reasonable tone for a woman who'd almost passed out from fright.

On unsteady legs, she turned to glare up at him.

He stepped away from her. "It would serve you right. That was a stupid thing to do. You had no idea if someone was in here and you walked right in. What the hell were you thinking, Rainbow?"

"I was thinking you looked like you might collapse in the snow. I was thinking one of us had to do something. And since I was the only one standing, I did it."

"I told you to wait for me." Alastair snapped the door closed, making her jump.

"And as you pointed out, I no longer do what people tell me to do."

"This is a fine time to get all independent. Couldn't it wait until after we're out of this mess?" He put the flashlight on the desk and flicked a switch that lit up another part of the torch. It gave off a diffused light, like a lantern.

"Yes. I'll get right on that. I forgot you're only interested in me when I'm meek, confused and easily malleable."

He spun towards her. "What the hell, Rainne? What's that supposed to mean?"

"Nothing," she snapped.

He took a step towards her. His bulk intimidating in the tiny space. "Not nothing. If you have something to say, spit it out."

"Fine." She glared up at him. "You chased me over half of Scotland when you thought I was a weak woman who would do your bidding. You wanted someone to protect. To cosset. It's no wonder you don't want me now. You obviously aren't interested in a woman who can think and act independently."

His lips tightened. "You are so far off the mark it's laughable. I don't want you because I don't trust you. When things get tough, you run. You abandon people. Why the hell should I give you another chance? So you can walk out again when the feeling takes you? Aye, that would make me all kinds of a fool. You women are all the same. I should have known better than to trust one of you. Can't make up your mind what you want, discarding people as though they were yesterday's paper. I don't need that. I don't need you."

Rainne took a step back from the sharp attack. The fury emanating from Alastair made her own anger crumble. This wasn't normal rage; this was something else. She stared into his darkened eyes and saw it. He was hurt. She'd really hurt him. And maybe not just her. She'd obviously stumbled on a deeper pain. One she'd helped to magnify by her thoughtless actions years earlier.

Before she could say anything, Alastair turned away. Everything about him screamed he was done talking. He pulled down the blinds on the small windows with sharp, angry movements. Rainne let out a sigh then looked around. There were a couple of office chairs, a desk with a huge computer monitor, another table with a coffee maker and microwave. A small fridge, a set of lockers and some shelves. The floor was wooden but had a thick rug. And there was a phone on the desk.

Rainne fell on it. No tone. It was a cordless phone and needed a power supply to work. What she wouldn't have given for an old rotary phone plugged into a regular old landline socket.

"It isn't working," she told Alastair.

"But this is." He hit the ignition button on the gas fire and it came to life.

Rainne almost cried with relief. They could get warm. She couldn't feel her toes any longer, even with the padded boots. And she wasn't entirely sure if her nose was still attached to her face.

Once Alastair had the fire going, he wedged one of the chairs under the handle of the door he'd already locked. He was moving slowly, favouring his right side. His teeth were clenched with what she assumed was pain, although it could have been irritation. Still, he didn't complain. Rainne doubted he would even if he was dying.

"We need to get out of these wet clothes and warm up." Alastair started undressing as he spoke, toeing off his boots.

Rainne looked away. It felt too intimate to watch. An intimacy couples shared. One she didn't have the right to anymore. Undressing around Alastair brought back memories of the last time they'd been alone together. Memories that made her ache with loss and longing.

"Maybe there's something we can wear in the lockers?" she said, trying to avoid undressing.

She pulled them open one by one. She found a few crime novels, a couple of packets of biscuits, cans of Coke and a Game Boy, but no clothes.

Alastair was watching her. "We'll hang our clothes over the chair in front of the fire. They'll dry in no time."

Yeah, and in the meantime, she got to flash her wares to the man who didn't want her. That wasn't humiliating at all. Yeah, right.

Alastair didn't seem affected by stripping in front of her. He tugged off his black woollen sweater to reveal he wore nothing underneath. The warm glow from the fire glinted off a set of abs he definitely hadn't had the last time she'd seen him naked. She swallowed hard at the sight. He'd been gorgeous then—now he was devastating.

"Rainne." His voice snapped her eyes back up to his face. "Get out of the clothes. You need to warm up."

She fidgeted with the zipper on her coat. Alastair watched her as though she was a bug under a microscope. He seemed to come to some conclusion, and smiled slowly. The first smile she'd seen on him since she came back to town. And it was devastating. The sharp angles of his face transformed, softening into something sexy and irresistible.

"What's the matter, Rainne? Shy? An ex-commune girl like you shouldn't be worried about getting her kit off. Didn't you grow up in a clothing-optional environment?"

"You're getting hippies mixed up with naturists. We didn't run around naked. We wore tie dye and Birkenstock. And we never, ever spontaneously undressed in front of each other."

Well, mostly never. She remembered a few late night campfires when she was a kid where she'd witnessed things she probably shouldn't have seen. And she wasn't just talking about the fact most of the people she lived beside didn't know the sharp end of a razor. There'd been one guy who looked like a yeti when he took his shirt off. The hair on his back had been long enough to plait. Rainne was all for getting back to nature, but drew the line at living life as a walking carpet. Seriously, how badly would it hurt the environment to shave your back? It wasn't like smooth skin hurt the ozone. There really was no excuse for it.

"You've slipped away again." Alastair sounded amused. "What's it going to be? Are you going to be sensible, and brave, and take off your clothes so you don't die of hypothermia? Or do I have to do it for you?"

Rainne's head jerked at his offer. No. Not offer. Threat. She gave herself a mental head slap. Wishful thinking was getting in the way of reality. Again. But then, reality was a nasty witch.

"Rainbow. Take off your clothes." His voice was low, and slid over her skin like hot honey.

His eyes darkened as he took a step towards her. "Strip." The low rumble vibrated through her body, making parts that should have frozen off in the cold snap to attention.

He reached for the zipper on her coat. His eyes held hers as he lowered it slowly. Rainne wanted to close her eyes and sway in place, but her vision was filled with muscled perfection and she couldn't look away. She clenched her fists at her side to stop from running her fingertips through the smattering of hair between his nipples.

The coat fell open. Alastair nudged it off her shoulders and she let it slide to the floor.

"Get rid of that useless hat," he ordered gruffly.

Rainne blinked up at him. "It's the Pink Panther."

He stared at her for a second, then his face closed up. She watched his eyes harden and his lips thin. The moment was broken. And Rainne felt bereft.

He reached for the hat, pulling it off her head in disgust. "It isn't meant for the cold. It's decoration. Not function." He threw it to the floor. "Get out of those wet clothes. We don't know what we're dealing with here. There's no time to mess around." Then he turned from her and continued to undress.

Rainne looked away as she picked up her coat and hung it on the hook beside Alastair's leather jacket. When she turned back, Alastair was unzipping his jeans. Her mouth went dry as he stepped out of them. He was wearing a pair of form-fitting black cotton boxers. Had his backside been that drool-worthy years ago? This was torture. Like a dieting woman being locked in a candy store. His thighs were like tree trunks, and each time he moved the muscles flexed. Rainne wanted to kneel in front of him and brush her cheek over his thighs. She was losing her mind. She looked away and wiped her mouth, just in case a little bit of drool had escaped.

"Rainne. Clothes," he snapped.

"Oh. Yeah."

Her pink fluffy sweater was wet around the cuffs, so she took it off while Alastair dragged the remaining chair in front of the fire and draped his clothes over it.

"Gimme that," he said, and she handed him the sweater. "I need the jeans and socks."

Like she didn't know that already. But taking them off would leave her exposed. And she didn't have washboard abs. She had a little pouch where her flat stomach should be. She looked like a freaking kangaroo.

Firm hands covered hers and her breath stopped dead.

"You're going too slow." His voice was thick molasses.

He flicked the button of her jeans and lowered the zip. *Breathe*, she told herself as she started to feel lightheaded. Slowly, Alastair pushed her jeans over her hips. She felt him crouch behind her. His breath warm on the small of her back through the thin thermal vest she wore.

"Lift." He clasped her ankle.

She lifted her foot so he could slip the leg of her jeans over it. The sock disappeared with it. His fingers ran up the soft arch of her foot before he placed it back on the floor.

"This one." He repeated the process with her other leg.

Her jeans were off. She stood in her pink Hello Kitty underpants and matching thermal vest.

"More cats," Alastair mumbled from his position

crouched behind her.

Rainne felt weak enough to crumble. For an eternity they stayed like that. Alastair behind her. Rainne waiting. Hoping.

"Alastair?" she whispered.

He shot to his feet and busied himself with hanging her jeans over the back of the chair.

Rainne worked to breathe steadily. She didn't have a clue what was going on. One minute he wanted to touch her, the next he didn't. Her head was spinning from the confused mess of signals he was giving off. She turned towards him, prepared to demand an explanation when she spotted the glint of glass on his neck.

Rainne gasped as her hand flew to her mouth. "You have glass embedded in your skin!"

"It's fine." He didn't look at her.

"It isn't fine, you idiot." Her eyes scanned over him. This time she didn't let his abs distract her. There was a large bruise blossoming at the side of his ribs. "Are your ribs broken?" Her voice trembled.

"Bruised. Maybe cracked. I don't think they're broken. I can breathe well enough."

Anger rushed through her. "And I suppose that's fine too?"

"Aye." He glared at her.

"Your wrist is swollen," she said. "Were you going to mention that?"

"Nope."

"No. Of course not. Because you might have to hand in your man card if you admitted you were hurt."

To stop herself from hitting the infuriating man, she went to fetch the first-aid kit she'd tucked into her coat. He might be able to ignore his injuries in the hope they'd disappear, but Rainne couldn't. She was going to take care of him if she had to kill him to do it.

CHAPTER 9

* MEGAN *

Joe insisted on untying the prisoner and carrying him, fireman style, up several flights of stairs to the tower. Megan didn't complain. She got to walk behind Joe and watch his manly show of strength as he took every step. Her prisoner stayed unconscious, which made her wonder just how hard her sister had hit the guy. Not that she cared either way. He was breathing, and that was all that counted.

When they reached the door to the master bedroom on the fourth floor of the tower, Joe banged it with the butt of his gun. Again—manly. Megan briefly wondered if all of Lake's guys were born with alpha genes, or if there was a class somewhere they took where they learned how to behave more manly.

"What's the password?" a female voice shouted—could have been any one of the retired women from Knit Or Die.

Joe hung his head for a second before answering. "There is no password. Let me in."

"How do I know you aren't compromised? Somebody might be holding you at gunpoint to make you say that."

"Good point," another woman shouted.

"It's okay," Megan shouted. "It's me, Megan. Joe's carrying the prisoner I captured."

The locks clicked over and the heavy wooden door swung open.

"Well, why didn't you say so?" Shona grumbled. "Who is he? Where's he from? What does he want?"

Joe marched past the curious women and unceremoniously dumped the guy onto the bed.

"He's unconscious at the moment," Megan said. "Claire hit him with a baseball bat."

The women stared at him. "Shouldn't he be awake by now? How long has he been out?" Margaret said.

Megan shrugged. "A few minutes. He's fine. He's breathing, isn't he?"

"He isn't fine," her mum said. "You two can't go around knocking men out. I didn't bring you up to behave like that."

Megan ignored her. What was she supposed to do? Ask him nicely to surrender? The guy was almost twice her size. How else would she get him where she wanted him to be if he wasn't unconscious? Sometimes her mother didn't think things through properly.

"Should we tie him up in the toilet?" Megan asked Joe. "You know, in case there's blood when we torture and interrogate him."

"One"—Joe counted off on his fingers—"there will be no torture. Two—there will be no blood. Three—there is no we. I will question him alone, but the chances of him telling us anything are less than zero. These guys have been trained. They won't talk."

"And four," her mother added, "we're not tying anyone up in the bathroom. How will we pee? I'm not going to use the room if there's a strange man tied to the sink. We could be stuck up here for ages and we've all had a lot of champagne. We need the toilet."

Megan frowned at Joe. "He's my prisoner. I'm going to interrogate him. And if that means torture, so be it."

Joe stared at the ceiling for a minute while he mumbled. "You're right—you found him. He's all yours. Have at it. Torture away." He sauntered over to talk to Ryan, who was peeking out the window from behind the curtain.

Megan narrowed her eyes as she watched him go. That was way too easy. Why didn't he protest more? She was missing something. She shrugged. Who cared? She got what she wanted. She had a prisoner to torture.

"Right, ladies," Megan said, with no small amount of glee. "Let's get him tied to the bed."

"Spread-eagled?" Jean asked as she patted her tight grey curls. Was she preening for the unconscious bad guy? No. Surely not.

Megan thought about it for a second then shrugged. "I don't see why not. Spread-eagled it is."

"Magenta, you're good with knots—come and help us," Kirsty's mum called.

"I think I'll just watch. I'm sure you'll be fine."

"Magenta Fraser," Margaret snapped. "You get your behind over here and help right now or I'll have a word with your mother."

Magenta dragged herself across the room. "I'm twenty-three. I'm married. I don't think my mother would care if I helped you tie up a guy or not."

"I care. You are part of this group and you have responsibilities," Margaret said.

The goth stared at Kirsty's mother before turning to Megan. "You owe me," she said. "You and your crazy twin cause me a lot of trouble."

"Suck it up," Megan told her best friend. "You don't need us to generate trouble. You cause plenty all on your own."

There was no arguing with the truth.

"Save me," Magenta mouthed to Kirsty, who was sitting on the sofa with Caroline, watching them like they were the night's entertainment.

"You're on your own," Kirsty said with a grin.

Abby and Jena gave her thumbs-up to encourage her, which made Magenta give them her own, less polite, hand gesture in return.

Megan ignored the laughter as she watched the women of Knit Or Die raid the closets for all of Josh's silk ties.

"Should he be naked?" Shona asked Megan.

"Why?" Megan stared at the woman.

"To make the torturing easier."

Jena Morgan snorted and hid her face in her best friend Abby's neck while she laughed.

"Shouldn't you guys be making Molotov cocktails?" Megan asked the peanut gallery. She gestured to the many alcohol bottles in the corner of the room.

"Turns out you make them with gasoline," Abby said. "Not beer and wine."

"I knew that," Jena said proudly.

"We can probably use the whisky, or the vodka," Abby carried on. "But we only have a couple of bottles of those. And we already made them into bombs." She pointed at the dressing table, and sure enough there were two bottles of whisky and one of vodka, each with a rag sticking out of the neck. "That's it for our arsenal."

"We have the prisoner's gun," Megan said. "It's not much, but every little bit helps."

"Enough of this—what are we going to do about him?" Shona pointed at their captive, who was now tied to the bed using a fortune in silk ties. "Do you have any ideas for making him talk?"

"I don't know how I'm going to torture him yet," Megan admitted. "I'm thinking about it."

"Why don't you sing?" her mother said. "That's always worked on me."

"Thanks, Mum."

"What?" Her mother held up her hands. "Singing isn't one of your talents. Remember that cat who used to run and hide under the bed every time you sang? And the dog who would howl? I'm not alone in my assessment. I'm sure if you sang to him he'd tell you anything you wanted just to get you to shut up."

"Great." Megan glared at her. "That's exactly what I'll do. I'll sing show tunes until he caves. Should I tap-dance too? I was never any good at that either."

"No need for sarcasm," Heather grumbled. "Just trying to help."

The women stood back and studied their work. The guy was still wearing the hand-towel gag Megan had fashioned for him downstairs. And he was still out cold.

"There's a strange man tied to my bed," Caroline said with bewilderment. "I never thought there would be a man tied to my bed."

Every eye in the room looked at her.

"What?" she demanded.

"Nothing." Kirsty patted Caroline's hand.

"I need to buy a new mattress." Caroline considered her bed. "And possibly move to a different bedroom. This one is kind of ruined for me now."

"We need to wake him up." Megan considered the guy before looking at Caroline. "Are you sure you're getting a new mattress?"

Caroline nodded. "I can't sleep on that one anymore."

"In that case"—Megan turned to her mother—"Mum, can you get a container of water and—"

"Waterboard him?" Heather looked excited at the prospect.

"No!" Megan stared at the woman. "Throw it at him to wake him up."

"Oh, right. Yes, I can do that." She disappeared into the bathroom.

"How does she even know about waterboarding?" Megan asked the rest of the women.

"Just because we're older than you are, doesn't mean we're ignorant," Shona said.

"I don't know what waterboarding is," Caroline said.

"It's when you cover someone's mouth with a cloth then pour water on them to make them think they're going to drown," Joe said.

"That is so wrong." Caroline was outraged. "There will be no waterboarding on my bed. Are we clear?"

There was a pathetic chorus of "yes, Caroline."

"And while we're at it." Caroline folded her arms and stared them all down. "No making him bleed, either. I might have to throw that mattress out, but it doesn't mean I want the visual of a bloody man on my bed stuck in my head."

"Great. Any more orders, or is that it?" Megan said. "It doesn't exactly leave us much to work with. Do you expect us to tickle the information out of him?"

"I guess we're back to you singing to him," Heather said as she threw a basin of water over the man's face.

His eyes jerked open. His muscles went tense and he fought his restraints. The Knit Or Die women gave each other congratulatory smiles when the restraints held.

Megan marched towards the man and stared down at him. He really was kind of cute with his golden skin and chocolate eyes. Pity he was the enemy. "You are going to tell us everything we want to know. You're going to tell us who you are, what you want and how many of you there are. If you don't, we will hurt you." She nodded towards the women.

As one, they all did what they could to appear meaner. The guy's eyebrows shot up high on his head.

"I'm taking off the gag. Don't scream or shout for help."

She untied the knot at the back of his head and peeled off the scarf and towel. He coughed when he was free of it.

"Right." Megan sat on the bed beside him. "Who are you?"

"*Je ne parle pas l'anglais.*" His voice was rugged, his accent sexy. Neither of which impressed Megan. She'd expected to deal with English. Now she was stumped.

"I love that accent!" Jena squealed. "It's so sexy. Make him talk more."

Megan cocked her eyebrow at the American. "Well, duh, Jena. That's the whole point of this."

"Why the heck are we being invaded by the French?" Margaret demanded. "Aren't we friends with the French? We sent them Mary, Queen of Scots when she needed a place to stay, for goodness' sake. Why would they attack us?"

"*Je ne parle pas l'anglais,*" the guy said again.

"Anybody here speak French?" Megan asked.

There was silence.

"This is exactly why Britain is going downhill. People are too arrogant to learn the language of their neighbours," Megan said.

"We could use Google Translate," Jena said.

Megan pointed to the candles. "No power, remember?"

"Oh, yeah," Jena said.

"Wait." Caroline shot to her feet. "I think I have a phrasebook from when we took a trip to Paris." She looked at Joe. "It's in the office. Can you get it?"

Joe shook his head. "Yes. I'll go downstairs, where it's probably teeming with mercenaries, to fetch a phrasebook so you lot can interrogate our captive with questions like 'when is the train to Paris?' and 'how much for a room for the night?'"

Caroline stared at him. "Does that mean you're not going?"

"Yes. It means I'm not going."

"Mum, didn't you study French in school?" Megan said.

"That was about a million years ago, and we learned really helpful phrases, like: *Il y a un singe dans l'arbre.*"

The guy on the bed burst out laughing.

"What did you say?" Megan said.

"There's a monkey in the tree." Her mother shrugged. "It's the only French I know."

"Well, that's freaking helpful," Megan snapped.

"Don't take that tone with me, young lady. It's more French than you know."

"Laydeez," the prisoner crooned in his sexy accent. "I have ze leetle ingles."

"Bloody hell," Shona said. "It's a sad day when the bad guy has to help you out."

Megan ignored the women and placed a hand flat in the middle of the prisoner's broad chest. She noticed his heart was beating steadily, as though lying tied to the bed didn't bother him at all. She ignored the amusement in his dark eyes and the way his bottom lip was fuller than the top one. He was a prisoner. She needed to remember that. And if he had some English, there was nothing to stop him from talking.

"Tell us everything you know," she said, and watched him smile widely.

CHAPTER 10

* RAINNE AND ALASTAIR *

"I can't believe you've been walking around with a face full of glass shards and didn't say anything." Rainne put the first-aid kit on the floor beside Alastair, where he sat beside the fire. She rooted around for a pair of tweezers.

"My face was frozen. I could barely feel it."

"That's not an excuse." She held a cloth in one hand and the tweezers in the other and reached for his face.

Alastair's hand snapped out and encircled her wrist. "I can do it. You rest and get warm. You're shivering."

Her breath quickened at the feel of Alastair's hold on her. "I'm right beside the fire. I'll get warm and deal with your face at the same time."

"I can do it." His jaw was locked.

"I know. But I'm here and I'm happy to help." Her shoulders slumped. "Just let me, okay? You can prove how capable you are when I'm done. Trust me, this doesn't make you any less of a man."

"You don't know what you're talking about." But he let her hand drop.

Rainne took that as permission, and gingerly reached for the first speck of glass embedded in his neck.

"Don't I?" She pulled the fragment free and moved on to the next one. "Even three years ago you were all about taking care of everyone around you. Your confidence was overwhelming. You knew what you wanted. You knew who you were. There wasn't an insecure bone in your body."

"And that's bad?" His sneer mocked her.

She stilled and stared at him. "You were twenty! What guy knows what he wants at twenty? What *person* knows who they are at twenty?"

"So you decided I was lying and made up my mind for me. Admit it, you didn't believe that someone would want you just for being you, instead of for something you could do for them."

Rainne flinched, his words a direct hit. "How could you want me for who I was? How did you even know who I was? I didn't. I didn't have a clue who I was."

"And now you do?" There was clear scepticism in his words.

"Yes. Now I do." She removed another piece of glass.

"Okay, I'll bite. Who are you, then?"

She let the question lie until she finished removing the last of the glass from his neck and face. She sat back on her heels and looked at the man before her. It was obvious he was in pain, but he hadn't said a word. Stubborn man. She left him for a moment while she fetched a mug of water for him, then handed him two painkillers.

"They're not massively strong, but they'll take the edge off."

She expected him to refuse the medication, but he surprised her by taking it.

"I'll clean out your wounds and then bandage your wrist."

"I can—" he started.

"I know you can," she snapped. "You can do everything. You're freaking Superman. Happy now? It doesn't mean you have to do everything. Now how about you shut up for five minutes and let me clean out your wounds? I promise never to tell anyone ever that Alastair Stewart had help."

He frowned. "If you want to do it that much, on you go. But how about you answer my question while you're at it. Who is this Rainne you had to run away to find?"

She ripped the packaging open on the antiseptic wipes and dabbed at his face. There was stubble on his jaw that scraped at her fingertips. His fists clenched on his thighs.

"Well?" he demanded. *Big, grumpy bear.*

She leaned close to him, aching at the sight of the gashes in his skin. She resisted the urge to press kisses to each one. He wouldn't appreciate them anyway. His breath slid over her bare shoulder, making her hyperaware of how close they were to each other. She cleared her throat and answered the question.

"I'm stronger. More capable. I have a business studies qualification now and work for an insurance company. I'm not the same ignorant girl who didn't know how to run a lingerie shop. If I was in charge of that shop now, it would be successful. I have my own flat, pay my own way. I make up my own mind about things. I don't let people around me sway me into agreeing with what they think. I'm more confident."

She spotted a gash at the base of his hair on the back of his neck and twisted over his shoulder to get to it. Her breast flattened against him and her hand stilled for a second. *Focus. Concentrate. This is medical help. That's all.* "I'm someone who can help now, instead of being someone who needs to be taken care of."

"Silly girl." Alastair's voice was a husky rumble. "You were always those things. You didn't find anything that wasn't already there."

Slowly, she leaned back to look at him. They were close enough to breathe each other's air. Alastair's eyes were dark. His expression brooding. Rainne blinked a couple of times before she dabbed at a cut on his forehead, at his hairline.

You didn't find anything that wasn't already there.

He couldn't mean it. Could he? Was that how he'd seen her? Her breast bumped his cheek as she reached for another antiseptic wipe. She stilled for a heartbeat before she pretended it hadn't happened. She lifted the new wipe to his face as strong hands curled around her hips.

Rainne froze with her hand poised in mid-air. She felt Alastair's thumbs gently caress the skin beneath the hem of her vest. Her heart beat so loudly she was sure he could hear it, but she didn't move. Afraid the moment would be shattered. Afraid he would stop touching her.

"You still smell so bloody good," he mumbled, as though talking to himself.

Rainne swallowed hard.

"Three years and I still remember exactly how you smell. It drives me insane. It isn't normal to have withdrawal symptoms from a scent."

He rubbed his nose against the crook of her neck. She shuddered.

"There." His lips moved against her skin. "It's stronger here. Like meadow flowers and rainy days."

He pulled her hips towards him. Rainne dropped the antiseptic wipe but didn't know where to put her hands. She was terrified he would stop. That he would retreat.

She looked down at him. "Alastair?" she whispered.

Dark eyes, tormented and burning, looked up at her.

"Alastai—"

A strong hand cupped the back of her head and pulled her

down to him. At the speed of light, his lips were on hers. Rainne moaned as she melted into him. Giving him everything, anything he wanted. She wrapped her arms around his shoulders, his skin hot to her touch. His kiss was part anger, part need. It overwhelmed her with its intensity. This wasn't the twenty-year-old boy she'd left behind. This was Alastair the man, and she revelled in him.

The firm pressure of his lips against hers. The scrape of his teeth over swollen skin. The wet urgency of his tongue as he feasted on her. She swayed in his arms, weak and desperate. Drowning in all that was Alastair. His delicious scent. The firmness of his muscles as they tensed to hold her in place. The rasp of his breath against her lips. He dominated. He controlled and he took.

Then suddenly he was gone. His hands dropped from her body. She blinked at him, slowly coming out of the haze of need he'd induced. His dark eyes were cold. His brow furrowed.

"That was a mistake."

Rainne's first instinct was to retreat. To hide. To agree and pretend he hadn't kissed her until she was delirious. She'd spent a lifetime smoothing over tense situations, making things easier for everyone around her. Not this time. Not with this man.

"And that's a cliché," she said.

He frowned at her. "What?"

Rainne pushed away from him, tidied the first-aid kit and walked across the room on wobbly legs to put it on the desk.

"I said it's a cliché. Every romance novel I've ever read has the hero getting physical with the heroine then saying it was a mistake. It's just him hiding from being hurt. Macho bullcrap. It wasn't a mistake, but it also doesn't have to happen again if your poor, wee, delicate heart can't handle it."

Alastair gaped at her.

"I'm going to use the bathroom," Rainne said, and hoped he didn't call her on running away, which was as much of a cliché as the rubbish he'd spouted.

ALASTAIR WATCHED RAINNE STOMP AWAY, her head held high with indignation, and his chest ached with the need to keep on touching her. He knew he was behaving irrationally. He didn't want to touch her, but he couldn't seem to stop. She drew him to her like a bear to honey. But he had to resist. He had to fight the pull. He had to remember all the reasons starting something with Rainne would be a bad idea—the top one being she couldn't be trusted not to rip his heart out all over again. He closed his eyes with a groan. He shouldn't have kissed her. All it did was make him remember how good it was between them.

He couldn't stop his mind from going over that one night they'd spent together. It'd been snowing then too. The Christmas market had been in full swing and the two lingerie shops were putting on a runway show. Rainne should have been there—she was manager of one of the shops—but instead she'd turned up at his door, cold and shivering. So completely devastated by something—he later found out her family had ripped her apart, but at that moment he'd been totally undone at the sight of her. He would have done anything, said anything, to make things okay for her. He'd felt helpless and panicked as he'd taken her up to his bedroom. He'd wished she'd pointed him at something to hit and let him go to it. Instead she'd stood there, trembling, eyes wide with unshed tears, cheeks stained with the evidence of tears already shed. And she had broken him in two.

"You want to talk about it?" He hoped she would tell him who to hit. No, who to break for hurting her.

She shook her head, but didn't utter a word. Leaving him at a loss. He hated feeling helpless. Hated it. Alastair glanced around the room as his mind ticked off all the things he should ask or do to make things better for her. None of them seemed to be right.

"What do you want to do?" he asked at last.

Her shoulders relaxed slightly as her wide blue eyes peered up at him. He felt like she was looking past his skin to deep inside of him. To a place no one else had ever seen before.

Without a word, she stepped in to him, stood on her toes and kissed him. He'd intended to keep the kiss short and comforting, but she wouldn't let him. Her arms wrapped around his shoulders as she ran her tongue over the seam of his lips. It was more than he could take. Kissing Rainbow was addictive. He'd never get enough. His hands settled on the small of her back as he pulled her tight against him. Soft curves flattened against his wiry frame. Curves he wanted to learn—first with his fingers and then with his tongue.

He thrust his tongue into her mouth, taking control of the kiss. He wanted to taste all of her. To feel all of her. She was perfection. He fought against the voice inside his mind telling him to throw her on the bed and brand her with his touch so that she, along with everyone else, would know she belonged to him. Struggling for control, he pulled back and did the sensible thing. The thing he had to do for her sake.

"Rainne," he said against her lips, his voice hoarse from wanting her. "What are we doing?"

He knew what he wanted to do, what he was desperate to do, but now wasn't the time to think with his dick.

She didn't answer. She didn't even look like she was listening. Instead she stepped out of his embrace and casually unbuttoned the straps on her purple dungarees, letting the bib fall to her waist. Her eyes never left his, as though in challenge, daring him to try to stop her. His mouth was dry, his jeans were too damned tight and his heart was beating so fast he felt giddy. Rainne didn't seem to care about the effect she was having on him. Or she was pleased with it. Alastair didn't get a chance to figure out what she thought, as she diverted him by bending over and removing her boots and socks. Alastair was momentarily distracted by the fact she'd painted each of her toenails a different colour, making them a rainbow to match her hair. He started to smile, but swallowed it when her dungarees fell to her feet. She calmly stepped out of them.

Words. He needed to find words. He needed to be sensible. The girl wasn't in a good place. He couldn't take advantage of her vulnerability. He was bloody well going to be honourable if it damn well killed him.

"Rainne. You're upset. This isn't the best time. You're not thinking straight."

She looked up at him with such undisguised need it almost made him crumble.

"I mean..." He stumbled over his words, feeling foolish that his will was weak where this woman was concerned. "I mean, I want to." Great. Now he sounded like he was twelve. Any other time and he would have told her exactly what he wanted to do to that glorious body of hers—in filthy, lust-filled detail. But this wasn't the time.

He took another breath. "You don't know what you're doing right now."

Rainne raised an eyebrow, which made her look sexy and cute, then reached down grabbed the bottom of her T-shirt and pulled it over her head.

Suddenly it was hard to breathe. He had to remind himself to suck in air. Her full breasts were cupped by the sexiest pale pink bra he'd ever seen. It made him want to suck her nipples through the lace. His eyes dawdled over the curve of her hip, to the flare of her thigh. Her mound was covered in more pink lace. A tiny, delicate triangle of the stuff that would rip with the barest tug. His fingers twitched to tug. To expose her to his gaze and touch. To get rid of the thin barrier between him and paradise.

Slowly, she turned her back to him, lifted her rainbow-coloured hair and waited for him to unclasp her bra. For a moment, Alastair was frozen to the spot. The woman was wearing a thong. The soft curves of her voluptuous rear were exposed for his pleasure. And it was definitely his pleasure to see them.

She glanced at him over her shoulder as though to prod him into action. No patience, his Rainbow. Couldn't a man appreciate the feast laid in front of him? Apparently not. He stepped forward, trailed his fingertips from the base of her skull, down her spine, to the clasp of her bra. It gave way under his touch, springing away from her back, leaving her bare to him.

She shook the lingerie off, let her long hair fall down her bare back almost to her hips and slowly turned towards him. Alastair let out a gasp at the beauty in front of him. Soft, firm breasts, creamy skin and dark pink nipples that were tight, hard and ready to be touched. She stood there, waiting as he looked his fill, completely at ease with being naked around him—as she should be. Because if Alastair got his way, she'd never wear clothes again.

He looked up into her warm eyes and opened his mouth, ready to ask again if she was sure about this. Rainne stopped his question with a nod that made him smile. He wasn't a saint. He didn't have the willpower of Hercules. He'd asked enough. Now he was going to take.

He pulled his jumper up over his head and threw it behind him, unconcerned about where it landed. His T-shirt and jeans followed.

"Come on, Rainne." He held out his hand. "I've been dreaming about getting you into bed. I don't want to waste a minute."

Rainne smiled and put her hand in his.

Alastair had planned his seduction of Rainbow Benson in detail. And it had all gone to hell when she'd turned up on his doorstep with tears in her eyes. He wanted her with a desperation that bordered on insanity.

He held her hand tightly as he led her onto his bed. He was nervous. How stupid was that? He'd wanted this woman since she'd first set foot in Invertary seven months earlier. He'd pursued her with relentlessness and patience. And now that she was here, where he wanted her most, he felt his hands shake with the pressure of the moment. He wanted this to be perfect for her. He wanted her to know this wasn't just sex for him. He had plans for Rainne. Long-term plans. And yeah, he knew she thought he couldn't possibly know what he wanted, because he was younger than she was. But he did. And tonight he was going to prove it to her.

Rainne lay flat in the middle of his double bed, her hair spread out over his pillow, a tiny smile curving the corner of her lips. She was a feast and he was a starving man. His eyes slowly roamed down her luscious body.

"I don't know where to start," he murmured.

Rainne shot upright, her arm covering her breasts. What the hell?

"I'm so sorry, Alastair," she said, her eyes wide with worry. "I didn't mean to push you. I thought you'd done this before."

Alastair couldn't help the laughter that burst out of him. "Aye, I've done this before. Not as much as I would have liked, but I think I can muddle through." He took her hand and moved her arm from his breasts. Because they belonged to him now and he wanted access. "I meant there's so much I want to do to you that I don't know what to choose first."

"Oh." Her shoulders sagged. Her smile was dazzling. "How about starting with a kiss?"

Her eyes went to his lips at her suggestion, and she licked hers in reflex. Alastair groaned, knelt in front of her, cupped her face with his hands and brushed his lips over hers. Soft. Delicious. Mine. He pressed her lips harder, asking for access, and she opened her mouth willingly for him. Soft hands curled around his hips as he deepened the kiss. She tasted of grape juice and sherbet, which made him smile.

A small moan escaped her as her fingers tightened on his hips, her nails biting into her skin. He kissed her long, hard, relentlessly. Wanting to consume her. To tie her to him in ways that would make it impossible for her to leave. She turned liquid against him, and Alastair felt his muscles tense in response. Slowly, he lowered her back onto the bed. He lay beside her, one arm arched over her head to tangle in her hair, the other caressing her throat.

"Alastair," she whispered.

He smiled before continuing their kiss. His hand slid over her collarbone to the curve of her breast. His heart rate spiked at the feel of her softness in his hand. She fit him perfectly, just enough to overflow. So incredibly soft. Except for that nipple, which was peaked and hard and demanding attention.

So he gave it some. He left her lips, red and swollen, to capture the puckered bud with his teeth. Rainne gasped and arched off the bed. Alastair held her breast where he wanted it as he tongued and sucked the rosy peak. Her fingers wound through his hair, tugging it tight. She gasped his name as he flicked his tongue.

"Mmm," he rumbled against the sensitive bud. "Delicious. Need more."

He turned his attention to her other breast, as his hand continued to caress and torture the one he'd already sensitised.

"Oh." It was long groan.

He looked up her body to see her head thrown back and her mouth open as she panted. Perfection. With one last tug at her nipple, he moved down her body, kissing his way. He swirled his tongue around her belly button and tugged at the piercing he found there. A silver hoop with a tiny star attached.

"Pretty," he told her, and smiled when she only moaned in reply.

The urge to rip off her lace underwear was too overwhelming to resist, so he hooked his thumbs under the delicate straps at her hips and pulled. They ripped free with ease.

"Alastair!" Rainne looked down at him, and he could have sworn he'd never seen anything so awe-inspiring. Her cheeks were rosy pink; her lips were full, wet and red. Her blue eyes were heavy-lidded with desire. She was a goddess. And she was here. With him.

"I'll replace them." He yanked the underwear out of the way.

He crawled up her body to kiss her, holding himself up on his arms as he pillaged and plundered. Her leg wrapped around his hip, reminding him that he'd stupidly kept his underwear on. He fell to her side, continuing to kiss her while he pulled his underwear over his hips and kicked them free. Better.

Nails dragged up his spine as Rainne tried to get closer. They were going to get closer, all right. He kissed a trail away from her addictive lips, down her throat to her shoulder. The heel of her foot dug into the back of his leg as she tried to manoeuvre him into the position she wanted him to be. He'd get there. In his own time. The last thing he needed was to live up to her expectation of twenty-year-old men. This was going to last, damn it.

"Please, Alastair." She ground against him.

His lips captured her nipple again as he worked his way lower. Just one taste before he gave her what she wanted. Just one taste. He pushed her thighs wide as she grasped the duvet, curling her fingers tight in the cotton. So beautiful. And all his. Alastair leaned over and licked his way through her wet centre. She bucked and groaned as he nipped and licked and sucked.

"I need, I need..."

He knew exactly what she needed. He took her clit in between his lips and sucked hard. She arched up in one curve of beautiful tension as she gasped his name.

"That's it, Rainbow," he told her as he gave her one last kiss. "You are so bloody beautiful."

He nabbed a condom from his bedside drawer and covered himself while he watched Rainne gasp for air. Her eyes were closed, her lips were parted and her pale skin shone with exertion. This was the way she should always look. Fresh from orgasm, sated and boneless.

With a satisfied smile, he worked his way between her legs and pressed into her. Her eyes shot open to look at him.

"Oh," she said on a gasp.

"Aye," he agreed.

Her hips rose to meet him; her legs curved around his thighs. Her hands clung to his biceps.

He leaned forward and kissed her as he eased into her. Had anything ever felt more perfect? He didn't think so.

"I love you, Rainbow," he said against her lips.

And then he moved his hips. His back tingled. His thighs clenched. Sweat ran down his spine. He stared down into the face of the woman he loved, her mouth open in ecstasy and her hair wild about her, and his control snapped. He groaned her name as he emptied himself into her and felt her clench around him.

"Alastair, Alastair, Alastair..." she chanted against his throat.

With great effort, he fell to her side, wrapped his arm around her and pulled her to him. Where she belonged. Where she would always stay.

Because he was never letting her go.

INSIDE THE TINY BATHROOM, Rainne splashed icy cold water on her overheated cheeks. She shook at the thought of their kiss. He was lying if he thought it was a mistake. Big coward. It meant something and she wasn't going to hide from it, even if he did.

She squared her shoulders, held her head high and stepped out of the bathroom to confront him. It was time to sort out a few things. To be honest with one another.

Or at least it would have been if she hadn't found Alastair fast asleep beside the fire. With a sigh, she crossed the space between them and brushed his hair off his forehead. He didn't have a fever. She felt his pulse and it seemed fine. It was probably just exhaustion from his injuries and dealing with the cold.

She debated whether to wake him.

"Alastair?" she whispered.

But he didn't stir. He was well and truly out of it. She

knew the sleep would help. She bit her lip as she studied him. What if it wasn't sleep? What if he'd slipped into unconsciousness? Should she try harder to wake him? What if his injuries were worse than he'd led her to believe? She wanted to wail with the frustration of not knowing what to do.

With a disgruntled sigh, she let her eyes fall on the faint outline of an old light switch by the door and cocked her head. Could it be? Maybe. Heart quickening, she hurried over to the panel and let out a whoop of joy. It was an old-style intercom system, connecting the guardhouse with the castle. An old intercom system that ran on the same basis as landlines. The power needed to operate a system like this was really low and usually came straight from the phone company, rather than locally—another piece of random information she'd picked up in the communes over the years. She thought it came from a guy who loved to protest against British Telecom. She mentally kicked her own backside. Like it mattered where her knowledge came from. All that mattered was seeing if the thing still worked. For all she knew they'd ripped out the cables when they renovated the castle.

Please, please let it still work.

She flicked the switch labelled "all rooms" and sent out what she hoped was a message that could be heard throughout the castle.

"Is anybody there?" she said. "It's Rainne here."

She looked over at Alastair, but even the sound of her voice didn't make him stir. Her stomach cramped with worry. She took a shaky breath and tried again.

"This is Rainne. We're holed up in the guardhouse. Can anybody hear me?"

CHAPTER 11

* LAKE *

Even a power cut hadn't managed to stop the bachelor party from hell. When the lights went out and the men cheered, Dougal had proudly announced he had a generator and told them not to worry—which made them boo. A minute later the lights had clicked back on and they got to watch as the Magic Mike wannabes started gyrating on Betty for the fourth time.

"Please, God, make it end!" Mitch shouted at the ceiling.

"Don't stop," Betty told the strippers. "If the power goes out again, I'll hum a tune, and you boys carry on. If it gets too dark, I'll feel my way."

"I'm going to be sick," Matt announced.

"Did you eat the prawns?" Josh asked.

"No, I watched Betty get a lap dance."

"Oh yeah, that."

"Don't worry, boys," Dougal boomed to a room full of men who were far from worried. "I have a backup generator. If this one fails, the backup will kick in. Nothing will stop this party."

"I'm totally okay with something stopping this party,"

Josh told the owner of the pub, who thought he was joking and laughed. Josh turned a miserable face to Mitch. "Do you think the women are okay? We don't have a generator at the castle."

"Yeah," Mitch said. "You have about a million candles in every room and the heating is gas. The women will be fine. They'll love the drama."

"I hope so," Josh said.

"Magenta's there," Harry told Josh. "She's a caving expert; she's used to the dark. She'll look out for them."

As one, the men turned to stare at Harry.

"What?" he said. "I was helping. I'm reassuring the guy. Magenta's got this. She likes the dark. Nobody needs to worry."

"She likes the dark because she's a freaking vampire," Flynn muttered.

"I'm telling her you said that. She is so going to kick your backside again." Harry seemed pleased at the thought.

Callum leaned towards Lake. "I think I'm going to pass on the partnership offer." He looked around the room, and if Lake hadn't known the guy so well he wouldn't have spotted the signs that he felt out of his depth. "I'm not cut out for this."

Lake cocked an eyebrow at him. If he had something else to say he'd better spit it out. Lake wasn't going to make it easy for him. Callum rubbed the scar on his chin. Lake remembered the exact moment he'd gotten it. A stray piece of shrapnel on a shitty job in Iraq. The operation had been a total screw-up from beginning to end, and they'd been lucky to get out with their lives.

"I don't do social," Callum said at last.

"No. You don't. You're a miserable, antisocial son of a bitch."

Callum frowned at him. "Last time I checked, so were you."

"I got over the fear. Found out socialising wouldn't kill me after all."

"Are you saying I'm a coward?"

Lake cocked an eyebrow at him. *If the shoe fits...*

Callum's jaw clenched briefly. "This isn't socialising. This isn't normal. Everybody's talking about their feelings and shit. The singer guy can't shut up about his wife. And he says you're part of a club that eats together once a week. Like you do this kind of crap regularly. Does that sound normal to you?" He shuddered. It was slight, but Lake noticed. "I don't know what's going on here. Maybe you sit around painting each other's nails when you're bored, but all this touchy-feely crap makes me want to vomit."

"Don't hold back, Callum, tell me how you really feel."

"I don't think I can work with your boy, Harry, either." His shoulders were still tense, as though it was physically impossible for the man to relax. And it probably was. They'd both spent a huge chunk of their lives on constant alert. It was a hard habit to break.

"Harry's the best in the business. He has governments crawling all over themselves to get him to work for them."

"He's wearing a Doctor Who T-shirt."

Lake's lips twitched. "His dress sense has nothing to do with his ability."

"He called me dude. Twice."

Lake couldn't help the grin that broke out. The startled expression on Callum's face made him smile even wider. Yeah, he smiled now. A lot. Well, a lot for him. It shocked the life out of anybody he'd known before he'd moved to the Highlands. Life in Invertary had changed him. Kirsty had changed him. In fact, some might even go so far as to say he'd mellowed.

"You won't be working with Harry," Lake reminded his friend. "You'll be heading up the London end of the business. You get to work with Harry's operations manager instead."

Yeah, and Lake would *love* to be a fly on the wall for that encounter.

Callum must have seen something in Lake's expression, because he became instantly suspicious. "What's wrong with the guy?"

"Nothing. *She's* called Rachel. Harry and her had a falling out a couple of years ago and he's only recently started talking to her directly. He used to communicate solely by email, Instant Message or through his wife, Magenta."

Callum rubbed his leg, once, caught himself doing it and folded his arms. Lake hadn't been there when Callum lost both legs—he'd already retired from the SAS by then—but he knew all about the car bomb that ended his friend's career.

"He was in a huff with his manager?" He let out a sigh. "How old is he again? Twelve?"

"Look." Lake leaned forward, put his forearms on the table in front of him and stared at Callum. "I'm not going to bullshit you. Benson Security doesn't do things the way we did in the service. We aren't staffed solely by military personnel. But each and every person who works with me is skilled and experienced. You won't find a better team anywhere. My team is the main reason I have to expand business or start turning people away. When someone hires Benson Security, they know they're getting the best. But I can't carry on unless I have someone I trust heading up the other office. I need someone who thinks the same way I do. That's you, Callum." He looked over at Harry, who was busy arguing the merits of *Babylon Five* over *Star Trek: The Next Generation* with his very bored older brother, Flynn. "You can put up with some eccentric behaviour. If you couldn't, I wouldn't have called you."

"I don't know." Callum wavered, running a hand over his sandy brown hair, which was still military short, even though he'd been over a year out of the service. "I can't do this social shit. It's taking all of my self-control to sit here right now. I'm torn between running or punching someone. It's taking a lot of energy to do neither."

"You don't have to do this social shit. You'll be in London. Far, far away from Josh and his breakfast club. All you need to do is turn up at the office, run the team, then go home to stare at your four blank walls until the next morning."

"I've never been any good at office stuff. I like to be out getting the job done, not telling someone else to do it."

Lake didn't point out that with two prosthetic legs, Callum's only real option was to be an office guy. His days of running the enemy down were over. Physically, anyway. That didn't mean he couldn't oversee a team. Or put his contacts and years of expertise to good use.

"You can manage a team. You did it for years. Julia will do the office admin stuff. She's a good assistant. She's only been with me a few months, but she's on top of the business. She'll steer you right."

"Julia?" Callum was obviously searching his memory. "Have I met her?"

Crap, that wasn't a question Lake wanted to answer, but the man deserved the truth. "No, you haven't met her. She's shy." *Terrified.* "Timid." *Borderline agoraphobic.* "Doesn't cope well with new people or forceful personalities." *Or any people. At all. Ever.*

Callum stared at Lake long enough for him to wonder if the man was going to get up and hike through the snow to get away from Invertary.

"You want this Julia to set up an office full of ex-military men. You want her to assist me. Are you insane? Our guys only come in one type—forceful and overwhelming. How exactly is she supposed to help me if she can't talk to the staff?"

That won't be a problem because she will never see them. She'll hide as soon as they set foot in the office. Lake thought it wise to keep that information to himself.

"She's an organisational genius. She's fantastic with computer systems. Amazing at project management and scheduling. She writes great emails and she can talk on the phone—mostly." *If pushed.*

"And she's scared of her own shadow?"

"Yeah." Lake grinned.

Callum shook his head. "Do you even realise how crazy this is? You want me to set up an operation with Julia the mouse and Rachel the bulldog."

"Look on the bright side. At least you won't have to be sociable. Rachel won't stand for it, and Julia will just hide if you invite her to anything."

Callum stared at him. He wasn't what you would call a silver lining type of guy.

"Okay," Lake said. "How about this? You'll make money and get to shoot things if the occasion arises. Plus, you're the boss. What you say goes. If you don't like working with Julia and Rachel, replace them. Only make sure you send Julia back here. I don't care that she occasionally hides in cupboards, she's indispensable." He leaned back in his chair and smiled at his friend. "So, what do you say, Callum; ready to get back into the game?"

Callum cursed. Lake reached for his beer, unwilling to acknowledge that he was anxious about his friend's decision. If he couldn't get Callum on board he'd be back to square one with the business expansion, and he couldn't do that. He'd barely had time to sleep these past few months. He needed this partnership just as much as Callum did—although Callum didn't know that yet. Being alone, staring at walls wasn't good for the man. He needed people around him. He needed a challenge. And Lake was handing him one on a silver platter.

Callum looked around the room as the muscle on his jaw flexed. At last he faced Lake.

"The crazy old woman stays here with you, right?"

"Absolutely." He held his breath and waited.

"I am going to regret this," Callum said.

Lake grinned widely. "Welcome aboard." He held out his hand for his new partner to shake.

From the other side of the room, Harry spotted the exchange and gave him a thumbs-up.

Callum saw the gesture and groaned. Lake just chuckled as he drank the rest of his beer.

* JOE *

"Is anybody there? It's Rainne here."

The women in the master bedroom screamed en masse when a voice boomed out from the wall. Joe swung in the direction of the voice. Gun out.

For a second nobody moved.

"This is Rainne. We're in the guardhouse. Can anybody hear me?"

"Caroline?" Joe barked.

"The intercom!" Caroline rushed for the old unit on the wall beside the bed. She flicked a switch. "We're here. This is Caroline."

"Thank goodness." Lake's sister sounded slightly tinny, and tight with emotion. "Is everyone okay? There was a guy out here with a gun. He shot at Alastair's truck."

"We're okay. We're holed up in the tower bedroom," Caroline said. "Are you okay?"

"Yeah, we're—"

Joe reached past Caroline and flicked the switch.

"Can they hear this conversation in the rest of the house?"

The last thing he wanted was to broadcast their situation to the enemy.

Caroline shook her head. "Not now that I've answered. Now it's just between here and the guardhouse."

Joe relaxed slightly. "Okay." He switched the intercom back on.

Kirsty pushed her way to Caroline. The redhead had circles under her green eyes that testified to weeks of sleeping badly. Tension radiated from her, and Joe suspected it wasn't only due to the situation and her ruined wedding.

"Ask her if they're injured," Kirsty said.

"I can hear you, Kirsty," Rainne said. "The truck rolled off the road. I'm okay, a few bruises, but Alastair is pretty banged up. He hurt his head. His wrist is swollen. I don't know if it's a sprain or something worse. His ribs are bruised too. He says they aren't cracked or broken, but I'm not so sure." Her voice was shaky. "He went to sleep a few minutes ago and hasn't stirred. I don't know what to do. What if he has a concussion? Should I try to make him wake up?"

"How's his breathing, Rainne? This is Joe." Joe stepped up beside them. He wasn't sure how good the mic was on the old system.

"Steady, I think."

"Is it raspy, slower than normal?"

"No."

"Okay. What about nausea? Vomiting? Is his speech slurred?"

"No nausea or vomiting. He slurred his speech a little when he first woke up, but it's been normal since then."

"Okay, that's all good. I think he's going to be fine, Rainne. Try not to worry. It doesn't sound like his lungs are impaired. Let him rest. It's probably just the warmth from the fire and the shock of his injuries that have wiped him out."

"Aren't you supposed to keep someone awake when they have a concussion?"

"Not anymore, honey. That's old advice. Now doctors say if there aren't any other symptoms, let them sleep. His brain needs time to heal. Along with the rest of him."

"Is it okay if I wake him later just to make sure he's okay?"

"Yeah." Joe smiled. He liked Lake's baby sister. The few times he'd checked up on her in Glasgow for Lake, he'd enjoyed their conversations. Although he could use fewer lectures on why his car was killing the planet. "When Alastair wakes again, don't let him move around too much—keep him as still as possible until someone gets to him. Otherwise he could make his injuries worse."

"How am I supposed to stop him moving around? I can't get him to do anything." The exasperation was loud and clear.

"Sit on him if you have to—but not on his chest. If those ribs snap they could puncture a lung. If he has a mild concussion, a hit to the head could turn it into something serious. Don't give him any aspirin or ibuprofen, they'll exasperate any bleeding he has."

"What about paracetamol?"

"That's fine, honey," Joe said.

"What about the guy with the gun? I can't get in contact with anyone but you lot. The phones are out. Do you want me to go outside? I can find out what's going on and give you an update."

"No!" everyone in the room shouted.

Joe held up a hand to silence everyone and barked at the intercom, "Do not go outside the guardhouse. Barricade the door and stay inside. Take care of Alastair. We'll deal with everything else. Claire has gone to town to get help. This will be over soon."

"But—" Rainne said.

"No buts, sweetie." Kirsty had gone as white as the snow outside at the thought of Rainne playing spy. "You have your hands full with Alastair. There are a lot of us here. We'll be fine."

"Okay." Rainne sounded resigned. "But if I spot anything from here, I'll intercom you and let you know."

"That's a good plan." Kirsty breathed a sigh of relief. "That would help. Just don't attract attention to yourself."

There was a pause. "I'm scared," Rainne whispered.

The looks the women shared said they understood totally.

"We all are," Kirsty told her. "Lake will be here soon, you'll see. We'll check in later and let you know what's happening. If anything changes, call us."

"I will." Then there was silence.

Kirsty stared at the silent intercom as Caroline wrapped an arm around her shoulders.

"She's going to be okay," Caroline said.

The two women headed back to the sofa where they'd been sitting. Joe looked around the rest of the women. He didn't like this situation one bit. Caroline and Kirsty were holding it together, but he didn't know for how long. Jena didn't seem to be worried, but he suspected she was pretending so as not to freak Abby out, which Joe appreciated—the last thing they needed was a freaked-out heavily pregnant woman. Meanwhile, the women of Knit Or Die were in proactive mode, dealing with the stress by trying to keep busy and feign control. Magenta was less sarcastic than usual. Julia was hiding in the bathroom. And Megan…

He looked over to the bed where Megan was questioning their captive, who was more relaxed and amused than threatened. Megan was in her element. Joe suspected that in her head she'd cast herself as Lara Croft in a big-budget action movie. There was no way she'd get any information out of the guy she'd captured. But if it kept her occupied and out of trouble, he was happy to let her try. And if that guy was French, Joe was a freaking Martian.

Jena had found a bag of cookies from somewhere and was dishing them out to the group when Joe held up his hand for silence. He was surprised when he got some. Maybe they could be trained after all.

"We need to barricade the door," Joe said to Ryan. "Help me pile furniture up against it."

"Not yet." Kirsty's mum pushed through the room holding two bottles of olive oil. "I need to deal with the stairs."

Before Joe could stop her, she was out the door pouring oil over the wooden stairs and floor. Then she shut the kiddy gate at the top of the stairs for good measure.

Kirsty watched her mother. "I don't think that gate will stop them getting past, Mum."

"Every little bit helps," Margaret said as she came back in the room. She faced the women of Knit Or Die. "Barricade the door, girls."

The retired women rushed to move furniture against the door. And Joe got the sense he'd lost control of the group.

"Aren't you going to complain about the oil on the floor?" Kirsty asked Caroline.

"Oil is good for wood," Caroline said. "I just hope the rest of the castle doesn't get damaged." She tugged Joe's sleeve to make him look at her. "You don't think they'll shoot my castle, or break anything, do you?"

Kirsty was shaking her head and waving her arms behind Caroline. Joe got the less-than-subtle message.

"I'm sure they'll respect this lovely historical building," he said.

Caroline smiled and everyone else sighed with relief.

"I like zis. It is like, how you say, a sleeping party, *non?*"

the prisoner called from the bed. "I have ze cookie, *s'il vous plait?*"

Shona looked at Megan to see if the prisoner was allowed a cookie. Megan frowned at her. "No, we're not giving him a cookie."

"We're not doing anything else with him either," Shona said. "So far you've just asked him questions and he's laughed. Or flirted. You need to up the torture. You need to inflict pain."

"I know," Megan wailed. "But this isn't as easy as I thought it would be."

"Twist his nipples. That's sore," Shona suggested. The prisoner looked like he might laugh again.

Megan glared at him, reached to the floor to nab a kitchen knife, then sliced his black shirt wide open. It hung to the sides of his chest, lying flat against his open suede jacket.

"Oh my," Shona said. "It's been a long time since I've seen a six-pack. Can I touch it?"

"No!" Megan leaned over, pinched a nipple and twisted.

The guy chuckled.

"Anyone else find this deeply disturbing?" Ryan asked. "I feel like I'm watching a really bad porn movie."

"Try candle wax," Shona said. "I bet if you pour it on his privates that will make him talk."

"This is painful to watch. I can't take any more," Ryan said. "Step aside, ladies."

He stalked across the room and punched the guy on the jaw. The prisoner's head came back around slowly as he licked blood from the corner of his mouth.

"You'll regret that," he told Ryan.

Megan shot to her feet. "Where did the French accent go? You're not French at all, are you?"

The guy gave her a sexy smile. "I can be anything you want me to be, baby."

Shona reached over and slapped him.

"Shona!" Megan shouted.

"What?" Shona said. "We're allowed to hit him now. Ryan did it."

"Tell us what you know," Ryan barked at the guy.

Joe shook his head. This approach wasn't going to work either.

"I don't think so," the guy said. "I think I'm just going to lie here and enjoy the fun."

"Bastard," Ryan said as he lifted his fist.

"No more hitting." Megan stepped between Ryan and the guy. "There has to be another way."

"Go ahead. Tickle the answers out of him. I'll be here when you give up." Ryan sauntered back to Joe.

"Feel better now?" Joe asked him.

"Being stuck in here is driving me nuts," Ryan said.

"Join the club." Joe watched as Megan ruined her tough-guy act.

"Are you okay?" she asked her captive.

"No," he said. "Want to kiss it better?"

Megan growled and turned her back on him.

Joe went back to looking out the window. The faint silhouettes of figures standing outside the castle hadn't moved since they'd come up to the tower.

"Why aren't they moving in?" Joe muttered.

"Maybe they're waiting for something," Ryan said.

Joe tensed. Of course.

"Waiting for what?" Kirsty said.

Joe looked over at her, his lips tight. "More men with transport out of here."

He watched as the blood drained from her face.

CHAPTER 13

* RAINNE AND ALASTAIR *

Rainne watched Alastair sleep as she paced the tiny room. Eight steps across. Ten if you included the minuscule bathroom, which she didn't. The gas fire had warmed the place to the point where she was glad she was in her underwear, although she didn't dare turn down the heat in case Alastair needed it.

She checked the clock on her phone for the hundredth time. Twenty-three minutes. He'd been asleep twenty-three minutes. She promised herself she'd wake him at the hour mark if he didn't stir before then. She couldn't leave him longer than that, not while she worried he would never wake up again.

She stopped dead in the middle of the room. What would she do if he didn't wake up? How would she get help? Everyone she knew was trapped either in the castle or in town. Even if she had a vehicle, she wouldn't be able to get it through the snow. And she couldn't leave Alastair alone long enough to fetch help. She wasn't even sure she'd *find* town in this weather. Her sense of direction was terrible in daylight with clear skies overhead. She didn't have a hope in hell when it was dark and thick with snow.

This was bad. It was very, very bad. Nothing in her life had prepared her for this. She knew how to organise a protest march, how to raise hens from eggs, how to buy environmentally sound clothing and, thanks to her recent studies, the basics of running a business. She didn't have survival skills. Apart from listening to Lake, what little knowledge she did have came from watching Bear Grylls on TV. Now that she thought about it, the skills he shared wouldn't be any use to her. There would *never* be an occasion where she'd need to filter her own urine through a sock to make it drinkable. She'd rather die of thirst before she got to that stage.

She bent over, put her hands on her knees and took steady breaths. She'd figure something out. She was capable. She was able. She'd come up with a plan if she had to. Right?

"You're stressing me out with all that worrying you're doing."

Rainne shrieked. She rushed to Alastair's side. He hadn't moved an inch, but his eyes were open a crack, watching her. She reached for him, caressing his face. Feeling for herself that he was warm and very much alive.

"You almost gave me a heart attack. I thought you were unconscious," she whispered. "I thought I'd have to get you some professional help."

He stared at her for a moment, the air charged between them.

"What kind of professional help?" he whispered back.

She cracked a smile. "That's the part where I got stuck. It's a long walk to the only doctor in town and I couldn't leave you alone while I did it."

"Did you have a plan B?"

"I was working on it. It might have involved making a

sledge from an upturned desk and sliding you through the snow."

His eyes twinkled in the firelight. "It's almost a shame I woke up and missed out on the ride."

Rainne smacked her hand on his stomach, letting it linger. "Don't joke. I was really worried."

"Just a wee nap." Alastair shifted out from under the intimacy of her touch, reminding her they weren't lovers. Or friends. Or anything at all to each other. He looked away and spoke to the darkness. "My head is splitting."

Rainne swallowed the rejection—after all, she was the one who'd rejected him first. And hers had been much worse. "I'm not allowed to give you aspirin. If your brain is bleeding, it will make it worse."

"My brain isn't bleeding." He lifted his right arm, forgetting it was injured, and winced. He studied the tight bandage she'd wound around his wrist while he'd been asleep.

"I really was out cold, huh?" Alastair's eyes snapped to hers. "Wait a minute. What to do you mean you're not allowed?"

"I spoke to Joe Barone; he works for Lake—"

"I know who Joe is. How did you speak to him? Are the phones back on?" He looked around the room as he spoke. "Still no power."

Rainne pointed at the wall. "The intercom works. We can talk to the castle."

"You might have mentioned that first."

"We've been talking one whole minute, Alastair. It isn't like I waited hours."

He shot her a look that said he thought otherwise. "What did he tell you?"

"Not to give you aspirin and not to let you move around too much in case you make your ribs worse. He said you could puncture a lung."

He stared at her for a second. "Not about my injuries. About the guy with the gun?"

"Oh." Her cheeks burned. "Of course. There's more than one of them. Joe doesn't know what they want. They haven't gone inside the castle. They seem to be waiting for something. Claire has gone into town to get help."

Alastair struggled to his feet. He still wasn't as steady as she would have liked. Rainne went to fetch him a can of Coke from the lockers while he checked to see if his jeans were dry. He turned them, as she'd been doing every few minutes, to make sure they dried evenly. Rainne tried not to look at him standing there in his underwear. But it was a small room and there wasn't anywhere else to look.

"You've changed," she blurted, then felt her cheeks burn.

"People do."

"You're bigger." Why, oh why, wouldn't her mouth stay shut? "Your shoulders." She pointed just in case he didn't know where he kept them. "Broader. You have more muscle, your body is wider and those weren't there the last time I saw you..." She trailed off before she said the word "naked."

Alastair looked down at the defined ab muscles she'd pointed to. He seemed at a loss as to what to say, which was new.

"Here." Rainne thrust the can at him. "The fluid and sugar will help."

Alastair took the can without comment, popped the top and drank until it was empty. "Got any more in there?"

Rainne fetched him another. She felt self-conscious and awkward as she wondered if she should mention the kiss. In the scheme of things, with everything they had to deal with, thinking about a kiss was really pretty stupid. Yeah. Maybe she'd keep her mouth shut. But the heavy silence was driving her crazy. She had to talk about something. Anything.

"So," she said. "How's your dad?"

Alastair stopped drinking to look at her. He wiped his mouth with the back of his hand. "We're doing small talk now?"

"It's just us, Alastair. Unless you want to sit in silence, then yeah, we're doing small talk."

"Okay." He stared at her long enough to make her think he was going to take the silence option. "My dad is fine."

Great. And there ended that conversation starter.

"And the business?" This was painful. She should just shut up and stare at the wall. But then she'd spend her time worrying about the guys outside and the danger everyone was in. Or if Alastair was going to keel over without medical attention. No. She needed to talk.

"The business is fine." He pointed to the window with the can. "Not really the weather for fishing."

She swallowed hard. It had only just occurred to her to ask about a girlfriend. What if he was in a relationship? She should have thought of that possibility before she turned up on his doorstep and declared her love. The thought was mortifying.

"Spit it out," Alastair said. "Whatever it is you want to ask that's giving you a constipated look."

She focused on the fire and felt her cheeks burn. "Seeing anyone?" she said as casually as she could manage.

"No," was the barked reply.

Relief almost swamped her. She scrambled around for something else to discuss.

"What about…"

"Enough," Alastair said. "I'm done talking."

Rainne let out a heavy breath. "Help me out here, will you? If you don't talk to me I'm going to drive us both crazy worrying about this whole situation. Distract me. Please. Talk about anything. Tell me about fishing. Or your dad. Or the shop. Or the football games you watch. Anything. I'll listen to anything."

He took a step towards her and suddenly the room seemed far too small for both of them. "You want me to talk, Rainne? You sure about that? You want me to chat with you like things aren't heavy between us? You want me to talk to you the way you wouldn't talk to me three years ago? Every time I look at you, I remember how it felt when you shut the door in my face." His face was stone. All emotion gone. No, that wasn't entirely right. There was anger. "What a fool I was. Running after you to Glasgow, hoping to convince you to come back. And you couldn't even bring yourself to talk to me. You would have thought I'd learned my lesson when I was a kid—women always leave. You can't trust them. My da learned that the hard way when my mum walked out on us when I was nine. And you reinforced the lesson when you tucked tail and ran three years ago. So you'll forgive me if I don't want to chat. The time for talking has passed."

He pushed past her and slammed into the tiny bathroom, snapping the door closed behind him. Rainne stared after him, shock flooding her body. She'd known his parents were divorced. He'd never mentioned his mother, and now she knew why. This situation between them was so much worse than she could have imagined. The damage she'd done to Alastair by leaving was huge. She'd abandoned a guy with abandonment issues.

The bathroom door opened. Alastair stalked out. He didn't look at her.

"I'm sorry," Rainne said.

He stared at the glow of the firelight. Rainne cautiously closed the distance between them. Her fingers itched with the need to touch him. To comfort him. But she didn't.

"I'm sorry," she said again. "I didn't know."

He turned his head slightly to look at her. "You never asked."

The words were a blow. The memory of their time together played out in fast forward in her head. They'd only had a few months together before she'd left, and they'd spent it dealing with her problems. He'd listened to her worries. He'd comforted her when she was upset about her family. He'd been there for her. And she couldn't remember ever asking about him. Not in any way that mattered. It had been all about her. She hung her head in shame.

"I was so selfish. All about me. My problems. My emotions." She barked a mirthless laugh as she took a step towards him, her heart heavy with the realisation of exactly how awful she'd been. She tentatively reached out to touch his arm. "I am so sorry, Alastair. For all of it. For being self-centred. For only caring about me. For not trusting that you knew your own mind. For not believing you when asked me to stay. For running away. I'm sorry."

She hung her head for a second. There was nothing else to say. She withdrew her hand from him, wrapped her arms around herself and turned away. They stood like that for an eternity. Alone, together in the same small space. Alastair staring into the fire. Rainne staring into the darkness. Rainne wanted nothing more than to be somewhere else. She was making everything worse just by being near him.

Not once when thinking about coming back to talk to Alastair had she considered the effect it might have on him. The memories she might bring up. The pain she might cause. She hadn't changed at all. She was still the self-obsessed girl who'd left years ago. The one who only cared about finding herself. The one who only cared about herself full stop. She wiped a tear from her eye. She didn't deserve to cry. Not when she was the one who caused the mess she'd ended up in.

"I thought it was my fault." Alastair's voice was low, as though he was thinking out loud.

Rainne turned towards him and saw he was still staring into the orange flames. She waited.

"I was a lot of trouble as a kid. Too loud. Too needy. I was always getting into scrapes. And I didn't sleep much. She was always telling me I needed to stay in bed and sleep, that she needed the peace. I didn't get it. I just wanted to be around her. She said I was too clingy. Always wanting attention." He paused, and Rainne's heart broke for the little boy who'd been abandoned by the mother he loved so desperately. She wiped another silent tear from her cheek, but didn't move and didn't make a sound. She didn't want to break the moment.

"I heard them arguing the morning she left." He folded his arms, his head bowed. "She said she'd never wanted to be a mother. She told him she'd never have married him if she hadn't been pregnant with me. We were holding her back. She'd planned a grand future and it wasn't going to happen in Invertary. Not with a needy wee boy clinging to her all the time and a husband who worked all hours. She packed her things and left. I never saw her again. We don't even know where she went. London, I think. Maybe."

Rainne waited. The silence a blanket around them.

"Da went into the sitting room and shut the door once she'd gone. I snuck past him and ran down the street after her. She was wearing her pink dress, the one she'd spent a week's shopping money on and made Da angry. I grabbed her round the hips and looked up at her. I can still see her face. Her lips were bright pink and her hair was white blonde. Bottle blonde, they call it. I begged her not to leave." He lifted his head and looked at her. "You know what her last words to me were?"

Rainne shook her head as the tears fell down her cheeks unchecked.

"They were: Go away, Alastair, and stop annoying me for once."

"Oh, Alastair," Rainne whispered.

"I never figured it out," he said, sounding genuinely confused.

She was terrified to ask, but the words tumbled out anyway. "Figured what out?"

She waited for the pain his answer would bring. Pain for the small boy who was unwanted. For the man who'd been rejected.

"How much you need to love someone before they stay."

Her heart crumpled. There were no words. And although Rainne knew she'd be unwanted and most likely rebuffed, she closed the distance between them and wrapped her arms around him. She held him tight. Pressing her cheek to his chest. Listening to that strong heart of his that loved so deeply and hurt so badly.

"I'm so sorry. I'm so sorry," she whispered.

She was sorry for her part in his pain. Sorry for the boy who'd been rejected. Sorry for the man who ached. There were no other words.

Slowly, she felt his arms wrap around her and he tugged her close. The warmth of his body engulfed her. She was wrapped in his scent and strength, once again taking from him when she was trying to give. Rainne sobbed against his chest. Wishing with all her heart that she could heal him. Wishing she could go back in time and protect the child. Wishing she could go back and change the day she ran.

Wishing she'd stayed.

CHAPTER 14

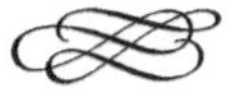

* RAINNE AND ALASTAIR *

Alastair couldn't do this. It was too much. A few hours alone with Rainne and he was kissing and holding her. Hell, he was spilling his guts to her. It wasn't right. He didn't want this.

He didn't want her.

His stomach clenched at the thought. But it was true. It had to be true. Only an idiot would let someone into their life so they could trample all over them again. And he wasn't an idiot. He'd learned his lesson three years ago. There was no point letting anyone close, because they always ended up leaving. He wasn't meant to be close to someone. He wasn't meant to be a part of a family. There was just him and his da, and that was the way it would stay.

It took great effort to step away from Rainne, but he did.

She looked up at him with tear-reddened eyes and his stomach lurched.

"We need to see if those clothes are dry." He turned his back on her and checked his jeans. Still damp, but wearable. Which was good, because he felt far too exposed being near-naked around Rainne. "We're good. Let's get dressed."

It was a subdued Rainne who took her clothes and went into the bathroom to get dressed. Alastair tugged on his jeans and hoped she didn't want to talk when she came back out. He was well and truly done with the talking part of their evening. In fact, if he never had to talk about his past or his feelings again, that would be great. Why he'd told her that stuff, he didn't know. It wasn't like he thought about his mother all the time. He'd dealt with it. He was over it. It was in the past. Where it belonged.

Like Rainne.

She needed to stay in the past. This time with her was muddying things in his head. He scrunched his eyes shut. He should never have kissed her. It must have been the pain. His head, ribs and wrist had ached, and it had been warm by the fire. Then she was touching him and her fragrance was everywhere. It was too hard not to taste her.

But he wouldn't do it again.

Once, because he'd been delirious with pain. That was it.

He looked at the door to the bathroom as it opened.

Aye. Once was enough. For old times' sake. To say a final goodbye. That's all it was. And he didn't need to do it again. His eyes lingered on her lips. Only the once…

"Okay, I'm dressed," Rainne said with that fake cheer she'd always used when she felt out of her depth.

"Good." He hoped that was all she had to say.

"How are your injuries?"

"Fine."

"Need more painkillers?"

"No." Yeah, this was going great. Nothing awkward about this conversation. "Look, we don't need to talk. I'm okay with silence."

She blinked those pale blue eyes of hers, and he noticed she'd tied her hair up in a messy bun with an elastic band.

Although it was strange to see her without the dyed rainbow mass that used to frame her face, he had to admit the soft brown colour made her eyes more luminous.

He watched those expressive eyes signal that something crazy was going on in her fluffy little mind. As long as it stayed in her head and didn't escape out of her mouth, he was fine with her thinking whatever she liked.

"I wish I hadn't been like your mother," she blurted. "I wish I could prove to you that I'm not a selfish witch, but the fact I'm even worried about this means I'm selfish."

What?

Alastair took a step back, dazed by the blow of her words.

"You're nothing like my mum."

"I left you. I rejected your love. I only cared about me. I never even asked you about her in all the times we were together."

"Bloody hell." He pinched the bridge of his nose and then glanced at the door. Was it too late to make a run for it? No, he couldn't leave her alone. She was too vulnerable if those guys came back. "Do we need to talk about stuff? I'm okay not talking."

"No, we don't need to talk." She held up her hands. "No. I'm sorry. It's okay. Really. You've been through enough and you've made your position clear. Okay, so the kiss was confusing, but you probably have concussion and can't think straight. I'm just doing what I normally do and thinking about myself."

Alastair let out a sigh. Aye. They needed to talk. There was no getting around it. Why did women always have to hash everything out? It was unnatural.

"You're nothing like my mum," he said again, hoping it would sink in this time.

She didn't seem to be listening. She'd shrunk in on herself

the way she used to do. Alastair stepped up to her and put a hand on each of her shoulders to make her look up at him.

"There's nothing selfish about you. You just get confused sometimes and make stupid decisions."

She scoffed. "Yeah. Right."

"Rainbow, when I first met you, you'd only just plucked up the guts to ask Lake to help you buy Betty's underwear shop. You were terrified of doing something on your own for the first time in your life—and you were twenty-six. You were worried about your parents and how they would cope without you. You felt guilty that you weren't there to run after them, because that's what you'd always done. I watched you do the same here. Anyone who asked got help, until it reached the point where you didn't have time to run your own business."

She shook her head. "I wasn't helping people. I was letting them walk over me."

"You were helping. When Caroline needed a volunteer at the library, you were first in line. When the church needed someone to take lunch to the shut-ins, you stepped up. When Betty was sick, you took her soup and made sure she got her medication—and nobody in town wanted to do that job." He stepped into her space. "Before Invertary you helped your parents, you ran your brothers' political protests, you put yourself out for anyone and everyone at the commune who needed something. Coming to Invertary was the first independent thing you ever did. It wasn't selfish. It was you trying to find your way."

"No." She wiped her cheek as a tear escaped. "I never asked you about your life. I was always talking about me."

"Because there was a lot going on with you at the time." He smiled at her as he wiped her cheek. "You need to cut yourself some slack. If you'd been here longer you would have known everything."

"I was here long enough," she scoffed.

"No, you weren't. I get that now. We really didn't have enough time to get to know all the little details about each other's lives."

"Yeah, like the fact your mum ran out on you. Maybe if I'd known that, I would have thought twice about doing the exact same thing."

"She ran because she didn't want us and because she only cared about herself. You ran because you were upset and confused. You were insecure and didn't trust the people around you. The people who said they loved you. You didn't leave because you didn't care. You left because you cared too much. You're nothing like my mum, Rainbow. Trust me, it's totally different."

Alastair felt as though he'd been knocked over the head as the words came out of his mouth. *It was different.* She hadn't been rejecting him when she'd left. She'd been scared, hurt, reeling from her family's betrayal. It wasn't like his mum at all.

Had he thought it was the same? The answer was a neon sign flashing above her head—aye, he had.

"No—" Rainne opened her mouth to argue.

Lights shone through the cracks at the sides of the blinds, startling them and cutting off her words.

"Get down." Alastair threw his good arm around her body and pushed her to the floor. "Under the desk." He quickly shut off the flashlight and the fire, before joining Rainne.

The room was suddenly pitch black. And then another beam of bright white seeped through the cracks. An engine. Two. Heavier than a normal car, they roared past.

"Snowmobiles," Alastair said softly when Rainne gave him a questioning look.

Her eyes went wide. Two sets of lights, two engines, passed the guardhouse on the way to the castle.

"They aren't coming in here," Rainne said with relief.

"No, but the castle's in trouble." He grabbed her hand and pulled her out from under the desk. "Show me how to work that intercom."

CHAPTER 15

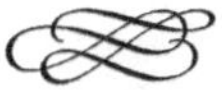

* LAKE *

"I can't take any more," Flynn complained. "Make it stop."

The men were staring in shock as Betty gyrated against a male stripper. She'd sat him on a wooden chair, announced she'd always wanted to give a lap dance then complained when everyone shouted that she wasn't allowed to take her clothes off. Instead she'd settled for being fully dressed in her usual tartan tent and dry-humping the poor guy's leg.

"I didn't even know if was possible for someone that old to move like that," Matt said in a disgusted kind of awe.

"Can we go be with the women now?" Josh whined.

Grunt pointed at Josh. "What he said."

Lake looked around the room. His friends ranged from bored to dazed. Yeah, it wasn't the best stag night he'd ever attended.

"What about Dougal's food?" Harry asked, halfway through a bowl of chips.

"Take it. I'll even pack it up for you." Dougal pointed at Betty. "Anything to get rid of her." He gave Lake a look of utter disgust. "I need to bleach everything they touched."

"In that case," Lake said as his friends hung on his every

word, making them seem even more pathetic, "I don't see why n—"

The door to the pub crashed open and one of the twins fell in, coming to a halt on top of a table. She bent over it shivering and gasping for breath.

"Baby!" Grunt ran to the woman, who had to be Claire, although Lake had no idea how the man could tell them apart. He scooped her up, his arm under her knees, and barged his way to the fireplace. "What are you thinking coming out here in this weather?"

The music stopped. Lake strode over to stand beside the couple as Grunt laid her on the floor in front of the fire. He peeled off her layers as her blue lips shook.

"Dougal?" Lake looked over at the man.

"I'm on it. Hot drink and warm clothes coming right up."

Lake nodded his appreciation. In the three years he'd been in town, he'd come to believe that Dougal could read minds.

"I…I…" Claire's teeth chattered as her eyes pleaded with her husband.

"Don't talk, baby. We need to get you warmed up." He ran a hand down her jean-clad legs. "You're soaked through."

A thick white terry-cloth robe materialised through the crowd.

"Turn round." Grunt ordered, and as one everybody, except Betty, faced away.

Fortunately, Betty was at the back of the crowd. "I can't see," she complained.

"Tough," Matt said, then grunted. Presumably because she'd kicked him. Betty was quick to dispense justice with her heavy-soled shoes.

"Cut it out," Matt said.

"Or what?" she said. "You'll arrest me?"

"Aye, I'll arrest you. If anyone could do with a night in the cells, it's you."

"If you arrest the strippers as well, I'll go quietly. Can you put us in the same cell? Can they stay cuffed?"

"Somebody please gag the woman," Mitch said.

"You can turn back now," Grunt said.

When they did, Claire was wrapped in the oversized robe and snuggled on Grunt's lap as he sat with his legs stretched out in front of him on the floor. There was some colour in her cheeks, but she still shivered. Grunt rubbed her hands and whispered to her as Lake felt the hair on his neck stand on end. The Donaldson twins were wild, but they weren't rash. They wouldn't walk through this weather if they didn't have a damn good reason.

"What happened?" Matt crouched in front of the pair, every muscle in his body on alert. It was clear he itched to take his younger sister from her husband and care for Claire himself. "Is Megan still at the castle?"

"Here." Dougal pushed through the sombre men. "This will help." He handed a large, steaming mug of hot chocolate to Grunt.

"Sip, baby." He held the mug to Claire's lips.

She sipped as they waited. Every second felt like a lifetime.

"They need you," Claire said between sips.

"Who?" Grunt said.

"Is it Megan?" Matt said. "Jena?" Lake put a hand on his friend's shoulder as he said his wife's name.

They all had the same fear. It was dark, the snow was thick and their women were cut off at the castle.

Claire looked up at her brother, then at Lake. His heart stopped beating. His breath froze.

"There are men at the castle. Megan and I were sent to get

you. We knocked out one of the guys, took his gun and dragged him back into the castle for questioning."

There was a collective intake of air.

"Oh my goodness," Dougal said with a tremble in his voice.

Claire shook some more. Grunt made her take another sip as they waited, tense and ready for action. None of the men voiced their fears. They didn't have to. They all had the same ones.

"I came on my own while Megan dealt with the guy. Joe sent us after we heard gunfire." Her bottom lip trembled as a tear escaped. "I think it came from the front gate."

"The other women?" Lake asked. Kirsty. Was Kirsty okay? A spike of panic zapped through him before deadly calm set in. He was in control. He would deal with this.

No one threatened his woman.

Claire looked up at him, shock in her eyes. "Joe moved them up to the tower bedroom. When I left they were fine— Mum was organising everyone to defend the castle. Ryan is in there with them too. Phones are down and the power is out."

The tears fell faster now shock had set in. Grunt rubbed her back with one hand as he held the mug of hot chocolate with the other. "It's okay," he murmured. "It's going to be okay. We'll take care of it. Don't worry."

He gave Lake a look that was pure fire. Lake nodded once. Absolutely—they would take care of it.

"How many men?" Lake heard the steel in his own voice.

"I don't know." Claire closed her eyes briefly. "At least three—including the one we knocked out." She looked up at him. "But I heard engines when I left. There might be more now."

"Think, Claire," Lake said. "More than one engine?"

"Yes." She frowned. "Yes, more than one. Definitely two. Are they going to be okay?" Her voice trembled.

"Yeah, they're gonna be good." Grunt tucked her head under his chin, put the mug on the floor and wrapped her in his arms. Cold eyes, filled with rage, turned to Lake. "Plan?"

Lake looked around the room and took note of the number of men who had combat or police training. It wasn't good. Most of his men were out on jobs. That left only Callum, Grunt, Matt and himself with the skills to deal with this situation. The other guys would be out of their element. Possibly more of a danger than a help.

"Don't even think about leaving us out." Josh read his mind. "That castle is my home. My pregnant wife is in there. Just. Don't." Fury emanated from the singer.

"I go where he goes," Mitch said.

"I'm in too," Flynn said. "Abby's in there. And our twins. You can't keep me away from them. I go with you, or I go alone."

Harry stood beside his brother. "I'm not much use, but I'm not going to hang out here while some losers threaten my wife."

Lake folded his arms and stared down his friends. "I understand. Our women are there. But we need to work as a team. Got it?"

They nodded.

Lake caught Callum's eyes and saw his own determination and worry staring back at him.

"We have to go in on foot." Callum cocked his head towards the window. "Too thick. Roads are covered. A snow-mobile would be good. Got one?"

Lake shook his head and vowed he was going to invest in at least one machine when this was over.

"Too noisy," Grunt pointed out.

"I agree. We don't know what we're dealing with—better

not to tip them off that we're there. We go in silent, on foot. We'll hit my office on the way and clear out the weapon stash." He looked at Matt, their resident cop. "You want to take over?"

Matt shook his head. "You're the expert at this sort of thing. My skills lean more towards rescuing cats and breaking up fights in the old folks' home."

They both knew that wasn't true; Matt was very skilled. But he was right about one thing: Lake had more experience with this sort of situation. He nodded his appreciation to Matt.

"What about police backup?" Lake said.

"Not in this weather. The town will be cut off until the heavy-duty snowploughs get through to us. Who knows when that will be. We're on our own."

It wasn't anything Lake didn't already know. "Is there a landline in the castle?" he asked Josh.

Josh grimaced. "Cordless phones. They all need power."

"Damn, there are times when technology doesn't help," said the hacker.

"Aye." Flynn patted his brother's back.

"Grunt?" Lake had to ask, even though he knew where the man's loyalty lay.

"I need to stay with Claire."

Lake nodded. Just as he thought. But he'd miss his skill.

"Hell no," Claire said, sitting up straight. "I'm safe here. They need you. You need to go—you're the biggest guy they've got."

Grunt smiled at his wife. "Bigger isn't *always* better, baby. You sure?"

She nodded. "Mum and Megan are there. I'll be happier knowing you and Matt are looking out for each other and for them. Dougal will take care of me."

"You can count on it," Dougal said.

"I'll help," Betty added, which didn't reassure anyone.

"I love you," Grunt said before kissing his wife. Hard.

"Okay." Lake looked around the room at his friends. "Dougal, Betty and the naked guys will hold down the fort here. Everybody else, wrap up and follow me."

As one, the men pulled on snow boots, padded jackets, hats and gloves. Silently, they stepped out into the blizzard and followed Lake the short distance up the high street to his business. The snow was thick underfoot, covering the cobblestone road and pavements, making the street one wide expanse of white. The wind howled, biting into exposed skin. Only the light coming from the pub's windows illuminated the way. The rest of Invertary was black. And silent. The eerie desolation filled Lake with a sense of foreboding.

He pushed open the door to the security shop part of his business. He sold home security systems and some survival gear. The shop made very little money, and he'd been thinking of shutting it down. Now he was glad he hadn't. He flicked on one of the demo security lamps he sold. It cast the room in a warm glow.

"Grunt," he said. "Get everyone armed."

The big guy headed for the locked armoury in the back office.

"Callum, comm units are on the shelf behind the desk. Get everyone kitted out and on the same frequency. I want us to be able to talk to each other while we're out there."

Callum went where Lake pointed.

"Matt, we need restraints and tape. I want these guys immobilised."

"Aye." Matt eyed each man in turn. "Immobilised. Not neutralised. Remember, this isn't an action movie. You can't go killing willy-nilly in the Highlands. We'll bag the guys, and when police backup gets here they'll take them into custody."

"What if they've hurt our women?" Josh asked.

Matt's jaw clenched. "I didn't say you couldn't inflict damage. Just don't kill anyone. The paperwork alone would be a nightmare. Plus the only people in this room with a gun licence either work in law enforcement or for Lake. The rest of you will be armed with stun guns and whatever else Lake has handy that's borderline legal. Got it?"

The men nodded. This was Invertary. They were cut off from the rest of Scotland by location and now by the weather. Everyone present had learned from experience that sometimes you had to take matters into your own hands. As Matt kept pointing out, he was the only cop for miles, and backup was an hour's drive away—in good weather.

"Mitch, Josh, flashlights, goggles." Lake pointed at them. "There are night-vision ones and normal ones for keeping out the snow. They're in back. Enough for everyone."

Mitch headed for the storeroom.

"Grunt, Matt, Callum, arm yourself with whatever you're familiar with. The rest of you stick to what Matt approves. Listen to his instructions on how to work the damn things. Consider it a crash course in safety."

"Batons?" Callum asked, holding up the extendible batons the police used. They were lightweight, solid and could easily crack a skull.

"Definitely." They would also be good for the guys who weren't used to weapons.

"Let's go," Josh said as soon as he was kitted out.

"Not so fast." Callum put a hand on his chest to stop him running out the door. "We need a plan. Easier to talk here than there."

Josh bristled and pushed against Callum's hand. "That's fine for you to say. It isn't your pregnant wife under siege in her own home."

"You're not the only one with a pregnant wife trapped out there," Flynn said. His jaw was tight.

"Calm down." Lake stood centre of the room. "Callum is right. Rushing off half-cocked will only get someone killed. We go in two waves. Callum, Grunt, Matt and myself first. The rest of you follow." He looked at Mitch, Josh, Flynn and Harry. "You four are on bag and tag. Secure the men we bring down."

"I don't like that plan," Josh said.

Lake stared at him for a beat. He understood his anxiety, his fear. It was the same one bubbling inside of him.

"It's the one that will work. You can't go cowboy and do your own thing. It will endanger the women and you could get us all killed."

Josh's jaw clenched, and Lake knew it gutted the guy to admit someone else was better able to protect his wife.

"No cowboy," Josh said.

"We'll get to our wives," Flynn said, patting Josh's shoulder. "We'll keep our babies safe."

Josh nodded and relaxed, slightly.

"Grunt and I will take the front," Lake said. "Matt and Callum, you're on the rear." He looked at each of them in turn. "The key here is to get in fast and immobilise them before they know what hit them. We'll use the cellar as a makeshift holding cell."

"Can't," Josh said. "It's packed full of furniture."

"We'll use another room for a holding cell, then."

"Isn't getting the women out of there the priority, rather than locking up these guys?" Flynn ran a hand through his overgrown hair.

"No," Matt answered his cousin. "Having the women walk to town in this weather would be dangerous. We make sure they stay safe and warm exactly where they are. It isn't just our wives in there—it's their mothers and friends too. The

Knit Or Die women are all retirement age. A trek through the snow to get into town would be too much for them."

Flynn nodded, but he clearly didn't like it. "I wish we could get them out of there to somewhere we know is safer."

Grunt put a hand on Flynn's shoulder. "By the time we're done, that castle will be the most secure place in town."

"We ready?" Lake said.

Determined stares were his answer.

"Then let's get out of here."

Silently, the men left the store and were swallowed whole by darkness and whirling snow.

Even at a run, in knee-deep snow, it would take half an hour to get to the castle.

Half an hour.

It was too long. Anything could happen in half an hour.

And none of it good.

* JOE *

"You heard Alastair," Joe said to the stunned room once the intercom went silent. "There are two snowmobiles on the way to the castle. Looks like they were waiting for someone after all. Playtime is over, ladies."

"Were we playing? I wasn't playing." Kirsty's hands shook in her lap. "Nothing about this is fun. I'm supposed to get married tomorrow. How am I going to do that when I'm trapped in here?" Her eyes went wide. "What if they break in and ruin the wedding setup? This is a disaster. It's a sign. All of it. The weather, the guys with guns, the barricades, the power cut, the fact Lake and I haven't had sex for three months!"

There was a chorus of outraged gasps Kirsty didn't seem to notice because she was too busy working her way into the middle of a hysterical meltdown.

"I should have paid attention to the signs. But no, I had to forge on. Forcing this wedding on everyone, including Lake —who obviously doesn't want it, or he would have at least taken an interest in the planning. He didn't care about any of it. Not one thing. Now I know why. He doesn't want to get married." She waved her arms around. "The universe doesn't want us to get married." She stood and glared at everyone in the room. "I'm making a stand. This is an official announcement. The wedding is off. Cancelled. Not happening. Once we're rescued and don't have to hide from scary gunmen in white balaclavas, you can all go home and pretend it never happened."

Everyone in the room gaped at her as tears started to run down her cheeks. Joe and Ryan shared a look of panic. Things were bad enough without dealing with a crying, hysterical woman.

"You don't mean that." Caroline wrapped her arms around Kirsty and rubbed her back.

"I do," Kirsty wailed. "Lake doesn't want me. The wedding is a disaster. We'll all be lucky to get out of this alive." She lifted her head to look at Margaret. "Mum, after we get out of here, I'm coming home with you."

Margaret rushed across the room to her daughter. "Don't be silly. Lake loves you. So we didn't plan for a siege or a blizzard. It doesn't mean you should call the wedding off. You're stressed and tired and overreacting."

Joe didn't want to point out that the wedding was probably off whether they cancelled it officially or not. There was no way the other guests would get through the snow. And he wasn't sure if the venue would make it through the next few hours. He doubted the guys outside would be careful of the wedding decoration. Either way, this wedding wasn't going to happen.

Caroline shot him a determined look. "Do something to hurry this up. We need to get the castle cleared out and tidied in time for tomorrow's ceremony."

Joe shook his head. "What do you think I should do?"

"I don't know." Caroline started to cry too.

Damn, it was contagious. Joe and Ryan started to back

towards the windows.

"Come here," Jena said, shooting him a glance that said he was pathetic. She led Kirsty and Caroline over to the sofa and sat them down. "Now you both need to calm down. Of course there will be a wedding. It just might not be tomorrow or in the castle. But wherever it happens, I'm sure it will be wonderful." She patted Kirsty's hand. "I got married in the hospital after I'd been stuck underground for hours when the mine collapsed, and it was still the most romantic day of my life. The most important thing is that you love Lake and he loves you."

"But he doesn't," Kirsty said. "He doesn't even touch me."

"Oh, honey." Jena waved a dismissive hand. "It's probably his age. They have little blue pills for that. Trust me." She looked around at the other women. "Trust all of us. Lake loves you."

The women nodded, and Kirsty sniffed back her tears. Big, bright, pleading eyes looked at Jena. "You really think so?"

"Yeah, I'm sure. He's been real busy, is all. Julia?" She called Lake's assistant out of the bathroom. "Tell her."

Julia nodded, but spoke in the direction of her ugly brown boots. "Jena's right. He's been really busy. Snowed under. I know he's been worried about work. But once he opens the office in London, things will ease off."

"He's opening an office in London and he didn't tell me?" Kirsty started to cry again, as though the lack of information was confirmation that Lake didn't love her anymore.

"He didn't want to bother you. He was worried that you were stressed enough with the wedding." Julia's soft voice was urgent, defusing Kirsty's fears. Joe liked Julia. She was pretty much the only sensible woman in the room—even with her many social phobias. "He was trying to get it all sorted to surprise you for your wedding day."

"See?" Jena said. "Everything's fine. As soon as you see Lake, you guys have a nice little talk and sort all this out. Right now, you need to dry your tears and concentrate on what's going on here. Okay?"

"Okay," mumbled Kirsty.

Joe wasn't sure if Kirsty was convinced or not, but he didn't care. The main thing was she'd stopped crying. And that was good.

The sound of engines cut through the mood in the room, and everyone turned towards the windows where Ryan kept watch.

"Snowmobiles are here. I'm counting at least nine men out there now, maybe more." Ryan's eyes were dark when he looked at Joe. They didn't need to communicate to be on the same page. This was bad. Real bad.

"We're secure in here and Claire should have reached the pub by now. We only need to hold them off until reinforcements get here." He hoped no one realised he sounded a whole lot more confident than he felt.

"I'd be happier if I wasn't working in the dark," Ryan said. "And I don't mean the power. I'd like to know what they want. Why they're here."

Joe couldn't agree more. He was barricaded inside a room with a dozen slightly tipsy women who were scared out of their minds, and he was planning for a siege while staring at delicate rose-print wallpaper. Having at least some idea why he was in this situation would make it slightly less surreal.

Megan let out an exasperated growl as she leaned over her captive. "Enough is enough. You heard the man. We need to know why you're here. Tell us what you want."

"For the two of us to be alone," he drawled. "I'm not shy, but what I have in mind would be better without an audience."

"Get your mind out of the gutter," Heather snapped.

"That's my daughter you're leering at."

"I can see she comes from good stock," the guy said.

"Oh, for heaven's sake." Megan threw up her hands. "Do I have to let Ryan hit you again?"

"Too late," Ryan said. "No time for that. The new guys are off the snowmobiles and they're heading this way. Looks like we're about to get some company."

"They're coming in here? Inside my castle?" Caroline sounded panicked. She shot to her feet and rushed for a window. Before anyone could stop her, she'd thrust it open and was leaning out into the icy night air. "Don't you dare break anything," she shouted down at the men with guns. "This castle was recently restored and I will not tolerate it being damaged."

Joe yanked her back into the room and slammed the window shut. "Thanks for letting them know exactly where we are."

Caroline straightened her shoulders, but her face paled. Her bottom lip trembled a little, making Joe panic that she would start crying again.

"I didn't think." She tucked a strand of her golden Doris Day bob behind her ear and smoothed her pale blue woollen dress. "I'm sorry, Joe." Water-filled eyes looked up at him. "This castle is a historical landmark. I want to make sure they respect it."

"While they break in?" Joe had to ask.

"Maybe now they'll be careful when they break in," she said.

Joe looked over at Jena and silently begged for her to deal with Caroline. Jena tottered over on her platform stripper shoes, wrapped an arm around Caroline and led her back to the sofa.

"Remember," Jena cooed, "things can be fixed."

Megan threw up her hands in disgust. She turned to Joe.

"You were right. He isn't going to talk." The blonde clenched her fists with clear frustration. "I'm putting the gag back on him. I really don't want to listen to him anymore."

"Admit it," the guy said to Megan. "You're just kinky. You like me tied up and at your mercy. After this is all over, I'll make sure you get another shot at me."

"Oh, I'll take a shot at you." Megan stuffed the hand towel into his mouth. "I just haven't decided whether it will be with a shotgun or a crossbow."

He was chuckling when she secured the gag with a scarf.

"Don't damage the walls or mouldings," Caroline shouted hysterically, making Joe spin towards her. The bloody woman was on the intercom. "And you had better not get a scratch on that flooring. If I find one bullet hole in my walls, I'll—"

Joe sprinted to her side and dragged her away. He took her to the couch and, gently as he could under the circumstances, pushed her into it. While she protested, he grabbed Kirsty's arm and thrust her into the seat beside her friend. He pointed at them.

"You two are staying right there. I don't care what happens." He pointed at Caroline. "No more shouting at the guys with guns." He pointed at Kirsty. "You have one job—keep Caroline away from the windows and the intercom."

He stalked away. This was a nightmare. He felt like Arnie in *Kindergarten Cop*.

"I don't think he's very happy with me," Caroline said behind him.

"No kidding." Kirsty muttered. "You know, someday this might be funny."

"If we survive," Caroline said.

"There is that," Kirsty said.

And Joe found himself considering whether it would be less stressful to surrender to the enemy.

CHAPTER 17

"We need to do something to help them," Alastair said. "You heard Caroline." He pointed at the intercom, in case she'd missed the hysterical rant. "They're inside the castle." He paced the small space, frustrated by the walls hemming him in.

"Help how? You can barely stand." Rainne folded her arms over her pink fluffy sweater. It undermined her determination to appear intimidating.

"What the hell am I doing now, then?" He *was* standing, damn it.

He watched her pause, take a breath then raise her jaw slightly before looking him in the eye. This was new behaviour. Something she'd learned these past three years. She was standing her ground, and he couldn't help the surge of pride that flowed through him as he watched her do it. Pride from the position of someone who used to know her. Not from the position of someone who was currently invested. Because he wasn't. Not at all.

He shook off his thoughts and got back to the main topic. The only topic. "I'm not going to sit in here like a scared princess and let my friends get assaulted by a bunch of *Die Hard 2* villains."

She looked blank. Some things never changed. This was what happened when you grew up in a commune: you missed the cultural references everyone else took for granted.

Cute little lines appeared between her brows as she frowned at him. "Is that a geek reference?"

"First, I'm not a geek. Second, it's a movie. Guys dressed in white with guns. Fights in the snow. One man out to save the world and eliminate the bad guys." Nope, she still looked blank. "Not important. The important thing is, I'm going out there to help. You stay here. Keep warm and safe."

Her eyes blazed, and damn if she didn't look even more beautiful. Now that he knew she had a temper, it was tempting to make her lose it just to see the passion in her eyes.

"You have got to be out of your tiny mind." She seemed shocked at the words coming out of her mouth, but it didn't stop her. Alastair found part of his brain was rooting for her. "You can't go out there alone. You're injured. What happens if you collapse in the snow? What happens if you get another blow to the head? At the very least, you need someone watching your back so they can drag you away when you pass out again." She gave him a determined stare. "You need me."

He was enjoying her little tirade until the last three words. They hit him like arrows. "No. I don't need you."

"Really?" Her hand shot out, lightning fast, and prodded him in the ribs.

Alastair saw stars. Real freaking stars. Right there. In front of him. The pain made his knees weaken, and he wobbled where he stood.

"It's okay, I've got you." Rainne was against his side, giving him something to lean on.

It took a minute to get past the surge of pain. When he did, he pulled away from her.

"What the hell, Rainbow?"

"I was proving a point." She blinked up at him, her eyes filled with stubborn determination. "I can prove it again if you'd like."

He took a step back from her. Which made her smile smugly.

Enough of this crap. "You won't be any help to me. You'll be a hindrance. You know nothing about this sort of thing. Bloody hell, Rainne, you're a pacifist."

"And I suppose you learned all about dealing with a bunch of armed intruders while you were standing about in a river with your rod in your hand!"

He couldn't help the smile that broke out.

Her cheeks went red. "Fishing rod. I mean fishing rod."

"I'm a guy," he said. "We know how to fight."

She threw up her hands in disgust. "You're trying to tell me it's a genetic thing? Really?"

"You've never hit a person in your life," he pointed out. "You think you can start now?"

"I hit you. Twice, if you include the demo just now."

He rolled his eyes. "Well done, Rocky. You're still not coming with me."

He could see her trying to figure out the Rocky reference, but she quickly gave up. Instead she looked up at him with an unholy gleam in her eye. "I don't have to hit anyone. All I need to do is cause a diversion to buy the women in the castle some time until help comes. I can blow up their transport."

Damn, she was sexy when she was smug. And, he had to admit, it wasn't a bad plan.

"Thanks for the idea. Now stay here while I implement it."

Fury again. Spectacular.

"No," was all she said.

"Fine." He sighed, and she looked triumphant for about a second. "I'll tie you to the desk until I get back." He took a step towards her and she squeaked.

He expected her to fight, but instead she ran for the intercom and put her finger on the "all rooms" button, ready to flick it on. Her eyes narrowed. "You let me go with you or I broadcast our whereabouts, and plan, to all the bad guys in the castle."

He stopped dead in his tracks and stared at her. Every muscle in her curvy body vibrated with tension. Her hand didn't shake. Her brow was furrowed in determination.

He wavered. "You wouldn't."

Her lips thinned. "I would."

"You could get us both killed."

"Better than watching you walk into the snow alone. Make your decision. You have to the count of five, then I'm talking. One." She cocked an eyebrow at him, exactly the same ploy Lake used to intimidate. On Rainbow it was cute.

He had a sudden flash of her with troublesome kids at her feet, counting down to get them to do what they were told.

"Two," she said.

He shook his head to clear it. He must have a concussion. It was the only reason he could come up with for the fact his mind kept wandering into territory he'd closed off long ago.

"Three," she gritted out.

Alastair ran a hand through his overgrown hair. Even lifting his arm to head height was painful. Maybe she had a point about him needing some help. But did it have to be her? What if she got hurt?

"Four." She pulled back her shoulders.

She was going to do it. The crazy woman would do it.

"Fine," he snapped. "You can come with me."

Her shoulders relaxed. "Good decision." She dropped her finger from the switch and gave him a sunny smile. "Now how do we blow up a snowmobile?"

CHAPTER 18

* JOE *

Three guns. Two trained men. One amused captive. Eleven insane women.

And a house full of gunmen with an unknown objective.

They were doomed.

It grated against every nerve in Joe's body to wait for help. He wanted to be proactive. He wanted to take the fight to the guys downstairs. Unfortunately, he couldn't leave the women alone. Who knew what they would do?

The crazy half of the Donaldson twins sidled up to him. "I'm gutted I couldn't make my prisoner talk. I don't know enough about torture. I need training. Does Lake run a class?"

He stared down at Megan. "Yeah. Every Wednesday night. Torture 101."

She studied him for a moment as if trying to decide if he was pulling her leg or not. It took her longer than he would have hoped. She narrowed her eyes at him. "Is now the best time for sarcasm?"

She had a point. The oldest women in the group, the ones who should have known better, were in the bathroom turning condoms into water balloons to throw at guys with guns. Kirsty was practically sitting on Caroline to stop her from taking over the intercom and lecturing the intruders. At least she hadn't noticed that the women had found her condom supply. Jena was working her way through the wine and cookies as she distracted Abby, who looked worried and kept patting her belly as if to reassure it. Julia was hiding in the bathroom, and Magenta was watching everyone with a sarcastic smile on her face.

At least the captive was gagged. Joe really didn't think he could stomach any more advice from the peanut gallery.

"What's the plan?" Megan said.

Plan? Oh yeah, he was in charge. Fan-fucking-tastic. "The plan is to wait to be rescued."

The blonde put her hands on her hips. "That sucks. Is that all you can come up with? I thought Marines were well trained. I thought you guys could deal with anything. Plus you're American—shouldn't you blast your way out of trouble?"

"How much TV do you watch, woman? These aren't stuntmen. This isn't a special effect. This is real life."

Megan let out a frustrated sigh. "I didn't think being under siege would be so boring."

Joe blinked at her. The woman was beyond insane. She was in a whole new category. "I don't have time to deal with your issues. We need to get this room properly secured. Get our guest off the bed. We need it for a barricade."

"What will I tie him to?"

"Use your imagination."

Her eyes actually gleamed before she walked away. Joe shuddered. Grunt had definitely lucked out in the twin department. His one was marginally sane.

"Listen up," he called to the women, and was surprised when they gave him their attention. "We're safe here for the moment, and I plan to keep it that way until Claire comes back with help. We need to reinforce the door barricade. The hinges are a weak point. We need to shore it up some more. No one can get through the walls; they're two foot thick and solid stone. The chances of them scaling the exterior to get to us are slim."

"What about coming down from the roof and in through the windows? There's nothing above this room, is there?" Ryan asked.

Joe looked to Caroline. "Where's the access to the roof above this room?"

"There's a metal ladder fixed to the exterior of that wall." She pointed to one of the walls without a window. "If you go out the landing window on the third floor, you have access to the ladder and it will take you up to the roof above this room. I know we call this a tower, but really it's only an elevated corner room. Access is easy."

Kirsty patted her hand as though to comfort her. "It looks like a tower to me, honey."

Caroline gave her a grateful smile. Joe wondered what dimension he'd fallen into when they were under attack but the homeowner was more upset that she didn't have a proper tower.

Joe brought her back to the problem. "Is there a chance they could get onto the roof, then come down and in through the windows?"

Caroline nodded. "The snow would make it more difficult, but with the right equipment it wouldn't be a problem."

"We need to barricade the windows," Joe said.

"No!" There was a chorus of protests as the women rushed out of the bathroom armed with water-filled condoms.

"How are we supposed to water-bomb them if the windows are blocked?" Kirsty's mother demanded.

"You're not," Joe said, and a water balloon hit him squarely in the middle of his chest.

Margaret covered her mouth with her hands. "Sorry," she said through them. "Reflex reaction."

Joe looked down at his soaked Henley and asked himself if that really just happened.

"Ooh, I just had a thought," Jena said. "We should be filming this." She dug around in her handbag and came out with her phone. She pointed the camera at him. "Do that again, Margaret. I'll get it this time."

Joe stared at Jena before turning his attention back to Margaret.

"Don't worry," she said. "I won't do it again."

"I need help with this guy's legs," Megan called from the bed. "He weighs a tonne."

"I'll help," shouted several women at once, and they all raced to the bed.

Joe almost felt sorry for the guy.

"Where are we taking him?" Shona said as they heaved the guy off the bed.

Joe watched his captive's shoulders shake and knew he was laughing. He also wasn't struggling. The guy wasn't even trying to escape or help his buddies outside. There was something seriously wrong about this whole situation.

"We're taking him into the bathroom," Megan said. "I'm going to tie him up in the bath. That way when we need to pee, we pull the shower curtain shut for privacy."

"Good thinking," her mother told her.

They hauled the man into the bathroom, forcing Julia to come back into the bedroom, where she lurked beside the wardrobe and tried to blend with the wood. Jena tottered after the women, filming them as they carried the guy out of the room.

"Why aren't you more worried about this whole siege thing?" Shona asked Jena. "You seem really relaxed."

Jena shrugged. "I have to get rescued a lot. I'm used to it. Plus it wasn't that long ago I was abducted and held at gunpoint by my ex. This seems kind of tame in comparison."

"Will you stop talking about being abducted?" Joe frowned at Jena. "You were never in any danger. We wouldn't have allowed it. In fact, we got you out of there at the first sign of trouble. It wasn't a real kidnapping. It was an unscheduled meeting."

"Says the guy who abducted me," Jena said to Shona.

Joe let out a growl before turning his attention to Ryan. "Help me lift the bed in front of the door. Then we'll shut the windows; lock them and block them too."

"At least wait with the windows until we've run out of balloons," Jean pleaded.

Joe counted their stash. The women had less than a dozen water-filled condoms between them. He eyed the windows. No one was firing back at the women. Yeah, he knew it was crazy, but he couldn't think of a reason not to let them finish.

"Fine," Joe said. "Have at it."

The women who'd helped carry the captive into the bathroom came rushing back into the room, eager to lob more balloons.

"What exactly is their plan here?" Ryan said as he watched the women lob water balloons at the guys with guns. "At best, they're just going to piss those guys off by soaking them."

"I think they're hoping they'll fall over and die of hypothermia," Joe said.

"Do any of them know how long it takes to die of hypothermia?"

"I don't think they care," Joe said.

"You know," Ryan said, "when I was with the army, I never imagined this was how my life would turn out."

"No one could imagine this," Joe muttered.

Together they heaved the heavy wooden bed upright and wedged it against the door.

As Joe got the bed into place, he felt a gentle tug at the sleeve of his shirt and looked down to find Julia beside him.

"What is it?" he said with a smile, worried he'd scare her off.

"You might want to do something about the dumb waiter." She pointed to what Joe had thought was a built-in closet. "It's big enough to fit a man and should probably be sealed."

Her face turned red as she scurried away.

"You know something, Julia?" Joe said as he went to check out the dumb waiter. "You are the only woman in here I'd pick for my team."

Two more balloons hit him on the back. When he spun around, lots of suspiciously innocent faces were looking elsewhere.

"Are those condoms?" Caroline came off the sofa. "Our condoms? Those are private. You shouldn't be touching private things. We shouldn't even be talking about them!" Her face went beetroot red.

"Take a nice, calming breath," Kirsty said. "Don't panic. Everyone in here knows you have sex. It isn't a secret. After all, you are pregnant. And let's face it, honey. You don't really need them right now, do you? Might as well use them for something else."

"This is so embarrassing," Caroline said.

"No, it's not," Kirsty said. "In fact, everyone will have forgotten all about this by morning. Won't you?" She glared at the women in the room.

"Forget what?" Shona looked down at the water-filled condom in her hand and faked a gasp. "You mean these aren't balloons?"

Kirsty rolled her eyes. "Not helping." She continued to soothe the mortified Caroline.

Sopping wet, Joe yanked open the door to the dumb waiter and stopped dead. Caroline was about to become a whole lot more embarrassed. He really hoped she didn't flake out on him. He had enough crazy to deal with already.

"Uh, Caroline," he said. "You want to come explain this?"

There was a moment of silence, then every woman in the room rushed to his side.

CHAPTER 19

They were dressed. Their clothes were still damp, but warm from the heat of the fire, something Alastair knew wouldn't last a second outside in the cold.

"You know, I actually think the snow's getting heavier." Rainne turned back from where she was peeking out from behind the blinds.

Alastair grunted as he rifled through the first-aid kit.

"Do you need more painkillers?" Rainne said. "I'm sorry I prodded you. But if you'd listened to reason, I wouldn't have had to."

"I'm looking for a lighter, or matches."

"And you think you'll find them in the first-aid kit?"

Rainne's eyes went straight to the shelf with manuals and folders to the right of the fire. She walked over and pulled a box of matches out from beside the books.

He found his eyes glued to the sway of her hips as she walked across the room. Those dark blue denims she wore cupped her curves like a second skin. Even teamed with a fluffy pink jumper and purple moon boots, she was still sexy as hell.

He was a fool for letting these thoughts seep into his brain. An even bigger fool for letting himself notice her. But he couldn't seem to help it. He put it down to close proximity—there was nowhere else to look. He had no choice but to notice the way her soft brown hair feathered around her oval face. Or the way her long lashes brushed her cheeks when she looked down. And those long, slender legs that ended in a round backside that would make any man salivate.

What the hell was he doing? There were guys out there with guns and he was waxing lyrical about the backside of the woman who'd rejected him. He was an idiot. An idiot who shouldn't have kissed her. One taste and his mind was filled with the memory of all that was Rainne. The taste of her skin on his tongue. The little gasps of pleasure she made when he touched her. It was all there now, front and centre in his brain. Along with the fragile hope in her voice when she'd asked for a second chance with him.

Memory of that hopeful look and the soft declaration of love she'd made ate like acid at the hard wall around his heart. Three years ago he'd been the one to declare his love, only to have it thrown back in his face. This time, he'd done the same thing to her. And he didn't like that feeling, not one bit.

"There was a guy at one of the communes who kept his matches on the shelf beside the fire," Rainne said, thankfully oblivious to his thoughts. She handed the box to him.

Alastair emptied the box onto the desk, divided the amount in half and placed them into two separate plastic money bags he'd found in the drawer. He ripped the matchbox in two, stashing half with each lot of matches.

"Take this. Put it somewhere safe." He handed her one of the bags.

"Why?" Her wide eyes blinked up at him.

"In case we split up, we should both be able to set the petrol tanks on fire."

She licked her bottom lip. A nervous habit he doubted she even noticed. "We won't split up. We're doing this together."

"Right." If he had his way, she'd be tied to the desk in the nice, warm, secure guardhouse. But no, she had to be a hero.

He shook his head then instantly regretted it as it started to throb again. It wasn't his problem if she wanted to go out into the snow and get shot at. He wasn't her keeper. Still… He eyed the desk. If he wasn't injured, he could have picked her up and put her where she was safe.

He handed over strips of her kitten-covered undershirt, which she'd cut for them. "Tuck the strips into your coat. Keep them dry."

She did as she was told while he watched her every move. He nodded when she'd zipped the coat up tight.

"When we get out there, communicating is going to be hard. We'll use hand gestures." He held up a fist. "This means stop and be silent."

She held up a fist to stop him. "Are you forgetting my brother is ex-military? I know every military hand signal there is, plus a few civilian ones I learned on demonstrations that are too rude to use."

"Don't think you'll need those ones, Rainbow."

Her answering smile made his mouth go dry. He cleared his throat. "Ready?"

She nodded, but her face had paled. Stubborn woman. "This will work, won't it? I mean, the bad guys will run out of the castle when they realise they've lost their vehicles, right?" She eyed the intercom panel. "Maybe we should tell the women what we're doing so they don't get scared?"

"What if the bad guys overhear? We'd lose the element of surprise." He brushed some stray hair from her cheek. "This will work, Rainbow. The distraction will buy some time until

Lake gets here. And they'll lose their transport." He smiled. "That will make it harder to run away."

She looked so hopeful that it made him ache. He took a deep breath, feeling the answering pain in his chest. "I really think you should stay here. Where it's safe."

"Don't make me hurt you again, Alastair."

It was like being threatened by a bunny. A very stubborn bunny.

He switched off the main beam of the flashlight, then turned on the faint, muted glow they'd use outside. It took a minute for his eyes to adjust. The first thing he noticed was the worried frown on Rainne's face.

"Take my hand." His voice was gruff.

When her fingers curled around his, he felt her shiver, and for a second he wished their gloves weren't between them.

"Hold on tight, Rainbow," he said softly. "The flashlight is dim. We'll only be able to see a little bit in front of ourselves, but it should be enough to get us to the castle."

He squeezed her hand to reassure her, then turned them both towards the door.

"Be careful, Alastair," Rainne said. "Please don't get killed." There was a pause. "I love you," she whispered, so softly that he doubted he was meant to hear.

Alastair stopped in his tracks and hung his head. His fingers flexed in hers. They were only words. She didn't mean them. People who loved you didn't leave you. An annoying voice in the back of his mind asked if she'd really left him, or had run from everything in general.

"Alastair?" Rainne said from behind him.

Oh, damn it to hell!

He turned to face Rainne. The temptation to touch her, to taste her, was too much. He didn't know what they were walking out into. He didn't know if he'd ever get to touch her again. And that felt like a crime.

"Don't make anything of this," he told Rainne.

He slid his hand up her arm until he cupped her cheek. He heard her suck in some air. A tiny shudder under his fingertips. Alastair blamed the memory of making love to her for his sudden, and persistent, need to touch and taste. She was in his head, under his skin, inside him. And the longer he was around her, the deeper she wormed herself into him.

"This is not a big deal," he said. "It's just for luck."

"I don't believe in luck anymore," she whispered.

"What do you believe in now?" He found himself entranced by the look in her eye.

"Hope," she said, summing up the very thing that had mesmerised him.

Softly, slowly, he closed the distance between them. Her lips were satin. She fit him perfectly. A tiny moan escaped her throat as she pressed into him. Delicate hands grabbed his leather jacket and tugged him closer.

What they planned to do was somewhere between dangerous and insanely stupid. If the bad guys didn't get them, the blast from the snowmobile might. That's if they didn't freeze to death in the snow first. He needed one moment touching Rainne, in case it was their last.

He slowed the kiss, until he gently pressed their lips together one last time. The cold was unbearable when he pulled back from her. Dazed eyes blinked up at him and he saw a flicker of hope in their depths.

"This doesn't mean anything." He wasn't entirely sure if the words were meant for her or for himself. Either way, they stuck in his throat like a lie.

He tugged the scarf back up to cover her mouth.

"Was that another mistake?" she whispered. "Or are we

calling that kiss something else?" Her eyes went wide. "We're not calling it goodbye, are we?"

"No." Alastair couldn't trust himself to say anything more. Not when his thoughts and feelings were jumbled up in one huge, confusing mess.

Alastair pulled open the door and a blast of freezing wind hit them hard.

Heads down, they stepped out into the thick snow. Sharp, icy flakes nipped at their exposed skin. Their eyes watered from the blinding cold. The kind that went through you to the bone and melded there. Alastair turned to check on Rainne but could barely see her through the thick falling snow. The silence was disturbing, made ominous by their purpose and the danger that awaited them. Each step they took was laborious. It felt more like they were wading rather than walking.

The snow ate at Alastair. It chipped away at his resolve, making him wonder what he was doing outside instead of staying tucked up in the warmth with Rainne. The pain in his side was a consistent dull reminder that he was one strike away from a punctured lung. His swollen wrist shot jagged spikes of pain through his body each time he moved it in the wrong way. His head throbbed with every step. His throat burned with each icy breath he sucked in. Yet through it all, he could only think about the taste of Rainne on his lips and warm comfort of her hand in his.

It felt right. Like he'd been missing a limb for three years and now it was back.

CHAPTER 20

* JOE *

"It's not what you think." Caroline stared into the dumb waiter from her spot beside Joe.

"I think it's a life-sized rubber doll that looks suspiciously like Josh McInnes," Joe said.

"And it's holding a box of illegal fireworks," Jena felt the need to point out. "Was the doll made in Japan? It looks like it was. They're experts at getting the face that lifelike."

All eyes turned to Jena.

"How on earth would you know that?" Abby asked her best friend.

"It's amazing what you learn working the nightclubs in Atlantic City. I know about stuff that would curl your toes."

"Josh promised me he wouldn't buy any of those fireworks. They're dangerous. People have lost limbs using them." Caroline was clearly outraged.

"Really?" Shona said. "You're worried about the fireworks and not about the sex doll?"

"It's not a s-sex doll." Caroline's face turned burgundy. "It was a joke gift. From Mitch."

"I don't see how it's funny," Kirsty's mum said as she stared at plastic Josh.

Caroline's shoulders went back, a sure sign someone was going to get a lecture.

"Mitch bought it for Josh years ago. He said Josh would never find a wife because he was already in love with himself. He told Josh this doll could solve all his problems, as he could take himself to bed."

"That is kind of funny," Heather said with a grin. "And smart."

"Is it anatomically correct?" Jena asked, and again all eyes turned to her. She shrugged. "It's a sex doll. Top of the line, custom made. It should have all its bits."

"I need to check." Shona reached for the doll.

"No." Caroline shoved herself between the women and the doll. "Hands off. That's my husband we're talking about. No one is seeing his private parts."

"Technically, that isn't your husband," Abby said. "It's a toy."

"A sex toy," Jena said, entertaining herself.

"Do you have three-ways with the doll and Josh?" Shona asked.

"Ooooh, no!" Caroline's horror was clear.

"Still, you can't tell me that the first thing you did when you saw it was pull down his pants to compare?" Jean inched towards the doll.

Caroline went into prim mode. Her back was ramrod straight. "I have never taken the clothes off the doll. If it was up to me it would be in the bin, but it has sentimental value for Josh."

"Are you sure that's the only kind of value it has for him?" Shona asked.

"I think this is taking narcissism a bit too far," Margaret said. "I worry about that boy."

"It was a gift." Caroline was clearly irritated now. "One he didn't ask for. One he doesn't play with. And no one is taking the trousers off the doll. Don't think I can't see you sneaking towards him, Jean." She put her hand up to stop the woman.

"Killjoy," the older woman muttered before backing off.

"Him?" Jena asked with a smirk.

"It! I mean it." Caroline looked like she was going to explode.

"Why is it in the dumb waiter?" Jena asked.

"Josh didn't want to store it in the cellar with everything else, and I didn't want it in the bedroom. This was a compromise." She sighed. "I was kind of hoping it'd fall down the shaft and I'd never see it again."

Kirsty came up to put her arm around Caroline. "Stop teasing her. She's with child and shouldn't be stressed."

As one, the women looked contrite.

"Quite right," Kirsty's mum said. "We're sorry, Caroline. I'd hate it if someone went poking around in my bedroom cupboards."

"Why?" Shona asked. "What you got hidden in there?"

"Please!" Kirsty held up her hands to stop her mother. "If you love your only daughter even a little, please don't answer that."

The grin on Margaret's face was mischievous. "I love you very much. These lips are sealed."

"You'll tell us later?" Shona said.

Her mum tried to nod without Kirsty seeing her. Kirsty just groaned.

"Okay." Joe took charge again, now that the shock of finding the doll had worn off. "If you lot are finished ogling fake Josh, let's get the dumb waiter sealed up."

"It doesn't work anyway," Caroline said.

"Yeah, but it's an access point and I want it sealed."

"Wait!" Heather said. "Take the doll out first. We might

need him. And grab those fireworks. They're weapons." She grinned with glee at her friends. One by one, the eyes of the women of Knit Or Die went wide.

"We can fire them at the intruders," Margaret said with awe.

"That's much better than balloons," Shona said.

"This is going to be great. You heard Caroline," Jean said. "These babies take off limbs."

Margaret grabbed the box of fireworks and headed to the corner of the room, followed by her cronies. Heather tucked the Josh doll under her arm.

"Put the doll back. There's no reason to remove him from the cupboard," Caroline said on a groan.

"We might need a decoy." Heather held the doll tighter. "I like the tux. Was it one of Josh's?"

"Can somebody bring the doll in here?" the prisoner shouted from the bathroom. "I want to see it too."

"No," everybody in the room shouted back.

Then there was a crash outside the bedroom door, a shout and the sound of a gun going off.

The women screamed. The doll was forgotten.

"Get that dumb waiter barricaded now," Joe snapped.

Ryan pulled a heavy wooden dresser over in front of it.

"Are they trying to shoot their way in?" Jean asked in a tremulous voice.

"No." Heather grinned. "Sounded like someone slid on the olive oil, fell and their gun went off. Here's hoping the bullet ricocheted off the wall and embedded in his head."

"Wow," Jena said. "Bloodthirsty. I like it."

Then there was a thud at the door and the barricade shook.

"Windows," Joe said. "Shut them. Lock them. Block them."

"But we need space to shoot the fireworks out," Margaret shouted.

"No time. Security first. Firing back later." *Hopefully never.*

The women rushed to carry out his order as the door thudded again.

CHAPTER 21

* RAINNE AND ALASTAIR *

"I see the snowmobiles," Alastair said.

The words were muffled by the hood of Rainne's jacket. She struggled out from behind his large frame, which he'd been using to block the wind from her, and spotted the snowmobiles immediately. One of them had been left with its headlights on.

"That's going to waste the battery," Rainne muttered.

Alastair tugged her behind a thin tree that did little to hide them, but fortunately the black night and thick falling snow made up for its shortcomings.

"I don't see anyone." Alastair spoke close to her ear, his breath warm against her cheek, making her shiver.

Her lips still tingled from his unexpected kiss. Although she knew it wasn't wise, she couldn't stop a little seed of hope from planting in her soul. She knew now, after hearing the story about his mother, that there was very little hope of a reunion with her boy. How could he trust her again? Life had taught him that people you love left. There was absolutely nothing she could do to reassure him it wouldn't happen again. Only he could deal with his fears. Only he could make the choice to take a chance on being hurt again. Rejected again. And she didn't think he'd be able to do it. His fears were too ingrained. And she was partly to blame for that.

"I think it's safe to go to the snowmobiles. I think the bad guys are in the castle. I'll take the one on the left," Alastair said. "You take the other one. Remember what I told you. You need to get the cloth wet with petrol before you wedge it back into the tank, otherwise it won't light. Not in this weather." He put his hand under her chin to angle her face up to his. For a second Rainne thought he was going to kiss her again, and her heart actually stopped beating. But he didn't. "Don't take any chances, Rainbow. First sign of trouble, run."

Hearing him call her Rainbow again shot little sparks of warmth through her chilled body. "Not without you."

"No, Rainbow. You run with or without me. Don't put yourself in danger. I can take care of myself."

Yeah, that was why his face was grey and he was swaying on his feet.

"I hear you," she said, and hoped he took that as her agreement to do as she was told.

He must have been feeling worse than he looked, because he seemed relieved at her answer and didn't question it further.

"It's time," he said.

"Yeah." Rainne took a deep breath and told herself to be positive. What could go wrong? Really? She had plenty of good karma stored. Oh, yeah, wait. She didn't believe in karma anymore. Or stones that emitted good luck. Or auras. Actually, since she'd turned her back on her hippy upbringing, her life had simplified immensely.

"Keep low," Alastair ordered. "Let's go."

He took her hand again and pulled her towards the snowmobiles. She tried to keep her eyes wide open and her mind alert. Adrenalin and fear helped keep her focused. She eyed each shadow, wondering if someone lurked there, watching and waiting. Really, what would she do if someone did step out and confront them? Her only valid option was to run screaming. In this snow, she wouldn't get very far. And no matter what Alastair might think, there was no way she would leave him to confront the intruders alone.

Stop freaking out. There are no men hiding in the bushes. Nobody is daft enough to hang around out here in this weather.

As pep talks went, it wouldn't win any awards, but it made her feel better. As they reached the snowmobiles, they separated. Alastair gave her hand one last squeeze, and she felt suddenly weak without him holding her. His strength, even when injured, was enough to take away the bulk of her fear. Without it, she found herself hesitant and trembling.

Each step through the snow was laborious. Each breath she sucked through the wet wool of her scarf hurt her lungs. But she kept on going. She had to. Her friends and family were in the castle. And Alastair needed her—whether he wanted to admit it or not.

She found the petrol tank cap where Alastair said it would be and unscrewed it. She pulled the zip down on her padded coat and reached inside for the strips of cloth. But she couldn't distinguish them with her gloves on, so they had to go. She pulled them off and stuffed them in her pockets, instantly feeling the bite of cold on her already chilled fingers. She took the fabric, twisted it to make it easier to get into the tank and then fed it through the opening. It took two attempts to get it wet enough to light. She threaded it back into the tank, leaving the petrol-soaked end hanging out, ready to be lit.

Her fingers were numb from the cold. It made holding the tiny matches difficult. She fumbled with them as she tried to get one ready to strike. A gunshot went off inside the castle. Rainne jumped. The matches fell to the snow.

No. No. No.

Rainne fell to her knees, scanning the dirty snow for tiny pieces of wood and seeing nothing. She ran her fingers over the surface of the snow, but they were too numb to sense anything.

It's okay. It's going to be fine. Just stay calm.

She cupped her hands in front of her mouth and breathed warm air onto them.

Loud thuds came from the castle. Screams followed. Rainne's heart pounded so fast and hard it made her dizzy.

Breathe slowly. Don't panic. Get the matches. Focus.

She spotted the faint outline of a match and pounced on it. There were two more beside it. She scrambled to her feet. Okay. She could do this. The rag was still poking out of the tank.

Okay. Okay. Slow. Steady. Think.

But her fingers wouldn't cooperate. They trembled and shook. They wouldn't bend properly, stiff with cold. She struck the match repeatedly against the rough piece of card. Nothing. She let it fall and tried the second one. The same result. Rainne blinked back pointless tears of frustration.

Light, damn it. Light!

She spotted Alastair heading her way. They'd talked about this. He was supposed to head to the tree line once his machine was lit. He staggered in the snow, corrected his aim and continued towards her.

More thuds came from inside the castle. Shouting followed.

Hurry. Hurry.

Rainne reached for the last match.

Make it work. Please make it work.

She sobbed with frustration as the second attempt to light

the match failed. They were just too wet. Alastair ran towards her. No. He had to go. He had to run.

"No," she told him, although there was no way he could possibly hear her.

Her head fell forward. Heavy with an overwhelming sense of failure.

She opened her eyes, and that was when she saw it. A dry match, snagged on her woollen scarf. With no thought other than to get the job done, she snatched it out of the wool, struck it and held her breath. The second strike and it was alight. With a stupid, grateful grin, she set the match to the petrol-soaked rag and watched it catch light.

She wanted to whoop.

"Run," Alastair shouted, no longer caring about the noise.

"You run," she shouted back.

She turned from the machine and ran as fast as she could through knee-deep snow. Which wasn't fast enough.

"Run, Rainbow!" Alastair was at her side, slowing to stay with her.

"No. Don't wait for me. Go!"

The stupid, stubborn man didn't listen. Instead he grabbed her hand in his good one and yanked her forward.

And that was when the first machine exploded. The second explosion followed quickly. The force took Rainne off her feet and propelled her forward.

She saw shadows flying towards her.

And then she saw nothing at all.

CHAPTER 22

The windows were barricaded using the rest of Caroline's heavy antique bedroom furniture. Fake Josh stood in the corner watching over them as they sealed the room. The floor was now empty, all of the furniture pressed against the walls, blocking windows and doors. Candles flickered, dotted at random spots on the floor. The women sat on the carpet, leaning against the walls. Nobody smiled. Nobody joked. As one, they jumped with each thud that came from the hallway outside the room.

There was no sign of Claire, or Lake and his men. Megan's stomach was tight with worry about her sister. She shouldn't have let her go into town alone. What if she was lying somewhere dying in the snow? No. She couldn't think like that. Megan eyed the captive as he sat quietly in the bath. She should have left him in the snow and gone with Claire.

"Identical twins, huh?" the captive said.

Megan's eyes shot to his. "How do you know about my sister?"

He shrugged. How he managed to look relaxed while tied

up to a metal shower rod, she didn't know. "Been in town a while."

Her stomach roiled. "Watching us?"

His expression was unreadable. "Watching everyone, Buffy."

She ignored the name. No doubt he meant it as an insult. But Buffy was a superhero with cool powers who could kick the backside of any guy. As insults went, it was pretty pathetic.

"Want to tell me why you've been skulking around spying on everyone?"

"No." His grin did strange things to her insides. It made her equal parts breathless and annoyed.

"Aye, didn't think so."

He really sucked as a prisoner. No doubt he would tell her something if she removed his fingernails, but the thought of harming him while he was defenceless turned her stomach. She took solace in the fact Buffy never tortured anyone either. It was beneath her. What she needed was a pet vampire. She was pretty sure Buffy got Spike to do her dirty work. Her captive would have cracked under the attention of the vampire in leather.

"I'd pay to know what you're thinking right now," the guy said, bringing her attention back to him.

She frowned at him. "Trust me. You don't want to know."

"Yeah," he grinned again. "I think I do. You zone out all the time, then get this scary look on your face. Makes a man wonder what's going on that head of yours, blondie."

"Right now I'm wondering if I have the guts to remove your fingernails to get you to talk."

Of course, he laughed. Megan ignored him and studied the pristine white tiled walls. There wasn't much else to look at. There were no windows in the bathroom, and she'd already snooped through the cabinets and the large antique armoire. All she'd discovered was that Josh had way more aftershave than one man reasonably needed.

"Any chance I can see the life-sized sex doll?" he said when he'd stopped laughing.

"Any chance you'll tell me why you're here?"

He shook his head, his eyes gleaming with amusement.

"Then I guess we're both out of luck," Megan grumbled.

His eyes crinkled at the corners as he smiled at her. She put his age somewhere in the early thirties, but his face had seen some living. It was tanned and lined from too much sun, and there was a small scar bisecting his top lip. Chocolate eyes with golden flecks almost hypnotised when you looked into them, even though they were perpetually amused. His nose was a tad too long, his cheekbones a tad too sharp and his hair was definitely far too short for his face. Basically, it was nothing more than a coating of brown fluff on his skull. Since she'd cut away his shirt, he was only wearing his suede jacket. The chocolate colour made his eyes pop and his shoulders bulge. His bulk would have been intimidating if he wasn't tied up in a bathtub. Right now, Megan wasn't thinking about how sexy he would be under different circumstances. She was thinking about her decision to remove his gag. Like every other choice she'd made since coming across the man, it had been the wrong one.

"Tell me why you're here," Megan said again. "Seriously, what difference does it make if we know?"

"A good operative never reveals his objective."

She rolled her eyes. If the power had been on, she would have filled the tub, then plugged in a hairdryer and lobbed it in to keep him company.

"Who do you work for?" she tried again.

"Wouldn't you like to know?" He sounded like a five-year-old.

"Well, duh, that's why I'm asking. You didn't get the brain in your family, did you?"

"Hey, I'll have you know I have a college education."

She looked at the width of his shoulders. "I bet it was in something really useful. Like football."

The annoying man smirked at her. "You might as well surrender. You aren't going to win."

"This isn't about who wins. People's lives are at risk here. This isn't a game."

"Life is a game."

"Ooookay." Megan hauled herself off the toilet. "The gag is going back in. I can't take any more of this. It's like trying to hold a conversation with Yoda."

"Happy to oblige, am I," he drawled.

Megan reached for the gag when an explosion went off. The room shook. Another followed. Megan held on to the sink.

"What the hell?" the captive said. The amused look was gone, and in its place was the intelligence and focus of a trained killer.

"Someone blew up the snowmobiles," her mother shouted. "I think Matt is here."

"The guys are here?" That was Caroline's voice. "Are we sure? How do we know for sure?"

"I can't see anything else," Heather Donaldson said. "It's all smoke and snow out there."

"I don't hear anything either." That was Kirsty.

"Caroline, get on the intercom. See what you can find out." Joe sounded intense.

A few seconds later, Caroline's voice rang out. "Alastair, Rainne, are you there?"

There was silence. She tried again. And again.

"I hope this doesn't mean someone got to them," Jena said softly.

"Try a house-wide call. See if anyone we know is in the house." Joe again.

"Hello, this is Caroline. Are any of our men here?" Caroline sounded desperate.

They all did. Because they *were* desperate. A good sense of humour could only take you so far when you were under attack.

"Hello, if you're there, answer me." Caroline again.

Nothing.

"I don't think your guys blew up the machines," the guy in the bath said.

"Then who did?" Megan asked him. "Is it your lot? Why would you blow up your own transport?"

"We wouldn't."

They stared at each other for a beat. She couldn't tell what he was thinking. Megan found herself mesmerised by his dark eyes. An unwanted flare of awareness went through her. His pupils dilated, telling her he felt it too.

"Tell me your name," Megan asked. "At least give me that."

"Dimitri." He gave up the name without any hesitation.

"Really? You don't look like a Dimitri."

"Tell that to my Russian parents."

"I thought it was a Greek name."

He cocked an eyebrow, surprised. Megan just about managed to resist rolling her eyes. *Oh yeah, Barbie has a brain. Booya sucker.*

"Greek origin. Russian version," he told her.

"Dimitri." She tried the name for effect. It suited him. "Tell me why you're here. Tell me something. Anything that will help us."

His eyes were hard as flint. "I can tell you one thing," he said quietly, making her take a step towards him.

"What?" Her heart raced as her focus became all about him. "What is it?"

"I can tell you you've overlooked something."

Her spine went taut. "What?"

He glanced up, and Megan followed his gaze. Straight up to the wide skylight above the bath. Her heart stopped. Her mouth opened to shout for Joe. The beam of a flashlight scanned over the glass before a hand appeared. It wielded the butt of a gun like a club.

"Get in the bath," Dimitri shouted. "It's going to shatter."

Without thinking, Megan threw herself into the bath on top of her captive. Dimitri pulled a bath towel over their heads. Just as they were covered, the glass shattered, raining down on them.

A heavy thump sounded on the floor beside the bath. The door to the room slammed shut.

"Down!" Dimitri ordered. He flattened her onto her back in the bath, lying on top of her. Shielding her body with his.

She heard gunfire from outside the bathroom, but the bullets hit the heavy wooden door. There was the scraping sound of furniture being dragged, and Megan knew the bad guys were blocking the door with the wooden armoire that sat in the corner of the bathroom.

She was trapped.

Barricaded inside the room.

With the bad guys.

Her mouth went dry. Her hands curled into the jacket of the man on top of her before she could question her actions. Fool. He was the enemy. His lips brushed against her ear.

"Trust me," he whispered. "Do as I do."

Before she could make sense of his words, the towel was whipped from their heads. She looked up, past Dimitri, into the cold grey eyes of a man wearing a white ski mask.

Arms tightened around her as Dimitri sat up in the bath, taking her with him. It took her a second to realise that

Dimitri was no longer tied up. He'd broken out of his bonds. How long ago, she didn't know, but it was before the guys came through the skylight. He'd been toying with her. Pretending to play captive.

"Meet Claire," Dimitri said. His voice was different. Hard. It also held a heavy Russian accent. "Claire, this is Reynard. He's come all this way to meet you, so be nice."

What the hell? Megan struggled against Dimitri's hold. He knew damn well she wasn't Claire. The man in front of her leaned forward and brushed the hair from her cheek.

"Pleased to meet you, Claire." He had eyes that were flat like a shark's. They made her shudder. "Our employer would very much like the pleasure of your company."

"I'm not…" Dimitri's hand slapped over her mouth and stayed there.

"What took you so long?" Dimitri said. "I've been trying to keep the target distracted until you showed up."

"Yeah." The other guy's accent was harder to place. European, but where? "I can see you suffered. I'm impressed you infiltrated the group. How did you manage to separate her from the others?"

"Charm." Dimitri stood and yanked her up with him, still covering her mouth. "And skill. We need to get out of here. Lake Benson and his men are on the way."

Megan struggled in Dimitri's arms, vaguely aware that being the captive was nowhere near as much fun as being the captor.

"We've got what we came for." Reynard motioned to Megan. "You've been a lot of trouble, Claire. This is the first time you've been away from your husband in weeks. I had intended for this job to be more subtle, but instead we were forced to start World War Three to get to you."

The pressure over her mouth increased. Dimitri really

didn't want her to tell his colleagues that she wasn't her sister. What the hell did that mean? Why did he want her to pretend? Who was after Claire? Who were these men? She was starting to hyperventilate when a rope ladder fell through the hole where the skylight used to be.

"I'll go up first. You follow with her," the masked man said.

Without another word, the man started to climb up the ladder into the black night.

"Don't tell them you're not Claire," Dimitri whispered in her ear. "Reynard will put a bullet in your brain and then hunt her down. There's more at stake here than your life." He stepped out of the bath, lifting her with him. "Your sister is pregnant. She was going to announce it after the wedding."

Megan jolted in his arms. He was lying. Claire couldn't be pregnant. She would have told her. Claire told her everything. She hesitated. Well, she used to tell her everything, until she'd married Grunt. Now things were a little different.

"Surveillance," Dimitri whispered. "She found out this morning. Trust me. These guys would love to take a pregnant woman. It would add to the fun. We can't let that happen."

"We?" Megan said against the palm covering her mouth.

"Play along. Do it for your sister. We'll figure the rest out later. I'll come up with a plan."

"Get a move on," the guy above them shouted down.

"Trust me," Dimitri whispered before shoving her towards the ladder. "Climb, Claire," he said loud enough for his colleagues to hear.

It was decision time. Did she pretend to be Claire, or call his bluff? She felt the warm length of Dimitri against her back as he herded her towards the ladder. She looked up at the faceless man above her, his handgun pointed at her head. Dimitri had said he'd shoot her if she wasn't Claire. She wasn't sure she could trust Dimitri. She wasn't even sure who he was, or whose side he was on.

But some things she did know for certain. She didn't want them hunting down her sister. And she definitely didn't want to die. That left only one choice.

She reached up, gripped the ladder and started to climb.

CHAPTER 23

Lake screeched to a halt at the castle gate as the night exploded. The men watched the balls of orange turn to smoke that faded into the blackness of the night.

"Was that the castle?" Josh sounded frantic. "It couldn't be the castle. Right?"

"Two small vehicles," Callum said. "Exploding one after the other."

Lake nodded. He'd heard the same thing. "Get a move on," he ordered everyone.

The men shook themselves into action and ran towards the flames in the distance. The glow from the burning vehicles clearly lit the exterior of the castle. Progress through the snow was slow, even at a run. Each step felt like a mile.

Gunshots sounded through the night, dulled by the thick stone making up the castle. Someone was in there. Where were the women? What were Joe and Ryan doing?

If he was too late. If Kirsty was hurt. Nothing would stop the havoc he would wreak.

"They're okay," Flynn said through the comm units.

Whether he was talking to himself or to everyone, Lake wasn't sure. "They've got to be okay. They're resourceful."

No one answered. Instead they picked up their pace, desperate to get to the castle.

Smashing glass. More gunfire. Shouting. Screaming.

Lake's fear compressed down inside of him, refining into pure fury.

"Split," he ordered, and they broke off into the three groups they'd previously arranged.

Callum and Matt headed to the back of the castle. Josh, Mitch, Harry and Flynn fell back and spread out, eager to pick up any strays Grunt and Lake left in their wake. Lake could have told them they'd be disappointed. No one was getting past him. With one sharp hand signal, Lake motioned for Grunt to move right, while he moved left.

Lake felt his breathing slow, his heart rate lower, his focus distil. There was nothing in his mind but the mission. Only eliminating the threat and securing Kirsty mattered.

Men ran out of the castle, straight to the burning snowmobiles. There were shouts. Cursing, followed by orders to find and eliminate the people who'd blown up their transport. Lake almost smiled. Instead, he crept towards the men, keeping to the shadows.

"I count five," Lake whispered into his mic.

A short, sharp shot to his right. The unmistakable guttural grunt of a man going down.

"One less now," Grunt said, his voice crystal clear through the headset Lake wore.

The men in front of him sprang into action. Guns were raised. They ran for cover. Some of them headed back into the castle. He saw the windows of the grand room blow as the men shot blindly into the night.

"Three more back here," Callum said. "Make that four."

Lake crept up behind one of the guys. He wrapped his

arm around his neck. A minute later he was unconscious in the snow. Lake disarmed him, then secured his arms and legs with cable ties.

"Two less," he stated calmly into his mic.

Each of the snowmobiles could have held at least two people, maybe three, and Claire had told them there were already three in the castle. That made at least nine, including the captive Megan had secured.

More shots and several grunts. "Three and four," Grunt said without a trace of emotion.

"Try not to shoot the assholes," Matt said.

"I didn't shoot," Grunt said. "And I didn't break any necks. These two are secured."

"Show-off," Matt said tersely. "More coming round the side of the house."

"Do we move the unconscious guys, or leave their asses in the snow?" Harry said.

"Leave them. They aren't going anywhere," Matt said. "We'll deal with them later. Make sure they're secured."

"What if they freeze to death?" Harry said.

"Anybody care, speak now," Matt said over the headsets.

There was silence.

Lake made it to the front door. It was ajar. He pushed it open with the barrel of his gun and listened. Nothing. Not so much as a creak coming from the ground floor. But noise reverberated through the building. It came from the tower bedroom.

Lake kept his back to the wall as he headed up the stairs, gun pointed in front of him.

"Need backup," Callum said in Lake's ear.

Lake changed direction and headed for the back of the house. Quickly, but silently, he made his way along the hallway to the kitchen. There was the sound of smashing glass. Gunfire. Screaming. Lake raced towards it all. He ran through the kitchen, grateful he was familiar with the layout of the house. As he came to the broken back door, he spotted Callum and Matt. They were hunkered behind the small wall surrounding the patio, pinned down by two guys in white snowsuits, armed with semi-automatic rifles.

Grunt appeared at Lake's side. They didn't speak to each other. With one hand motion, Lake communicated where he wanted Grunt to go and the man was off, moving silently into the shadows.

Lake stepped out into the back patio and took aim at one of the guys who had Callum pinned. Then he felt a thud on his upper arm, making him jerk backwards. He'd been hit. He spun in place and spotted three more assailants rounding the corner of the building. Lake crouched behind the only cover available, a metal patio chair, and fired. The men dodged, hiding beyond the corner of the building.

"Five down," Grunt muttered as he came up behind Lake. They crouched, back to back.

"Stop them!" A high-pitched scream came from above them.

Lake fired off three shots at the corner of the building, pushing the remaining assailants back. When they ducked out of sight, he looked up. The women were hanging out of the windows.

"They've got Megan," Jena yelled, her arm outstretched, pointing.

Lake's head snapped in the direction she pointed. Two men, dragging a woman between them. Shots rang out, making Lake and Grunt flatten to the icy ground.

"Stop shooting at my castle," Caroline shouted. "You. You in the white. Put that gun down at once."

Lake had no idea who she was shouting at. All of the men wore white. There was another gunshot and the sound of shattering glass.

"Not the conservatory!" Caroline wailed. "We just had that installed."

Then something heavy flew through the air and landed on the head of the guy who'd shot the conservatory. He crumpled under it.

"Good shot, baby," Josh shouted. "Wait. Is that Josh Mark Two? Couldn't you have thrown the lingerie drawers?"

"Six. Flattened by a life-sized Josh doll," Grunt said.

"Status?" Lake barked into his mic.

"Two with Megan," Matt said, his voice vibrating with fury at the thought of his sister being taken. "Two pinned to the back patio."

"Everyone else secured," Mitch said.

"And tasered," Harry added. "Just in case."

"You just like using the taser," Flynn said.

"I'm getting one when this is over," Harry agreed.

Matt had taken advantage of the commotion to sneak up on the gunman who'd pinned Callum down. "Seven. Secured and disarmed," he said.

The last remaining attacker fired rapidly at Matt as he ran for cover in the spot where his cousins were crouching.

"Matt!" Jena screamed. "Don't get shot, baby."

"Don't worry," Matt's mother shouted. "We've got this under control."

And then all hell broke loose—and it took the form of whizzing rockets, blasts of light and bursts of sparkles.

"Crap," Josh said. "They found the firework stash."

Lake watched in amazement as the back garden exploded around them. "Take cover," he snapped. "They have no control over these things."

He ducked back into the kitchen just as a massive rocket took out a planter. The explosions and blinding bursts of light carried on for a couple of minutes as fireworks flew randomly across the yard instead of into the air. When the noise died down, the air was filled with smoke and the snow had black burn tracks through it.

"Eight," Grunt said. "Taken out by a flying Roman candle."

"Ow," Flynn said. "That had to hurt. The guy looks like he's been scalped."

"Burnt off his balaclava," Grunt agreed as Lake came up beside them.

"Get Megan," Lake ordered Grunt, and the man mountain was instantly gone.

Shots hit the snow behind Lake and Flynn, making them dive for cover.

"No!" Harry shouted. "I've been hit, I've been hit. They killed my laptop. It's okay, baby, it's okay. Papa's going to dig out the nasty bullet and you'll be good as new."

"You're embarrassing me," Flynn said.

"It's my favourite laptop," Harry said.

Lake kept low to the ground and crept back into the kitchen. He ran across the room, aimed at the guy pinning Harry down and fired through the glass window. Twice. One in each leg. The guy went down with a howl, firing wildly. As soon he was on the ground, Matt rushed out and removed the gun, but ignored the writhing man.

"Nine," Matt said.

Lake watched from his spot beside the kitchen door as Matt produced some plastic ties from his pocket and secured the fallen guy's arms and legs.

"Clear this side," Callum said.

"Clear out front," Mitch said.

"I'm pissed I didn't see any action," Josh said.

"Go find your wife," Mitch told him. "That'll cheer you up."

"I'll scout round the perimeter," Matt said, and took off at a run.

Harry and Flynn came out from their hiding spot and

headed towards the castle. Flynn walked up to the injured men lying bound in the snow and tasered each of them.

"Just in case," he said.

"Is it over?" Abby shouted. "Did you get them all?"

Flynn looked up at his pregnant wife, the relief plain on his face. "It's over, sugar. You okay? The babies?"

She looked down at her belly then smiled at her husband. "We're fine." She looked behind her into the master bedroom. "We've made a bit of a mess in here, though. Jean accidentally set off a firework in the wrong direction. Where's Megan?"

Matt came running up as Abby asked about his sister. He looked at Lake. "All clear."

Lake nodded. "Boys, get the prisoners and the wounded inside. Matt, you're with me. Let's get your sister."

They took off at a run after Megan.

CHAPTER 24

* RAINNE AND ALASTAIR *

Alastair landed face first in the snow. Pain surged through him. Aye, those ribs were definitely broken now. He focused on breathing slowly, hoping to ease the pain. That was when the gunfire started. Lots and lots of gunfire.

Rainne...

He scanned around him, blinking away the daze in his head. The snow glowed orange in the dimming blaze of the still-burning snowmobiles.

Rainne?

There.

The silhouette of a body lying against a tree.

She wasn't moving.

Rainbow!

Alastair swallowed panic that felt a whole lot like terror, and struggled to sit up. The world swayed and tilted. He fell to his side on the snow and pure agony racked his body. More gunfire rent the air. Who was shooting? Was Lake here? Alastair worked on breathing calmly as stars danced in front of his eyes.

He saw the shadow of a figure, crouching low to the

ground and moving fast towards the castle. Enemy? Friend? He didn't know. Adrenalin coursed through him, dulling the pain and clarifying his thoughts.

He had to get to Rainne.

He had to get her out of harm's way. He didn't know who was firing. And no one knew he was out there with Rainne. If they weren't being deliberately targeted, they could still get caught in the crossfire. They needed to get inside. Now.

Slowly. Agonisingly. He crawled across the snow. Every breath was a knife to his chest. He could barely feel his fingers, which was probably a good thing, as it meant he also couldn't feel his wrist. It had lost its bandage and was now bent at an unnatural angle. Bloody hell, he was a mess. No use to anyone.

And he was all Rainne had.

Nausea assaulted him, but he struggled onward. *Got to get to Rainne.* An eternity later, he collapsed at her side. He put his hand on her back.

"Rainbow. Baby," he whispered, afraid to attract the wrong attention. "You need to wake up. We need to get out of here."

She didn't move.

No. No. No. No. No...

Panic made Alastair sway in place. She had to be fine. There was no other option.

"Please be okay, Rainbow. Please be okay." His whispered pleas were swallowed by the black night.

Women were shouting. He could almost taste hysteria in the air. Alastair blocked out the words. It sounded like the world was exploding behind him in bursts of luminous colour, but everything he cared about was right in front of him. He brushed her hair from her forehead and caught sight of his hand. He lifted it to the dim light.

Blood.

No. This wasn't happening.

He wrapped an arm around her waist and tugged her up so she was leaning over his legs. He propped his back against the tree and pulled her into his lap. She was a dead weight.

No. Not dead. Never dead. Don't think it. Don't say it.

Her face was as white as the snow. Her lips were blue.

"Rainbow. Wake up."

He unzipped her coat and thrust his hand inside, splaying it over her heart. He waited.

There! A heartbeat. A breath.

"Don't scare me like that." He buried his face in her hair. Inhaled her scent.

His cheeks felt wet, and it took him a second to realise he was weeping.

She was okay. She was going to be okay.

There was another short burst of gunfire. He thought it came from the back of the castle. More shouting. Male and female voices. Was it over? Were they okay? He looked down at Rainne, so limp and lifeless in his arms. His brave girl. Braver than he was, willing to try for a second chance with him. Willing to put herself and her heart out there for him to stomp on.

And he had. He'd stomped all over her because he'd been too scared to take a chance on getting hurt again. Pathetic bloody coward. Too stubborn to see past his pride until it was too late. No. Not too late. Never too late. She was breathing. She was going to be fine. She had to be.

"Sorry, Rainbow. Please be okay, baby." He kissed her hair.

He needed to get them out of the snow. He needed to carry her to the castle. It didn't matter if the place was full of nutters with guns. If they stayed where they were, they'd die of hypothermia anyway. Better to try for the warmth of the nearest building.

"Don't worry, Rainbow. I've got you."

Alastair clasped her tightly and tried to get to his feet. A brutal, nauseating wave of pain had him falling back to the ground and gasping for air.

"It's okay. It's okay." He wasn't sure who he was trying to reassure. Probably himself.

Right, he had to do this differently. He gently placed Rainne on the snow beside him and got to his knees. Bending over, he lifted her to cradle her in his arms. She was so small. Had she always been this small? Delicate. Fragile. So damned fragile. He glanced at the castle. It was quiet. No more gunfire. Good. That was good. Right?

He took a breath and raised his leg until his foot was flat on the snow in front of him. His weight still rested on his knee. Now was the hard part. Tensing his muscles and holding Rainne tight, he transferred all of his weight onto his foot and pushed upright. With one agonising surge, he was on his feet. Rainne clutched to his chest. He wanted to roar in victory, but instead he bit his bottom lip and swayed with pain.

For a moment he concentrated on breathing and staying upright. At last the dizziness faded, although he still felt weak and his jaw was at breaking point from clenching his teeth.

Slowly. Agonisingly. He turned towards the castle. He didn't know who was in there. He didn't know who was in control. But he did know Rainne had to get out of the cold. She wouldn't survive if she didn't. There was nothing for it but to take the chance and head for the castle. He just hoped he'd find help waiting for him, instead of a firing squad.

"It's going to be okay," he whispered to Rainne. "I've got you."

And he was never letting her go.

That was where he'd been going wrong. He'd let people walk away and hoped they came back. Not this time. Not again. This time he was going to superglue the woman to his side if that was what it took to make her stay. It was amazing the clarity that came with life-threatening danger. His objections and fears now seemed petty beside the vastness of what he could have lost.

And he wasn't going to lose Rainne.

He wasn't.

Black spots appeared in his vision as he tightened his hold on his girl. At least she wasn't lying in the snow anymore. He drew in another agonising breath.

He took a step. It jarred his side, making his eyesight blur. He shifted Rainne's weight slightly until she was resting on his forearm rather than his wrist. Only sheer brutal determination kept her in his arms. Another step. Another agonising burst of pain. The snow sucked at his boots, trying to keep him in place. Alastair fought against it. He kept his eyes on the building in front of him and kept on walking.

Another step closer.

He heard a gunshot from further away. Over near the west gate, he thought. But no more shots from the castle.

Another step closer.

Rainne was silent in his arms. There was no way for him to check if she was still breathing. Not without letting her go. And he wasn't doing that. Not ever.

Another step.

He saw movement through the windows of the castle's grand room, but couldn't tell who it was. Candlelight flickered to life, making the room glow. Shadows moved about.

"Nearly there," he told Rainne.

He'd lost count of the steps he'd taken. His lung felt like someone was holding the sharp tip of a knife against it.

Damn, he was a hair's breadth away from a punctured lung.

Another step.

He'd lost feeling in his frozen fingers. His arm muscles cramped to keep Rainne tight against him.

One more step.

One more step.

Just one more step.

He reached the snow-covered front stairs to the castle. The door at the top lay open. Voices wafted out from inside, but he couldn't make out what anyone was saying. Sweat trickled down his brow. This was it. He was going in. He hoped to hell he'd meet a friend instead of a bullet.

He took the first stair with a groan. Four more. He could do it.

Four. *Bloody hell, the pain.*

Three. *Breathe. Slow. Shallow.*

Two. *Hold it together. Nearly there.*

One. *Swallow the pain.*

There. He was there. The sharp agony under his ribs was stronger. Stars burst in front of his eyes. He stepped into the hallway, boots heavy on the wooden floor. He was past stealth. He didn't care who heard. He took a step towards the grand room. Someone came through the door.

Alastair froze. It took a second for him to realise it was Caroline. She turned towards him and gasped.

"Rainne needs help," Alastair said. His words seemed to be coming from far away.

"Help!" Caroline shouted as she rushed towards him.

Joe appeared beside her, his face stern. His eyes went wide and he ran at Alastair.

"Help Rainne," Alastair said. Damn, his words were slurred and he was finding it hard to see.

He felt a pop in his side. A bright flash of white-hot pain surged through him. His eyes rolled back. And he was falling.

Still holding Rainne tight to him.

CHAPTER 25

* MEGAN *

To say Megan was annoyed would be like saying the Hulk felt slightly grumpy.

She'd been hauled into the darkness and dragged through the snow without even a coat to wear, and she was freezing her bum off. Her silver sweater had been chosen for pretty, not practical. Not to mention she'd changed back into her high-heeled fashion boots with their smooth sole which kept slipping in the snow. On top of that, a seriously scary guy stalked two paces in front of her and her former captive was pressed to her back. Trust him, he'd said. Yeah, she'd get right on that.

Megan scanned around her. The snowfall was easing up —slightly. There were no other men near them. It was just the three of them. And from the sounds of it, the bad guys back at the castle were having their backsides handed to them by her brother and his friends.

Good. She hoped they suffered.

She tripped over the snow and head-butted Reynard's spine.

"Watch it," he snapped. "Keep hold of her. We need to

speed up. I have a couple of snowmobiles stashed at the west exit."

"What about the others?" Dimitri's left hand wrapped around her upper arm.

"They're on their own. I don't get paid enough to save their asses."

Charming.

Dimitri motioned for her to speed up, using the gun he held in his right hand. "Hurry," he ordered.

Was he an idiot? She scowled over her shoulder at him. No way was she hurrying to get to whatever Reynard had planned for her. Dimitri bugged his eyes at her, as though to remind her of what he'd told her. Like she'd forget. He'd told her to follow the scary guy and he'd come up with a plan to save her—later. That did not instil confidence. She wasn't even sure what side the guy was on. Dimitri had his own agenda, and Megan figured she'd become dispensable if she got in the way of it. So, no. She wasn't going to wait around for him to rescue her. What was this, the eighteen hundreds? Did she look like she was wearing a corset and would faint at the first sign of trouble? No. She didn't need to be rescued by some man.

She was going to rescue herself.

She looked down at Dimitri's hand as it held the gun loosely at his side. It was the only type of gun she recognised—a Beretta M9. She'd been given a lecture on it from Grunt one night when they were watching an action movie and she'd called it a toy gun. Grunt had retrieved his Beretta and talked her through how it worked, all to make the point that no gun was a toy. At the time she'd thought he was being anal; now she thought he deserved a thank-you hamper, because Dimitri was holding the only gun on the planet she knew how to use. Now all she needed to do was come up with a plan to get her hands on it. She looked at the gun. Then at the scary guy in front of her. Then back to the gun.

Oh, to hell with having a plan.

She never did have the patience for planning anyway. Without a second thought, she grabbed Dimitri's hand, and gun, pointed it at Reynard, flicked the safety off with her thumb and squeezed the trigger.

"What the—" Dimitri started.

Before he could say, or do, anything else, she turned and kneed him in the balls. He howled and bent double, leaving Megan time to turn to Reynard. He was out cold, face down in the snow. She grabbed his gun—some sort of automatic thing she didn't recognise. She swung around and pointed it at Dimitri's head, hoping she didn't have to shoot, because she wasn't even sure her finger was on the trigger.

"Drop the gun." Then she kicked him in the balls again for good measure.

His gun fell to the snow, followed closely by the man, who writhed in agony.

Serves him right.

The guy had been nothing but trouble since she'd captured him. Megan tore her eyes from the groaning Dimitri and looked down at the overly complicated gun in her hand. She wasn't quite sure how it worked, so she tossed it over to the trees and picked up Dimitri's discarded hand-gun. Much better. Point and shoot. She could do that.

"You gonna leave anything for me?" a voice said.

Megan reacted before she realised it was her brother-in-law. She had to lower her gun to let him walk forward.

He looked down at the two men and grinned. "I came to rescue you."

"Thanks?"

Grunt crouched beside the scary unconscious guy as the weight of the situation began to sink in. She'd shot someone.

Had she killed him? Her hands began to shake, and she worked to hide her reaction from Grunt. She didn't want to tarnish her newly acquired street cred.

"Is he dead?" At least her voice was steady.

Grunt looked positively delighted. "No. You shot him in the ass. I think he passed out from the shock of it." He pointed at Dimitri, who had turned green and was muttering something about never having children. "Why didn't you shoot him?"

Megan shrugged, although inside she wanted to weep with relief. No dead bodies. Yay for her. "I'm not sure what side he's on."

"I would rather have been shot," Dimitri wailed.

Lake and Matt appeared out of the darkness. Megan let her older brother pull her into a tight hug.

"Good job, Grunt," Lake said.

"Hey!" Megan complained into Matt's chest.

"Wasn't me," Grunt said. "By the time I turned up, she'd sorted them out."

Lake and Matt gaped at her.

"What?" She was seriously offended by their disbelief. "I have skills."

"No you don't," her brother said.

"Fine. I might not, but I watch a lot of action movies."

"You're telling me I was taken down by a woman whose only experience comes from action movies?" Dimitri shouted. Megan noted he was back to using a vague North American accent.

"Can I kick him again?" Megan asked her brother.

"Unfortunately," Lake answered. "We need him. We have some questions that have to be answered."

"He won't answer," Megan said. "He's the one we were interrogating in the castle."

Dimitri started to laugh, while still holding his balls. "That was an interrogation?"

"I really want to hit him again." Megan took a step towards the guy, but Matt pulled her back.

"He'll answer the questions I ask," Lake said to Megan. His cold eyes were on Dimitri.

Yeah, she bet he would. Megan would answer anything Lake asked her too. There was something about his controlled, calculated stare that was chilling.

She cleared her throat. "He said they were after Claire. He told me to pretend to be her." She looked at Grunt, who had gone eerily still. "He said they'd kill me if I told them I wasn't Claire. They've been watching you for a while. That one"— she pointed at Reynard—"is being paid to take Claire to his boss. I don't know who the boss is, though."

Grunt stood slowly and seemed to morph into someone even bigger than his usual colossal size. He loomed over the men who'd attacked them, and Megan got the distinct impression he was a hair trigger away from turning their bodies into Swiss cheese.

Dimitri's eyes were on Grunt. He wasn't amused now. "I'll tell you everything. Just as soon as I can stand. Buffy's right— I'm one of the good guys."

"We'll see," Grunt said. It was a clear threat. If Grunt didn't like what he heard, Dimitri wouldn't like the consequences.

Lake stood with a sigh. "Everyone back to the castle. Then we'll sort this mess out." He picked up the discarded weapons. Megan expected him to ask for the one she held, and was surprised when he didn't.

"Just in case you need it, hotshot," he told her.

Grunt bent over, lifted Reynard and tossed him over his shoulder as though he weighed nothing. He pointed at Dimitri. "You're walking. Don't try anything funny."

Dimitri struggled to his feet. "Trust me, the last thing on my mind is anything funny. All I can think about is getting to an icepack." Dimitri glared at Megan.

"Stop whining," Megan said. "If you want ice, lie down and press your balls into the snow. You totally deserve the pain. I'd kick you again for caving after two seconds with Grunt, when I asked you questions for hours."

"Face it, Buffy, the big guy is scary. You're just amusing."

Megan narrowed her eyes. "Now I really want to hurt you."

Dimitri moved closer to Lake. "Keep her away from me," he said as he limped towards the castle.

CHAPTER 26

* RAINNE AND ALASTAIR *

Alastair wasn't out more than a few seconds. He came to, lying on the floor in the castle hallway as Joe was taking Rainne from his arms.

"Help, we need help," Caroline shouted.

"She won't wake up." Alastair gasped for air. It was so damn hard to breathe. "She—"

"I got her, don't worry. We need to warm her up." Joe turned as more women rushed into the hallway. "Someone light the fire in the office. We need to warm them up. Caroline? Hot water bottles?"

"Of course. I'll have to fill them from the hot water tap, but it's better than nothing." She rushed off.

Someone thudded to his knees at Alastair's side.

"I'll get blankets," Kirsty shouted as she ran after Caroline.

Alastair panted through shallow, painful breaths as he looked up to find Ryan. "She." Gasp. "Hit." Gasp. "Her." Gasp. "Head."

"We're on it." Ryan pulled at Alastair's shirt. "Looks like broken ribs. Probable punctured lung. He's turning blue."

"Rainne." Pain made Alastair's eyes close. His lungs flexed and he coughed, making it worse. His vision blurred.

Someone else came to his side. Alastair panted as he turned his head. Flynn. When did Flynn get here?

"I've got a comm line to Callum," Flynn told Ryan. "Callum was a medic in the SAS. He's digging a bullet out of some guy's leg right now. He can tell me what to do." He touched his ear. "Callum, we've got a problem here. Broken rib. Punctured lung, we think. We're not sure."

Alastair fought the urge to cough. Panic bit at him. He couldn't breathe. There wasn't enough air. Damn it, he was going to suffocate when he hadn't sorted things with Rainbow.

He wrapped his fingers around Ryan's arm, uncaring that his grip was tight.

"Rainne?"

"Don't worry about her," Ryan said.

"No." Alastair coughed hard, but never let go of Ryan. "Rainne?"

"We've got her," Margaret Campbell said from behind Ryan. "We're warming her up. We think she's still unconscious because she got too cold. Don't worry about her. She's going to be fine."

Alastair relaxed slightly, and then lost consciousness for a few seconds as agony spiked through him.

"Blue around the mouth," Flynn was saying when Alastair was able to focus again. Flynn was looking at his wife. "I need a scalpel and a sanitised tube."

"I heard," Caroline said as she appeared in Alastair's view. "I'll get you something."

"What?" Alastair said. It hurt to talk. Hurt to breathe. He was drowning. It felt like someone was sitting on his chest and every short breath was pure agony.

"You're going to be okay," Flynn told him. "You'll be breathing fine in a minute. Try not to panic."

Aye, that was exactly what he'd do. Right after he punched Flynn for the stupid advice. His chest spasmed as the urge to cough hit him and he fought it.

"What are you going to do?" Abby sounded shaken.

"I need to insert a tube into his chest cavity, near his ribs. It will let the air out and take the pressure off his lung. Right now the air he's sucking in is seeping out into his chest cavity and it has nowhere to go. The more air in the cavity, the less can get into the lung. That's why he's going blue, baby—he isn't getting enough air. We need to relieve the pressure." Alastair stared at Flynn as he smiled at his wife. "Callum is going to talk me through it. But it seems simple enough. It's good practice for the future."

"Flynn." Abby rested her forehead against his for a second. "You're going to be a vet."

"Horses, people, same difference," Flynn said.

"Not." Gasp. "Reassuring." The words sent Alastair into another hacking cough.

"Stop talking," Flynn ordered. "Nothing you say is going to be helpful anyway."

Alastair made a mental note to hurt Flynn Boyle once this was over. The ex-football player had it coming.

"Rainne is doing great," Joe said as he crouched beside Alastair. "The head injury was small. Once she warms up, she'll wake up."

He sounded sure. Alastair wanted to believe him. Rainne had to be okay.

"Here." Caroline rushed back into the hallway. She thrust a thick plastic drinking straw and a paring knife at Flynn. "That's the best I can do."

Flynn told Callum what they had then nodded to Caroline. "It's good. I need antiseptic wipes and bandages." He looked at Alastair. "I'm not going to mess with you. This will hurt. You can't move. I'm going to get Ryan and Joe to hold you down. Don't panic, okay? I can't risk you jerking when I use the knife and causing more damage."

"Do." Gasp. "It."

Joe secured Alastair's legs while Ryan held his arms. He was trapped. Gasping for air. In agony. Trapped. He clenched his teeth hard and fought the instinct to struggle free.

"Now," Ryan said to Flynn.

With no word of warning and no hesitation, Flynn put his hand on Alastair's bruised ribs and came at him with the knife.

The pain was searing. Alastair tensed against the men holding him. His neck arched upwards. His teeth clenched hard enough to break, and a low growl came out of his mouth.

"I've made a small cut," Flynn said. "The worst is over. Honest. I'm feeding the tube into the space. Nearly done."

Although he knew the whole thing happened in a matter of seconds, it felt like a millennium. Abby handed Flynn the wipes, bandage and tape. Alastair felt the straw being secured to his side.

Alastair gasped in a breath and didn't cough. His second breath was easier. The pain began to subside.

"Better," he rasped.

And it felt like everyone in the room was breathing alongside him.

"You did good," Abby said before kissing her husband.

"What. About. Me?" Alastair said, feeling lightheaded.

"You did good too." Abby smiled down at him.

Alastair felt Joe and Ryan release his limbs. He didn't move. He couldn't move.

Flynn was talking to Callum through his headset. "The

blue is fading. The rasp has gone, but we need a doctor and a hospital. He's breathing better. And talking. No more coughing." He grinned down at Alastair. "You're going to be okay."

Alastair couldn't say anything. Once this was over he was going to punch the guy, then shake his hand for saving his life.

Flynn paused while he listened to Callum. He looked up at the women around them. Alastair hadn't realised the hall was crowded. Most of the women from the hen night were staring down at them.

"Callum said he heard from Lake. They've got Megan. She's fine. She'd freed herself before they got there." He paused and grinned widely. "She shot her kidnapper in the backside."

"That's my girl!" Heather shouted, and then burst into tears. Caroline wrapped her arms around the woman and cooed to her.

"He also says that there are a couple of snowmobiles parked at the west entrance." Flynn pressed another button and spoke again. "Lake, we have Rainne and Alastair in here. Collapsed lung. Broken ribs. Possible concussion. We need a doctor." He waited, then nodded. "I'll tell him." Flynn turned to Ryan. "Can you go get a snowmobile and run into town to fetch the doc?"

"I'm on it." Ryan ran from the room.

"You okay?" Joe said to Alastair.

He started to nod, but it hurt too much to move. "Aye. How's Rainne, really?"

"You can ask me yourself," said the voice he loved.

Alastair turned his head slightly to see Rainne rushing towards him. She was wrapped in a duvet and wasn't steady on her feet. Jena was running after her, slowly, in her platform heels.

"She escaped," Jena said. "She insisted on seeing Alastair, and when I turned my back she was gone."

Rainne collapsed to her knees on Alastair's left side. One hand poked out of her wrapping. She moved to touch him and then jerked back as though remembering her touch would be unwelcome. The pain of watching her uncertainty made Alastair ache more than all of his broken bones. Biting back a moan, he lifted his hand, took hers in his and wound their fingers together. Her eyes went wide as she watched him do it, then they went glassy with unshed tears. But she held him tight.

"I was unconscious," she said softly. "When I woke up, you weren't there." Her eyes scanned down his body and she trembled. "There's a pink plastic drinking straw sticking out of your side."

"It's Flynn's fault," Alastair said, pleased it no longer hurt to talk.

"Hey," Flynn said. "I saved your ungrateful backside with that straw."

"I'm grateful," Rainne said. "I'm glad you saved him, Flynn." A tear ran down her cheek and Alastair lifted his other hand to brush it away. Pain stopped him and he winced.

"Your wrist!" Rainne looked over at Joe. "Check his wrist. It was badly sprained before the blasts sent us flying."

Alastair felt Joe gently pull back his sleeve.

"Yeah, it's broken now." Joe glared at Alastair. "Why didn't you mention it?"

"I forgot," Alastair said his eyes on Rainne.

Joe started muttering something about insane Scottish men, while he went to fetch something to splint Alastair's wrist.

"This just goes to prove what I've been saying all along,"

Margaret said. "There are no tougher men in the world than the Scots."

"Aye," Shona said. "The proof is in the wearing of kilts in winter. Takes a real man to do that."

Rainne started to giggle, and Alastair felt his heart melt. He held on tight to his woman.

"Are you really okay?" he asked Rainne.

She rubbed her thumb over the back of his hand. "I might have a teeny, tiny concussion. I feel a little bit nauseous. Apart from that, I just feel weak. I want to get warm and stay warm for the next sixty years."

Alastair was grateful when the deep breath he took didn't send him into agony. "I can help with that," he said.

Rainne's eyes shot to his and he watched her swallow several times. Everyone around them fell silent. Alastair hated being the centre of attention, but he didn't want to break eye contact with Rainbow long enough to demand privacy.

"Alastair," she whispered. "You're injured. You don't know what you're saying."

Joe knelt at Alastair's other side and started bandaging up his wrist.

"This will hold it 'til the doc gets here," Joe said.

"Joe," Margaret said. "Shut up, they're being romantic."

Alastair couldn't help but smile. He was lying on his back, in the middle of a torn-up castle, with a plastic straw sticking out of his side, and Margaret was worried about romance. Now he knew where Kirsty got her flair for the dramatic.

"We'll talk about this when you're better." Rainne's cheeks flushed under the attention.

"I think we should talk about it now." Alastair bit back a curse as Joe was less than gentle with his wrist.

"Aye, now is a good time," Margaret said.

Rainne glanced at the woman before shaking her head.

"Later," she told Alastair. "We'll talk when you know what you're saying."

Alastair wanted to object, but he held his tongue. What he wanted to say to Rainne was better said in private. In a room with a bed. A nice, big, soft bed. He smiled at his girl as his eyes slowly closed.

CHAPTER 27

The castle was in chaos. There were people everywhere. Lake was pleased to note that his friends had taken Matt's orders to heart and hadn't inflicted any life-threatening injuries on the fools who'd assaulted them. That didn't mean the guys weren't suffering. He almost smiled when he realised the women of Knit Or Die had forgone their usual caring attitudes and were administering first aid without dealing out pain meds.

"I know it hurts," he heard Shona say as he passed her in the kitchen. "But that's what you get for attacking my friends. You're a big tough guy, right? If you're tough enough to attack a bunch of unarmed women, you're tough enough to deal with this."

He scanned the dining room as he moved through it, making sure every captive was secured. There was nothing to do but guard the men until the police from Fort William took them off their hands.

"This is why there should be more cops in town," Matt grumbled at his side. "Things like this keep happening. This town is too much for one man." He glared at Lake. "Although it never used to be until you foreigners started turning up. I blame you for all this. You started the trend."

"As Shona said, you're a big tough guy, suck it up." Lake almost smiled at Matt's silent, one-fingered reply.

Jena squealed when she walked into the kitchen and spotted Matt. She ran in her stripper shoes and threw herself into his arms.

"You didn't get shot," she told him. "I'm so proud."

Matt grinned at his crazy wife, picked her up until she'd wrapped her legs around his waist and left the room with her.

Lake wandered through the house until he found Kirsty in the grand room. She was standing alone, and dejected, in the middle of what was supposed to be their wedding venue. To his shame, Lake hadn't seen any of the plans for their ceremony. And now he was seeing it for the first time in the aftermath of a battle. Bullet holes gouged the cream and gold wallpaper. The bay windows were shattered. Tattered purple material was strewn about the floor. There was snow and mud on the cream carpet. The white material covering the chairs was torn and filthy, and some of the chairs were broken.

"This is a sign," Kirsty said, letting him know she'd heard him come in. "The last in a long line of signs." She turned to him. Her eyes were glassy with tears. "We shouldn't have organised this wedding. We shouldn't be getting married at all."

To hell with that.

Lake closed the distance between them in three long strides. He wrapped his arms around his woman and his mouth covered hers. She was alive. She was fine. She was his. Lake kissed her for every minute they'd been apart these past few months. He kissed her for every second he'd feared he would never see her again. He kissed her with everything he had, body, mind and soul. Letting her know, by touch, by taste, that he was hers. Always hers.

With a low moan in the back of her throat, Kirsty wrapped her arms around his neck and held on tight. Their kiss was brutal. Tongues, lips, teeth clashing in a desperate tango of need. Lake swallowed each sound she made with pride.

He backed her through the debris until she was pressed against the inner wall. Snow swirled through the destroyed windows behind him. The temperature of the air plummeted with each minute the room was exposed to the elements. Lake didn't care about any of it. He was on fire for the woman he loved.

"I need you," he said against her lips. "Now."

"I thought you didn't want me anymore."

Her words were an arrow to his heart. "Daft woman. I leave you alone for five minutes and your imagination goes wild."

"Not five minutes, three months. Three months of you absent in every way except bodily."

The pain in her eyes said everything she didn't put into words. He'd hurt her. Neglected her. Let something else become more important than the woman he loved. *Never again.* He tugged on her hair to arch her neck, nuzzling in the curve of her throat, breathing her scent and revelling in it.

"I've missed you," Kirsty said on a moan.

"I'm here now." He nipped the tight muscle at the top of her shoulder, making her weaken in his arms.

"We haven't made love in three months," she whispered. "I thought you didn't want me."

Want her? What he felt went beyond want, beyond need into the realm of desperation. He wound his fingers through the russet-coloured curls that swept over her shoulder. He'd met her when her hair had been pixie short and she had been the most beautiful woman on the planet. Now, she was devastating. All long limbs, glorious curves and flowing red locks that made him weak at the knees.

Lake stopped and leaned his head back while the rest of his body kept hers pinned to the wall. He resisted the urge to grind his hips against her just so she could feel how much he wanted her. He looked down into those wide blue eyes of hers and ached with how much he loved this woman.

"Is that what's been bothering you?"

She nodded as she pulled her bottom lip between her teeth. Lake groaned, swept his mouth down and took over the task of teasing the spot she'd been worrying. It took great control to stop again, and when he did his breath was uneven and shallow and his need for her was almost out of control.

"I thought you didn't want to marry me."

"Kirsty Campbell—soon to be Benson—you think too much. It shouldn't be allowed. It leads to nothing good." He waited until she looked back up into his eyes before he spoke again. He wanted her to know he meant every word. "I love you. No. It's more than that. Without you I can't survive. You're essential to me. My thoughts are filled with you. Only you. Saying I want you doesn't even come close to how I feel. I don't just want you. I'm desperate for you. And we are definitely getting married." He cocked an eyebrow at her as his lips twitched. "Maybe not here, but it's happening."

"Oh, Lake," she said on a sigh. "Then why haven't you made love to me?" Her words were soft, but the pain behind them was loud.

Hell, he'd made her feel rejected and unwanted. It was the last thing he'd intended to do. He let out a sigh. "Too tired. Too busy. Too stupid." He flattened his hands against the small of her back and pressed her into him. "I'll make up for it. Starting now."

He kissed away any protests she may have made as he

fisted his hands in the knit dress she wore and inched it up those long legs and over her hips.

"I need you now," he said against her mouth, then kissed her again. Tasting her passion, making her moan with need and lose herself in him.

"Uh, Lake," a voice said in his ear, making him freeze. It was Flynn. "Your mic is on."

Lake cursed loudly. "One second," he said to his beautiful woman. "Flynn's in my ear." He kept his body flush against hers and tuned out the confused look on her face, preferring to focus on the dazed glint in her eyes and the lips swollen from his kisses. "I'm switching off," he barked at Flynn. "Guard the door."

"Lake!" Kirsty slapped her hands on his chest as he ripped the comm unit from his head and threw it over his shoulder. "We can't do anything in here. Not now."

She might be protesting, but he noticed her fingers had curled into his sweater to hold him closer rather than push him away. He heard laughter as the grand room door closed firmly. Someone would be standing guard. And he damn well wasn't going to waste his time worrying about what people might think or overhear.

"We can," he told Kirsty. "And we are."

Then he stopped all conversation. His tongue licked up the side of her throat before his teeth nibbled on her earlobe.

"My mother is out there somewhere." Her voice was breathless.

Lake continued to inch her emerald-green dress up over her hips.

"I don't care." He captured her mouth again.

He felt worry leave her as she lost herself to sensation. Lake hooked his hands under her backside and hauled her up.

"Wrap your legs around me," he ordered.

Her ankles hooked behind his thighs. He pressed his hard length against the heat of her core and ground into her. Her breath hitched and her head fell back to rest on the wall. Lake had never seen anyone more beautiful. Her cheeks were pink; her lips were full and parted. Long, dark lashes rested on her cheeks as she moaned.

"This is going to be fast," Lake said. "I'll make it up to you."

Her eyes opened but they were heavy-lidded with desire. "After the wedding?"

"Possibly during, too."

Her bright smile made his whole world align itself. He slid his hand over the satin skin of her hip, hooked a thumb into the side of her panties and felt a ribbon bow. He grinned.

"They were my new line," Kirsty said. "I'm calling it 'easy access.'"

Lake tugged at the bow and felt the underwear fall away.

"Have I mentioned lately how much I love your lingerie designs?" He shifted to balance her weight between the wall and his hips. His fingers sought her centre, and he groaned to find her wet and ready.

"You want me," he whispered as his forehead fell against hers. His eyes closed as he concentrated on the feel of her, silken and delicate to his touch.

"Always," she whispered back. "Always, Lake."

He couldn't wait a second longer to feel her around him. Moving his hand away from her, he smiled at her moans of protest as he unzipped his jeans and released himself. He was hard and desperate to get inside her. Three months? It couldn't have been that long since they'd been together. He *was* an idiot. But he wouldn't be one ever again. With no hesitation, he surged inside Kirsty. Her moan of pleasure and completion mirrored his own.

"Love you," he said before capturing her lips with his.

His tongue plundered as his hips rocked his length into her. He needed her. He needed all of her. She was his. With a gasp and a whine, Kirsty wrenched her lips from his. His name was a moan as she tightened around him, making him lose his own control. They sagged against one another, panting and sated.

"I do love you." Kirsty kissed the side of his neck.

"Then marry me."

She made a great effort in lifting her head to look over his shoulder. "Not here."

"No. Not here."

"I really wanted a Leap Day wedding."

He smiled. "I'm not waiting another four years to make you my wife." He'd waited too long already, putting it on hold while they both got their businesses up and running.

Kirsty ran her hands over his shoulders and down his arms. She stopped dead. Damn. He'd forgotten about the bullet wound.

"Lake? What's this?" She pushed at his shoulders, making him back up a little. Then she looked down at her fingers. They were covered in blood. Her face paled. "Lake?"

He inwardly cringed. This was not going to go well. "I might have gotten a little bit shot." He aimed for levity.

"Lake Benson, you've been shot and you didn't tell me?" Kirsty's face flushed with outrage. "Let me down. Let me down now."

He winced as she slid off him and down to the floor. She tugged down her dress and bent to pick up her underwear. She pulled the panties back on as she glared at him.

"I can't believe you let us do that when you were bleeding." Now it was fury making her eyes glow. He preferred when it was desire.

"It's nothing. Don't worry about it."

Her eyes narrowed. "Get that jacket off. How bad is it?"

"It's fine. Seriously. I'm okay." In truth, he wanted to get back to the kissing part of his evening before there was more crap to deal with and the kissing would get delayed. It seemed to be the story of his life these days—work and obligation pushing out all the good stuff. A sense of peace flowed through him as he thought of Callum taking on half his burden. Hopefully he'd never again go three months without touching his woman.

"Jacket off. Now." Kirsty pushed away from the wall and stalked towards the door. She yanked it open. "Flynn, Abby," she said with dignity to the people who knew exactly what they'd been doing.

Lake could only imagine the look Flynn was throwing her way. He winced as he pulled off his jacket.

"Lake's been shot. I need the first-aid kit." She frowned at Lake. "I'll be back in a minute. I need to visit the bathroom. Don't go anywhere. We're dealing with that gunshot wound when I get back."

"No way." Flynn pushed past Kirsty to step into the grand room. He scanned the devastation, then focused on the blood still dripping from Lake's arm. Flynn's grin was slow and wide. "You are a legend. Not that we heard much—the walls here are thick and the doors are solid wood—but I can imagine. And all that while wounded. Kudos."

A hand yanked Flynn back into the hall. "What?" Lake heard Flynn protest. "Tell me you aren't impressed."

Lake hung his head and counted to ten.

Then things got worse—his mother-in-law appeared.

Margaret Campbell frowned at him. "Is this really the best time for hanky-panky?"

"Mum!" Kirsty's face turned the same colour as her hair as she came back into the room. "Lake's been shot. Where's the first-aid kit we're using for our own men?"

"We have separate kits?" Lake said, hoping it would be enough to distract attention away from what they'd been up to.

"We kept the good stuff for our boys," Margaret said. "This kit has painkillers in it." She glared at him. "Although I'm not sure you deserve them."

Lake tried not to smile. "We've been living together for three years. You know we have sex."

"Lake," Kirsty wailed.

"I know," Margaret snapped. "But this isn't the time or the place and I don't need to know about it when it happens." She stomped off, hopefully to get the kit.

Lake looked down at his arm. There was a gouge that ran across his bicep. It wasn't deep, but it was still bleeding. Kirsty grabbed his arm to study it.

"You could have been killed," she said, as though it was his fault.

"No. I couldn't. I'm good at what I do. It's only a flesh wound. No big deal."

"No big deal." Her voice went into hysterical territory.

Lake looked at a still-grinning Flynn for help.

"It's only a scratch," Flynn said. "He'll be fine."

Kirsty frowned at Flynn. "It's time for you to be gone." She turned back to Lake and folded her arms over her luscious breasts, making his mouth water. They needed to find a bed, and soon. "You and I are going to have a proper talk about this later," Kirsty threatened as she cleaned out the wound.

"Yes." He leaned forward and kissed her again. "We're going to have lots of proper talks from here on out. I'll try to communicate better in future."

Her eyes filled with tears, but she smiled up at him. "Damn straight you will."

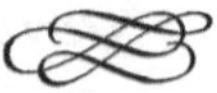

CHAPTER 28

* RAINNE AND ALASTAIR *

Rainne was curled up in front of the fire in the office when Ryan arrived back at the castle with Doctor Murray. He took one look at Alastair, lying on the couch with a straw in his side, and declared he needed to be taken back to his clinic. It wouldn't be possible to get Alastair to hospital, but thanks to Josh, Invertary's clinic was probably the best-stocked rural practice in Europe. As soon as Josh found out Caroline was pregnant for the first time he'd bought an x-ray machine, an ultrasound, a crash cart and anything else the doctor could think to ask him for.

Before the orange haired doctor went off to assess the rest of the castle's wounded, he examined Rainne.

"You're fine," he said. "A bit bashed up, that's all. You need to stay warm and rest. No need for you to come to the clinic."

"No!" Alastair protested from his position on the couch. "She needs to be checked out properly. She was unconscious. She hit her head."

"She is also sitting right here, feeling fine," Rainne pointed out.

"There could be internal bleeding." Alastair glared.

"Who's the doctor here and who's the fisherman?" Doctor Murray demanded. "When I want help with my fly casting, I come to you. I don't tell you how to do it. You're the one with the awards on your wall. It's the same with medicine. I'm the one with the degree and the experience. There's no internal bleeding. Rainne is fine."

"And you know this how?" Alastair asked. "With your x-ray vision?"

Doctor Murray stood, grabbed his bag and headed for the door. "I need to see other people. Deal with him," he said to Rainne. Then he was gone.

"I'm fine," Rainne said to the grumpy man on the sofa. "No symptoms of anything. I don't need to go to the clinic."

"Aye. You do. You can't take a chance with your health, Rainbow."

"I'm not the one with a broken wrist and a plastic straw sticking out of me."

"You had blood in your hair." He sounded so outraged it was hard not to laugh.

"Nothing a good shower won't fix."

His mouth tightened. "You're coming to the clinic. And that's final."

Rainne got up and walked over to Alastair. She stroked his hair, feeling the soft brown strands slide through her fingers. "You can't decide that, Alastair. There are people here hurt a whole lot worse than I am. I'm going to stay and help Caroline clean up while we wait for the police to get here. Lake said the main road has been cleared, so it shouldn't be long now."

"No. It's too dangerous. You can't stay here with all these guys in the castle."

"They're being guarded. I'll be fine." Her hand dropped back to her side. "I should go see what I can do."

Alastair's good hand shot out and his fingers curled

around her wrist. Dark, unreadable eyes looked up at her. "I want you in the clinic with me. We have things to talk about. Things to sort out."

It took all of the energy she had left to smile at him. "We can do that once you get better."

His grip tightened. "I mean it, Rainne. We need to talk. If you go running away again, I'll chase you down."

Her heart skipped a beat, but her brain knew better. "You're only saying these things because you've been badly injured. Before you were hurt, when you were in your right mind instead of delirious, you made it clear you didn't want me. That you would rather I left."

"I've changed my mind."

Stubborn, foolish man.

"No, you haven't." She pried his fingers from her wrist and stepped away from him. "You feel responsible for me after everything we've been through. It's to be expected. You spent the past few hours worrying about keeping us both alive. But you don't want me, Alastair. Not really, and not in the way I need you to want me." She took another step towards the door. "When you're well and thinking straight, you'll agree with me. It's best if I don't go with you to the clinic."

She turned her back on him and walked towards the door.

"Don't you leave me again," he said.

"I'd have to be with you to leave you," Rainne said softly, and then stepped into the hall.

"Rainbow!" Alastair shouted, but she kept on walking until she hit the kitchen.

Every eye in the room turned to watch her. Most of them filled with pity. Three years ago, Rainne would have burst into tears and fled in shame. But as she kept telling everyone, she wasn't that girl anymore. Instead she held her head high and looked at Heather Donaldson.

"What can I do to help?" she said.

She was grateful when Heather smiled, linked her arm through hers and led her off to where she was needed.

ALASTAIR CLOSED his eyes and lay back on the sofa. She'd done it again. She'd walked away. And he was in no state to chase her.

What was it about him that made women eager to escape him?

"She didn't believe you," a female voice said from the door.

From his position Alastair couldn't see who was speaking, and he didn't recognise the voice.

"It's not that she doesn't want you," the woman said. "She doesn't believe you."

"Who are you?" Alastair wished she would step into the room so he could see her.

"I'm Julia." She didn't come into the room. "I work for Lake. I've been talking to Rainne on the phone for the past few months. We've become friends. Well, as much as you can from phone calls." There was silence.

Alastair was almost afraid to speak in case he scared the woman away.

"She told me about you." Julia sounded wistful.

"What did she say?"

"She told me how much she loved you."

Alastair's heart ached and he closed his eyes.

"She told me you wanted to marry her and start a family." Alastair heard her take one step closer. "She didn't believe you then either. It's hard to believe someone really means it when they say they want you just as you are. It's even harder when experience teaches you that people only want you for what they can get from you."

Julia sounded like she knew what she was talking about.

Alastair cleared his throat. "I wanted her regardless of what she could do for me. I'm nothing like her family. My feelings weren't conditional on what I'd get from her."

"Weren't they?"

He felt like he'd been punched in the gut. "No. I wanted her here, making a life with me."

"And when she wanted to do something else, you withdrew your love. Withdrew yourself."

"That's not what happened." *Was it?* "I went to Glasgow. She shut the door in my face."

"You went to Glasgow to bring her back here." Julia stepped closer, and Alastair could feel her standing just out of sight behind the sofa. "You went because you wanted Rainne, not because you wanted what was best for Rainne."

He flinched. "She said that?"

"No, but I heard it. You were only twenty. You two were together such a short time. A few months of listening to you, against twenty-six years listening to her parents. Are you really surprised she didn't believe you meant what you said? Especially when your actions said your love was conditional on her doing what you thought was best?"

Alastair fell silent, and the mysterious Julia turned towards the door. "She really does still love you," she said. "Don't make her suffer because of it." And then she was gone.

Leaving Alastair alone, wondering if Rainne hadn't been right to leave him three years earlier. Wondering if he'd been the immature boy she'd accused him of being, expecting her to give up her life to be with him after a few months together. He scrunched his eyes closed against pain of a different kind. The past was a mess. They'd both made mistakes. But they had a chance to fix them now. To start again. To do things differently.

And he, for one, wasn't going to throw that chance away.

CHAPTER 29

It was close to midnight. The snow was easing off and Megan was once again stuck in a room with her captive. At least this time she wasn't alone. Lake, Grunt, Claire, Joe, Callum, Matt and Kirsty sat around Caroline's guestroom on the second floor of the castle. The room was huge, outfitted with a massive bed, desk and chair, sofa and armchair, all in shades of blue with white. It was gorgeous. But the décor wasn't the reason they were there.

Candles flickered on the tops of the desk and dresser, and Megan wished the electricity was back on, because she would seriously have killed for some coffee. Especially since the first thing Claire had told her when Grunt brought her back to the castle was that the pub had a generator. Megan bet Claire had coffee. But then, Claire had also been stuck with Betty, so she guessed that evened things out.

"Talk," Grunt ordered from where he was standing beside the armchair Claire was curled up in. Normally he would have been sitting in the chair with his wife in his lap. Megan could only assume he was standing because he expected Dimitri to make a run for it and he wanted to be ready.

Dimitri let out a sigh, ran a hand over his hair then looked around the room. "I'm an independent contractor."

"You mean a gun for hire," Kirsty said, making Lake smile.

"I'm a gun for hire, love," he said.

"No you're not." She wriggled closer to him on the sofa. "You're a security specialist."

They shared a secret smile that sent shivers through Megan's body. It took her a minute to realise it was envy she felt.

"Anyway," their captive said, "I was in the army until about six months ago."

"Which army?" Grunt asked.

"US Rangers," Dimitri said.

Grunt grunted, and Megan didn't know if that was a good grunt or a bad one.

"So you're American?" Megan asked.

"Sometimes," Dimitri said. "Mostly. That's not the point. The point is this, about a year ago my sister went missing in Eastern Europe."

Megan felt her heart miss a beat and wondered at the calm, even tone Dimitri was using to tell his story. What exactly did it hide? She looked over at Claire, only to see her own worry mirrored back at her. If Megan's sister went missing, she would rip the world apart looking for her. And she knew Claire would do the same.

"When the authorities came up with nothing," Dimitri said, "I resigned my commission and went hunting on my own."

It sent a chill up Megan's spine when he said "hunting" instead of "investigating."

"I followed rumours, hitting dead ends, until I heard the same name whispered over and over."

Grunt looked at his best friend Joe, and they seemed to

communicate with the telepathic link Megan had always wanted with her twin.

"Rudi Abramovich," Joe said.

Dimitri's lips thinned as he nodded.

Lake turned to Joe. "Fill us in." It was an order.

"Rudi runs a crime ring out of Eastern Europe—Romania mostly, but he moves around. He has a base in London. His speciality is skin trade." He looked at Dimitri. "Slaves."

Dimitri nodded. His fists clenched beside him, where he sat perched on the end of the bed. Megan had the insane urge to rush over to his side and rub his back, as though it would somehow help ease his pain.

"He snatches young women," Dimitri said. "Tourists, locals, runaways, then sells them off to the highest bidder."

"You think he sold your sister." It wasn't a question. Lake already knew the answer.

"Sold or killed." Dimitri's voice was flat.

Megan couldn't take it anymore. She walked across the room from where she'd been standing beside the window and sat on the bed beside Dimitri.

"I'm sorry," she said. "That's awful."

She covered his clenched fist with her hand. Dimitri stared into her eyes for a moment, then surprised them both by turning his hand and linking their fingers. Megan faced her friends and family and mentally dared them to say something. It was only hand holding. A little comfort for a distraught man. Nothing more.

Lake eyed her thoughtfully before talking to Dimitri. "What's this got to do with Claire?"

"Rudi wants Claire delivered to him. I don't know why. But he ordered her specifically. I got in on the job because Reynard was an idiot. A rank amateur who was hiring guys without checking them out. He's worked with Rudi before and wanted to curry favour to get higher in the organisation.

He didn't have a clue what he was doing. Most of the guys he hired were wannabe soldiers. He put together a mini-army for one snatch and grab."

Megan stiffened beside him. "You weren't actually going to help him take my sister, were you?" Because it sure as hell sounded like he wasn't impressed by their professionalism.

Grunt made a loud growling noise from deep in his chest. It went a long way towards proving Megan's theory that he was related to King Kong. She noticed her frowning sister did nothing to soothe the beast. From the fury in her eyes, Claire was pretty close to growling herself.

"No," Dimitri said hastily, his eyes on Grunt. "My plan was to foil his attempts while gathering intel."

"You know you're really crap at planning." Megan remembered his promise to come up with something when she was taken. She hadn't been impressed.

Dimitri shrugged. "There were plenty of times in the past week where we could have lifted Claire. I made sure it wasn't possible."

"And we should thank you?" Megan was really beginning to regret holding the guy's hand.

"No. But you should listen." He looked at Grunt. "He's got it in for you. Reynard told me that Rudi wants Claire to get back at you. He had a buyer set up for her. A guy in the Middle East who is known for going through slaves. He planned to put Claire in place and then feed you the information. There was talk of photos and video."

Grunt stepped away from the armchair, turned and put his fist through the door. He then retracted his fist, perched on the chair beside Claire and wrapped his arm around her as though nothing had happened.

"Nobody touches my wife," he said.

Claire smiled and snuggled into her husband. They were both nuts.

"Yeah," Joe said. "We're all getting that, big guy."

"Why is this Rudi guy after you?" Lake asked as Kirsty and Megan shared a wide-eyed look over Grunt's show of strength.

If Megan was reading the girl-look correctly, and she was fluent in girl-looks, then Kirsty was just as impressed, and slightly disturbed, as she was.

"It was one of the first jobs we took when we went out on our own," Joe answered for Grunt. "A client in the US wanted us to escort his daughter home from Romania. He said she was in a bad relationship and feared for her life. He wanted protection for her when she made a move to leave the guy." Joe let out a sigh. "We went to Bucharest, met up with the woman in a back-street café. She had a black eye and swollen lip, and that was just the damage we could see. She wanted to go back and pack her stuff, but we intervened. It was clear she had to get out of there straight away. She didn't even have a passport on her, said the husband kept it in his safe. We figured we could smuggle her over the border into Moldova or the Ukraine, then contact some people we knew and get her papers made up so we could get her on a flight to the US."

Joe looked at Grunt, who was staring, stony-faced, into the distance. Every muscle in his body was tense while Claire petted his chest and made cooing noises.

"She had guards," Joe said. "She didn't even know she was being followed until they attacked when we left the café. I got her out of there while Grunt dealt with the guards. One of them got away." He looked at Grunt, whose jaw was tight. "It wasn't your fault. The cops turned up and the whole situation went to hell." He looked back at Lake. "We found out later that the girl was Rudi's wife. And Rudi had Grunt's face on camera. It stands to reason he would have eventually tracked him down. He'd want payback. The sick bastard would see it as quid pro quo—we took his wife, he takes Grunt's."

"I don't like his thinking," Claire said, stating the obvious. "I don't even know this Rudi guy. I don't want to be his pro anything."

"I won't let him take you," Grunt promised.

"I know." Claire looked perfectly relaxed as she snuggled closer to her man.

"As much as I appreciate your declaration," Dimitri said to Grunt, taking his life in his hands and proving he wasn't the sharpest tack in the box, "Rudi isn't going to quit. He'll keep coming until he gets what he wants."

"Or gets dead." Grunt's dark eyes dared Dimitri to object.

"I don't hear anything about anyone killing anyone," Matt said into the silence that followed Grunt's declaration. Megan's brother rubbed a hand down his face. He looked beyond tired after an evening gathering statements and sorting out prisoners. Invertary was far too much work for one cop. He stared Dimitri down. "You're going on the record, saying this was a kidnapping for hire. That will sort out a lot of my paperwork. The last thing I want to see are charges brought against Lake and his guys."

Dimitri shook his head. "I can't." Everyone in the room became instantly tense. "I can't blow my cover. I need to go back to Rudi. I need to find my sister."

"We'll find your sister," Joe said. "We'll do it when we deal with Rudi." He looked at Grunt, who nodded his approval.

"No," Claire said, looking slightly green. "You can't go away. I need you here."

Grunt leaned over to kiss her forehead. "We won't be gone long. You'll be safe. Lake will look after you."

"No. No, Lake can't. I need you."

"I understand, but..."

"No buts." Claire started to cry. "You have to stay here."

"For goodness' sake," Megan said. "Just tell him already."

Claire's bottom lip pouted as she stared at Megan. "I wanted it to be special." Then she blinked. "How do you know, anyway?" A wide smile lit up her face. "Did the twin bond kick in?"

Megan shook her head and pointed at Dimitri. "He was snooping."

"Oh." Claire's shoulders fell.

"Claire, baby, what's going on?" Grunt looked about five minutes away from going postal on everybody in the room.

Claire looked up at her husband as she patted his chest. "You need to stay here because we're going to have a baby." Her smile was tremulous.

Grunt didn't move. Didn't speak. He just stared at Claire. People began to shift nervously.

"Did you hear me, Samuel?" Claire tried again. "We're going to have a baby."

In one lightning-fast move, he hooked his hand on the back of her neck and pulled her lips to his. The kiss was not PG rated. Megan was about to fetch a bucket of water when they came up for air.

"I'm having a kid," Grunt told Joe with a loopy grin. "I can't go to Romania." His whole demeanour darkened. "And Rudi better not come here."

He sat in the armchair, hauled Claire into his lap and held her tight. "Mine," he growled.

"Yours," Claire said on a sigh.

"Okay." Dimitri's eyes went wide at the sight before him. "So the big guy isn't going to Romania." He looked at Matt. "I need to go."

"What makes you think you can get close enough to Rudi to find out what you need to know?" Joe asked. "You're just one of the guys Reynard hired. You never even met Rudi."

Dimitri's hand tightened on Megan's as he looked at Joe.

"He'll see me because I'm going to bring him the thing he wants. I'm going to take him the woman."

Grunt started that scary growling sound again. Dimitri ignored him as he turned to Megan.

"I'm going to take Megan to Romania and tell him she's Claire."

"Hell no!" Matt shouted as he shot to his feet.

"Grunt, sort him out," Claire demanded as she sat up. "He's not taking my sister to a slave trader."

"No, he's not, baby." Grunt climbed to his feet.

Matt and Grunt stood shoulder to shoulder as they faced off against Dimitri. Megan's head reeled. She was barely aware that she was still holding Dimitri's hand—the hand of the man who wanted to sell her off.

"You want to set up an op, don't you?" Joe said calmly. "Use Megan to get inside, find the information you need then bust out with Megan."

Dimitri blanched. "You thought I wanted to give her to him?" He shook his head in disgust.

"An operation like that would need coordination." Lake looked over at Callum.

"We need to eliminate the threat," Callum said. "This might be the most effective way."

Megan shook off Dimitri's hand and walked to the window. The snow had stopped entirely. Outside was a world of beauty and peace. Nothing like the state inside her head, where thoughts raced and jostled for position.

"You can't be serious about sending my sister into a situation like that?" Matt demanded of Lake. "She doesn't have a freaking clue about guys like Rudi. She has no training, no skill. It would be like leading a lamb to the slaughter."

"She can take care of herself," Dimitri said. "And she'll have backup."

"I'll go," Joe said. "This is our mess and Grunt needs to stay here."

Grunt grunted.

"You've run situations like this before," Lake said to Callum, who nodded.

"We need more men," Callum said.

"I can set up a team," Lake told him.

"Is anybody listening to me?" Matt demanded. "She isn't going. Sort this out another way. And while we're at it, Dimitri is staying here to testify. Nobody is going anywhere."

Grunt's hand came down heavily on Matt's shoulder. "Rudi won't stop. He'll keep coming until Claire is taken or dead."

"I agree we need to stop him, but not with Megan. One sister isn't more important than the other," Matt said through clenched teeth.

"Hear, hear," Claire shouted. "My sister isn't going to Romania."

"Yes," Megan said evenly, and everyone in the room gave her their full attention. "Yes, I am."

There was a moment of stunned silence before everyone started shouting at once. Megan's eyes found Dimitri. He was silent, staring at her, and he looked almost proud. He nodded his thanks to her and Megan inclined her head in acceptance. A strange sort of exhilaration swept through her body. For years she'd been looking for her calling. The career that suited her. She had a strange feeling it had just found her.

She straightened her shoulders and smiled at the group.

She was going to be a gun for hire.

And she was going to kick ass.

CHAPTER 30

On the morning that should have been Lake's wedding, Rainne found the only member of her family who ever gave a damn about her in the war room, making plans. Okay, so it was the kitchen, but from the look on Lake's face he was definitely scheming about something. Rainne stepped straight up to her brother and wrapped her arms around his waist.

"How you feeling?" Lake said as he pulled her to him.

"Good, I'm good. Love you, big brother."

He smiled down at her, squeezing her tight. Those smiles were new. Thanks to Kirsty, Lake let himself show emotion a whole lot more than he ever did when they were growing up. Although there was twelve years between them and her memories of Lake were those of a child, she remembered him as a wary man. Always watching, assessing and analysing.

It wasn't surprising considering their parents had made it clear from early on exactly how much they disapproved of Lake—all because he had a different ideology. Their rejection of him had taught Rainne at an early age that if she wanted them to accept her, she needed to do as she was told.

"You're thinking hard, Rainbow. What's up?" Lake patted her back as she clung to him.

This was new too. He never used to be good at showing or accepting affection. Rainne had a lot to thank Kirsty for.

"I'm so pleased you found Kirsty," she said.

"So am I." She could hear the laughter in his voice. "Now, do you want to tell me what you're after?"

She grinned against his chest. "Can't I just give my big brother a hug?"

"Absolutely. Anytime. Now what do you need?"

She stepped back from his hug. "I need to check on Alastair at the clinic. I'm worried about him. Can you spare someone to take me into town?"

She knew better than to take a snowmobile and go on her own. The guys were all on high alert after the attack and watching the women like hawks. Lake would be the worst. Years of experience had taught her that sometimes it was best to humour his overprotective streak. It made him happy.

Lake cocked an eyebrow at Mitch, who was leaning against the breakfast bar, nursing a mug of coffee. It was clear from Mitch's rumpled appearance that he was still getting over the night before. His usual suit was replaced by faded jeans and a crinkled grey T-shirt. His hair was a mess, his feet were bare and he was obviously thinking too hard about something.

"You ever ridden a snowmobile?" Lake said.

Dark thoughts cleared from Mitch's face and his eyes lit up. "How hard can it be?"

Lake nodded to Rainne. "Give her a lift to the clinic and back, will you?"

"My pleasure." Mitch put his mug on the counter. "Meet you outside." He practically ran from the room, eager to get on the machine. All sign of the troubled man he'd been a moment earlier had disappeared.

Rainne shook her head as she watched him go. "Boys," she said.

They followed Mitch down the hall and out the front door. He was wrapped up against the cold and stroking the snowmobile like it was a cat.

"Let's go," he said to Rainne.

Rainne ran down the front steps of the castle, careful not to slip on the snow, and climbed onto the machine behind Mitch.

"Oh," Lake called after them with a grin. "Pick up Betty as well. She's been calling every ten minutes saying she needs to be here."

"Damn it," Mitch grumbled. "I knew there was a catch."

Lake was still grinning when he went back inside the castle.

"I've never been on one of these," Rainne said.

"Neither have I." Mitch started pressing buttons.

Worriedly, Rainne looked over at the burned-out wrecks of the other snowmobiles making a black mess of Caroline's front lawn.

"Maybe we should fetch someone to tell you what to do before we go?"

"It's like riding a bike," Mitch said as the snowmobile sputtered to life and lurched forward.

They bounced over the snow towards the gate, stopping and starting randomly. Rainne held on tight and wondered if after everything she'd been through she'd meet her demise taking a ride with Mitch.

"See?" Mitch shouted, sounding far too pleased with himself. "Easy."

They rode through the snow-covered streets into town. The storm had passed, leaving an icy white world in its wake.

Power was still out, but cell phones were working. Only the main roads were cleared, which for Invertary meant the road to Fort William. The rest of the town was snowed in.

The picturesque beauty of the small Highland town made Rainne sigh with pleasure. A clear blue sky over a blanket of white. The loch glistening in the sun. Kids playing in the street, wrapped up tight and using tin lids as makeshift sledges. They whooped with laughter when the snowmobile drove past, throwing snowballs at Mitch. Cars were buried to the point that they'd lost their shapes and looked like massive white bubbles. Trees bent under the weight on their boughs. Roofs were piled high with snow, just waiting to fall and bury anyone standing beneath them. There were snowmen outside some of the houses. All of them looked happy. There was something comforting and peaceful about the aftermath of a storm.

They came to a halt in front of Invertary clinic and Rainne climbed off.

"I need to go get Satan. I'll come back for you once I've picked her up."

Rainne eyed the snowmobile. "Will we all fit?"

Mitch looked behind him. He seemed to be trying to figure out a way to get them all on. Rainne decided to intervene before he had Betty sitting on her lap.

"Is there any chance you can take Betty to the castle then come back and get me?"

His sigh was heavy and clearly fake. "Fine, but only because you're the groom's sister."

"And not at all because you get to play with the snowmobile for longer." *Yeah, right.*

The American grinned before gunning the engine and heading up the street. Rainne shook her head as she watched him go. It was hard to believe Mitch spent most of his time in business suits and board meetings.

She pushed through the door to the converted Victorian house that was now the town's only medical facility, and the noise hit her. Shouting, complaining, swearing. Rainne raised her eyebrows at the nurse, and doctor's wife, who was behind the desk.

"What's going on?" Rainne said.

Janice rolled her eyes. "It's a guy called Reynard. Megan shot him in the backside and he's *not* happy. The police were in to question him. They want to move him to Fort William now that the road's open but we need to wait for an ambulance and a police escort to take him." She grinned. "He can't sit in the standard police van. The seats are too hard and would hurt his sore bum. We wouldn't want the mastermind behind the attack on our women to get uncomfortable in any way now would we? While we're waiting for his ride, I'm making sure to take *really* good care of him."

"He's getting a lot of sympathetic treatment, then?" Rainne said.

"Oh, aye." Janice nodded solemnly.

Rainne grinned at the woman's faux innocence. "Where can I find Alastair?"

"Room two, and he's grumpy as well. Men. Whether it's a broken limb or a paper cut, it's all the same. If they spent five minutes dealing with labour pains they might have a better understanding of what real agony is."

With a laugh, Rainne headed to Alastair's room, attempting to tamp down her nerves by counting backwards from twenty while breathing slowly. It didn't help. She pushed open the door to find him lying in bed, eyes on the wall-mounted TV, remote in hand. He didn't look happy.

"Hey, how you doing?" Rainne said as she entered the room.

She stood a couple of feet from the bed, unsure of her welcome.

"Rainbow, am I glad to see you. Get me out of here." He started to sit up, but a machine attached to his thumb by a clip began beeping and the door banged open.

"Stay in bed," barked the doctor.

"I feel fine. I want to go home. With Rainne."

Alastair's skin was grey, his eyes were tight with pain and his hair was matted. Yeah, he looked fine.

"Not going to happen." Doctor Murray put a hand on Alastair's shoulder and firmly pushed him back into the bed. "Stay," he ordered. "You have a tube in your chest, your arm in a cast and you have two broken ribs. You're not going anywhere. Not before the chest drain comes out."

"When will that be?" Rainne asked as Alastair growled like a trapped animal.

"Tomorrow, probably," the doc said. "The damage to his lung was minor. It should be healed by then. Well, healed enough to stop from leaking air. His ribs will take a lot longer to mend. And moving around won't help." He glared at Alastair.

"I hate being in here," Alastair said.

"And we hate having you in here." The doc slammed the door when he left.

Alastair watched him go. "He's a bastard when he doesn't get any sleep."

"Or he's fed up dealing with unreasonable men who are clearly injured and won't listen to expert advice."

He scowled at her, and Rainne ignored him. Instead she tugged at the white cotton blanket and tucked him in.

"You've only been here a few hours. Talk about a drama queen. This is pathetic. Just sit back, watch TV and you'll be free soon enough." She refilled the plastic beaker beside his bed with ice water as she wondered why every hospital room she'd ever been in was painted mint green. She imagined someone thought it would be soothing. It wasn't.

"When I see this colour now, I think of hospitals," she said. "Don't you think a nice patterned wallpaper would be much more welcoming?"

"I don't want to be welcomed. I want to go home." His head thumped back onto the pillow.

There was more shouting and cursing from the room next door.

"Maybe once that guy goes you'll be able to relax," Rainne said.

"I'm never going to make it." Alastair looked up at her. "I'm going stir crazy. And we need somewhere private to talk."

She really wished he'd stop saying that. It made her want to put her fingers in her ears and sing la, la, la until he gave up.

Rainne stepped back from the bed. "No we don't. Everything is fine."

"I've been thinking." Alastair completely ignored her. "Last night brought clarity. I've been an idiot." His eyes were dark with emotion. "I'm glad you came back, Rainbow."

She shook her head. "No. Don't be. I shouldn't have come back here. It was selfish of me. I didn't think it through. I didn't realise my actions would rake up so much pain for you."

The damn man rolled his eyes at her. "Don't over dramatize this Rainbow. I'm fine. I've dealt with it. Part of me thought you were like my mum. I realise you aren't. Issue closed."

Rainne gaped at him. "That's just...nuts. You can't get over a revelation like that in a matter of hours."

"You want me to go into therapy for years, only to come to the same conclusion when I'm done?"

"You don't know what..."

"If you tell me one more time that I don't know my own

mind, I'm going to lose the plot entirely. I'm not an idiot. I know what I damn well think!" He took a deep breath, winced and then scowled at her. "I'm glad you came back. I'm glad you had the courage to ask me to try again. I want to. I want you."

The words sounded more like a threat than a romantic declaration.

"Even if that were true." She ignored his frown. "How could it work between us? I didn't think this through before I came here. I didn't think about the practicalities, let alone the emotional baggage we'd need to deal with. Your life is here and mine is in Glasgow."

"We can figure that out," he said.

It was her turn to roll her eyes. "You made it clear years ago that you never want to leave Invertary. You dreamed of a life here."

"What if I want more?"

"Is that even possible? We'll never get past our trust issues. Let's face it. You'll always be waiting for me to leave you. I can see that now. I could promise you forever and you wouldn't believe me. You don't trust me. And that's on me. I hurt you." She bit her bottom lip for a second, aware he was watching her intently. "It was a dream," she said at last. "You were the dream. Those few months we had together were the dream I kept coming back to, wondering what might have been. But there are some things that are better left in the past. I realise that now."

"No—"

"Yes. At least coming back gave us a chance to talk things through." She tucked her hair behind her ear as she backed towards the door. "It's good to get closure."

He let out a rumbling growl. "Closure?" He jerked towards her but grunted and plopped back down, his face even greyer than before. "What the hell are you talking about, woman?"

Whatever Rainne would have said next was lost when the door crashed open. A guy she didn't recognise rushed in. He had a knife in his hand. Rainne froze. The man grabbed her arm and pressed the knife to her throat. His eyes were cold and sharp. There was a scar across his cheek, making his mouth seem lopsided. He was dressed in medical scrubs and his feet were bare.

"Get away from her!" Out of the corner of her eye she could see Alastair struggling to get out of bed.

Rainne wanted to tell him to stop. He was going to injure his lung again. But she was frozen. She felt a sharp sting at her throat, which made her whimper.

"You," the man said. He had an accent. European. "You're the one who came on the snowmobile. Where is it?"

Rainne stared at him. Her brain couldn't comprehend what was happening. Her limbs were limp. Her voice wasn't working. All she could think was that Alastair needed to stay in bed. She had to tell him to stay there. Everything else was blank. Confused. Blocked.

The sharp bite of pain at her throat intensified. She whined.

"Leave her alone!"

There was a crash to the right of Rainne as something toppled to the floor, but she couldn't turn her head to see what. She couldn't take her eyes away from the terrifying man.

"Don't touch her. Get away from her, you bastard."

The guy turned his cold eyes on Alastair. "One more step and I slit her throat." He sounded calm, as though he was asking for sugar in his tea rather than talking about killing someone.

Not someone.

Her.

She started to pant. Her hands were tingling. "Alastair?" Her voice was a shaky whisper.

"It's okay, Rainbow, I'm here. Stand still. We'll sort this."

The guy gripped her arm tighter as he looked back down at her. "Where is the snowmobile?"

She swallowed, and it caused the knife to press into her. She felt something wet run down her throat. Blood. She was bleeding. He'd cut her and showed no remorse. In fact, his face showed only brutal determination.

There was a roar and Alastair rushed the man. The knife left her throat as the guy swung at Alastair. He knocked Alastair across the room, where he hit his back on the edge of the bed and crumpled to the floor.

"No!" Rainne screamed. She struggled to get to Alastair.

He was lying on the floor, clutching his ribs.

"Alastair!" She couldn't see blood. He wasn't stabbed. But his ribs. His lung.

"Stop moving. Your boyfriend is okay. For now." The knife pressed back to her throat. "I need the snowmobile."

"What did you do with the doctor and nurse?" Rainne whispered.

He ignored her. "Where is the snowmobile?"

There was the unmistakable sound of an engine. Mitch was back. Early. Inside Rainne's head she was screaming. Her mouth was dry. Her hands were numb. Her body shook. She had to get to Alastair. She had to make sure he was okay. She had to warn Mitch. He couldn't come in here.

The guy spun her around, pulling her back against his chest. He covered her mouth with his hand.

Alastair was a groaning heap on the floor. "Damn it to hell," he snapped. "Let her go."

"One more word," the guy said. "And she pays for it."

Alastair made a strangled noise and Rainne struggled against her captor.

"I have no problem killing you," he said against her ear in a voice so cold it made her freeze.

The door opened. Mitch stepped in. "I came to get you first," he said before he saw her. "Betty was busy with the strippers. I couldn't watch. I'm traumatised enough already. I'll go back and get her later when she's finished whatever the hell she's doing. I hope those guys got paid a bundle for dealing with her."

He turned and spotted them. Shock registered on his face as he took in the scene. In a split second he'd morphed into someone else. Someone bigger. Stronger. He launched himself at her captor, but he wasn't fast enough.

The man shoved her to his side as he swung the knife. Rainne hit the wall. She saw the knife go into Mitch. He stopped mid-lunge as though he'd been pulled back by an invisible rope. Then he collapsed.

The guy crouched over Mitch, rifled through his pocket, came out with the key to the snowmobile and ran. Without as much as a backwards glance.

"Help!" Rainne screamed. "Help!"

She rushed to Alastair. "I'm okay," he said on a groan. "Deal with Mitch."

She pressed a palm to his cheek before turning to Mitch.

There was a knife sticking out of his side. There was blood. So much blood. She took a deep breath and screamed as loudly as she could. She fell to her knees beside Mitch, sliding in his blood.

"Don't. Remove. Knife," Mitch said through gritted teeth.

Rainne heard a clatter outside the door. She didn't know what to do. She didn't know how to help.

"Help!" she shouted. "Please help!"

The door crashed open and the doctor ran in. He took in the scene in front of him before rushing into action.

"Find my wife," he ordered Rainne as he leaned over Mitch.

Rainne nodded and hurried from the room. She opened exam room one and rushed inside. The nurse was gagged and tied to the bed. She didn't seem hurt. Rainne's fingers trembled as she worked on the knot of her gag.

"He got free from his cuffs," Janice said as soon as the gag was gone. "He grabbed me when I came into the room. He's gone. We need to stop him."

Rainne untied her legs. "He stabbed Mitch and took the snowmobile. Alastair is injured again. I think it's his lung."

"Where's Hamish?"

It took a minute for Rainne to realise she was talking about Doctor Murray. "He's with Mitch."

"Hamish went to the pub to pick up lunch," his wife said as she shook off the bandages binding her wrists. "There should have been a police officer guarding that guy. I don't know why there wasn't. I met him earlier. He came from Fort William. I have no idea where he's gone." Her fury made it clear she planned to find out.

Rainne followed Janice as they ran into the other room. The look of relief on the doctor's face was heart-melting.

"You hurt?" he asked his wife as she examined to Alastair.

"No. Just bloody angry. We're missing a cop and now we're missing a patient. I hope he bursts his stitches and gets an infection in his backside."

Doctor Murray's answering smile said it all. "We need an air ambulance," he told his wife. "This is too much for me. Mitch needs surgery."

Janice scrambled to her feet and reached for the phone. "They both need to be taken to the hospital."

The doctor turned to Rainne. "Call Matt. The police need to get that guy and find out where the guard went."

She nodded and pulled her phone out of her pocket. She fumbled as she dialled the castle.

"It's Rainne," she said to the person who answered. "We need Matt at the clinic. There's been an escape and Mitch has been stabbed."

CHAPTER 31

* KIRSTY *

Kirsty spent what should have been her wedding night checking up on the injured men in Fort William hospital. A visit to the hospital seemed a fitting end to the day. It was ten o'clock at night and her chance to get the wedding she'd dreamed of was over. At least everyone she cared about was in one piece. She was thankful for that.

Alastair's chest drain had been replaced. His lung hadn't been punctured again, but his wrist had needed to be recast. Mitch had needed surgery. The knife had penetrated his body low on his right side, missing everything major, but damaging his intestines. He'd been stitched up and put on antibiotics. He was going to be fine.

Kirsty sighed heavily as she watched the snow covered scenery pass in the darkness. They were part of a convoy of cars, filled with friends, heading back to the castle.

"I wish Rainne had come with us to see Alastair," Kirsty said.

"She might go tomorrow," Lake said, but Kirsty didn't think so.

Rainne was preparing to leave. Kirsty recognised the

signs. Unfortunately there was nothing she could do about it. Rainne and Alastair had to sort things out for themselves.

"I'll make it up to you, you know." Lake reached for her hand. "About the wedding. I'll help plan the next one. We'll make it wonderful."

She glanced over to where he was driving and smiled. "Yes, we will."

His answering smile was full of promise. Up ahead she could see the tail lights of Josh's and Matt's cars disappear as they turned into the castle driveway. The lights were on in the castle, although the boarded windows and circle of burned wreckage on the lawn made the place less welcoming than usual.

"Guess the power is back on," Kirsty said. "Caroline is going to go insane fixing this mess."

"Josh already spoke to me about increased security."

"With a generator to keep it all running?"

"Two." Lake pulled up in front of the castle. "And a panic room."

As they got out of the car, the castle's front door opened and her mother raced out. Kirsty felt her stomach clench and fear rise at the look on her mum's face. She rushed to her side.

"What's wrong? Is everything okay?"

"You need to come with me, right now." Her mother turned and hurried back into the house.

Kirsty flashed a worried glance at Lake and saw he had his head together with Ryan and Dougal. He caught her eyes and nodded at her. A reassurance. Heart racing, Kirsty followed her mother into the castle.

"Come on," Margaret said from the top of the stairs.

Kirsty ran up them and followed her mum into the blue guest room. And stopped dead.

"What's going on?" she said.

Her wedding dress was out of the bag and draped over the bed. Her shoes sat on the floor beside it. Her makeup bag was set up on the dresser.

"Quick." Her mother tugged her into the room and closed the door behind them. "You need to jump in the shower. Make it fast—we have less than an hour to get you ready."

Kirsty was rooted to the spot. "For what?"

"Your wedding, silly girl." Her mother shooed her in the direction of the bathroom. "Get on with it."

"But how?" Kirsty's head was spinning as she let herself be herded where her mum wanted her to be.

"Buts and hows later. All you need to know is that Dougal and I took care of everything. We commandeered a snowmobile and picked up supplies. You wanted a Leap Day wedding and you're going to get one." She reached up and cupped her daughter's cheek. "It's the least you deserve. Now, hop to it. Shower. Time's ticking."

Kirsty felt hope surge inside her, but it didn't feel right. "I can't get married when Mitch and Alastair are in hospital. It seems like a callous thing to do."

"Don't be daft," her mother snapped. "You think those boys wouldn't want you to have your special day? You can call them if you'd like, but I know what they'd say. They'd tell you to listen to your mother."

"But…" Kirsty wasn't so sure.

"No buts." Her mother pushed her into the bathroom. "You know I'm right. It's time to stop waiting and marry that man."

Kirsty found herself alone with the bathroom door closed firmly behind her. She stood staring at herself in the mirror for a minute wondering what the heck was happening. How could she get married when the castle was a bombsite? All the food would be ruined by now, and she wasn't even sure if the vicar stayed awake this late.

"I don't hear the shower running," her mother shouted. "Don't make me come in there."

With a giggle, Kirsty started to undress. Excitement began to froth through her veins. She was getting married. It was actually happening. At last.

Years of performing quick changes on fashion shoots meant Kirsty was ready for her ceremony in forty-five minutes. She'd parted her hair in the middle and left it loose around her shoulders in gentle, spiralling waves. Her lips were a pale pink, to match her cheeks. Her eyes were dark and smoky, in shades of purple to make her dress pop and her green eyes luminous.

Her dress was the same blue/purple of the Campbell tartan. Kirsty had it made for her by a friend from her days as a model. It was a form-fitting fishtail shape that flared out gently from mid-thigh to fall to floor length. It was sleeveless, with one shoulder uncovered, and the other had a large chiffon flower pinned to it, in the exact same shade as the dress. The material came down from the shoulder to wrap around her body, following her curves into the fishtail. She'd matched the dress with simple metallic silver sandals with a high pencil heel and thin straps that wound around her ankle and toes. Drop earrings in silver, two oversized silver bangles around her right wrist and her engagement ring were her only jewellery.

Her mother saw her and covered her mouth with her hands. Her eyes welled up.

"You are so beautiful." She rushed towards Kirsty, stopping an inch in front of her. "Am I allowed to touch you? Will I ruin the look?"

Kirsty laughed and pulled her mum into a hug. "It's all really simple. There's nothing to ruin."

"I can't believe you're getting married," her mother said on a sob.

"I can't believe it either. I thought we'd missed our chance to do this today. I keep thinking this is all a dream and I'll wake up to find my wedding dress was trashed in the raid."

"This is definitely real, although you might wish it wasn't when you catch sight of Betty."

Kirsty narrowed her eyes. "What's the old witch done now?"

Her mum looked slightly panicked, which wasn't reassuring. "Forget I said anything. We have more important things to deal with. Like getting you downstairs for the ceremony." She sniffed back a sob. "I wish your dad was here."

"The makeup is waterproof, but if you make me cry, I'll have to get married with a bright red nose."

Her mum laughed. "We don't want that." She stepped back to look up at Kirsty. "I am so proud of you. You've been through a lot and look at you now. My beautiful daughter is getting married. In a sleeveless dress." That set her off again. "After the accident, I never thought you'd show your skin again. I kept telling you nobody noticed the scars but you. I was right, wasn't I?"

"Aye, Mum, you were right." She smiled down at her. "Lake likes my scars."

"Lake loves you."

Yes. He did. "Now, want to tell me where I'm getting married? Last I checked, the grand room was a dump."

"You'll just have to wait and see." Her mother stepped back, looking gorgeous in her forest-green two-piece suit. "Ready?"

"More than ready." Kirsty wanted to run into Lake's arms. She wanted to say her vows, change her name and let the world know she planned to spend every second of her life loving that man.

Her mother led her down the stairs and through the

unusually quiet castle. When they reached the closed door to the kitchen, Margaret Campbell paused.

"Here we go." She squeezed Kirsty's hand then pushed open the door.

Kirsty heard the music before anything else. Josh sang "The Way You Look Tonight" as she walked into the kitchen. Her gaze took in the spectacular buffet laid out on the breakfast bar. Behind the bar, staff from Dougal's pub were quietly busy manning the ovens and waiting to serve people. They smiled widely at her when they saw her.

She turned into the dining room and saw Caroline and Rainne, her beaming bridesmaids. They were wearing the tartan dresses Kirsty had made for them. The purple tartan shifts fit like gloves and made them glow. Caroline stepped forward and handed Kirsty her bouquet of irises and roses. It had been stored safely in the fridge and hadn't fallen victim to the carnage like the rest of her wedding flowers.

"You are beautiful," she said.

"So are you." Kirsty gave her a quick hug.

"There's no flower girl," Caroline told her. "It's past her bedtime."

"We'll manage," Kirsty said.

"Yes, we will."

Rainne was next, hugging Kirsty tight.

"I am so pleased my brother found you," she said. "You make him happy. He smiles around you. You've shown him what having a loving family means, and I am really proud to have you as a sister."

Kirsty blinked back tears as she hugged Rainne again. "It will happen for you," she whispered. "Don't give up hope."

Rainne nodded and stepped back. Kirsty reached out and ran her finger over the flesh coloured dressing at Rainne's throat. It could have been so much worse.

"I'm proud to have you as a sister too, Rainne," she said and watched as Rainne blink back tears.

Kirsty took a deep breath. This was it. It was really happening. She was getting married. Her smile was so wide she felt like she would burst.

She held on to her mum and followed her bridesmaids through to the new conservatory. The room was packed. Two blocks of chairs, in rows, were filled with smiling faces. The chairs were draped in white, with purple sashes—just as she'd planned.

"How?" Kirsty said.

"I own a material shop, remember?" her mum whispered. "Just don't look too closely. Nothing quite matches."

Kirsty ran her eyes over the decorations and spotted the different shades of purple and different patterns in the white.

"It's perfect, Mum, really. Thank you." Even the broken and boarded windows had been covered with white satin and purple bows.

Her mother sniffed again.

The music changed as Kirsty fought to take in all the details. The room was decorated with thousands of fairy lights. Through the huge windows she could see the snow sparkle under trees filled with the same lights. Jars with candles lit up the patio outside the room. More jars with candles were dotted around inside, making the place glow.

It was fairyland.

At the front, in the corner of the room, Josh stood dressed in a suit, singing for them. At the end of the aisle, the aging vicar waited. He stood in front of large planters filled with bare branches wrapped in yet more fairy lights.

Kirsty sucked in a breath as Caroline started walking down the aisle followed by Rainne. She watched as her bridesmaids reached the bottom and took up positions to the left of the vicar. And then a figure stepped out from behind the crowd to stand at the end of the aisle. Everything else in the room faded away. Kirsty could only see Lake. And he was gorgeous. He was dressed in traditional Scottish garb, complete with a purple and green Campbell tartan kilt. His broad shoulders were mouth-watering in his tailored black jacket. He was perfect. And he was hers.

"I'll go sit down. Love you, honey," her mum said.

"No." Kirsty hooked their arms together. "You need to walk me down the aisle."

With a wide smile and tear-stained cheeks, her mother held her head high and accompanied her daughter.

Kirsty couldn't keep her eyes from the stunning man who waited for her to get to him. His luminous blue eyes glowed with warmth and love as she walked towards him. The closer she got to him the darker his gaze became, making promises he would definitely be keeping later.

"I'm in a skirt for you," he told her as he reached for her hand.

"It's only fair," she said. "I'm in a skirt for you."

"You won't be in it long." His grin was filled with lascivious intent.

"Lake!" Her mother smacked his arm and everyone burst out laughing.

Red-faced, she gave the crowd a finger wave, kissed both Kirsty and Lake on the cheek, then took her place in the front row beside her friends from Knit Or Die.

"If we hurry up we'll still be married on Leap Day," Lake said.

Kirsty started to smile until her eyes hit Lake's best man. Betty McLeod grinned widely. This time at least she'd remembered her teeth. Instead of her usual tartan tent, she was wearing a tent made out England's flag. The red and white of the St. George's crosses made Kirsty's jaw drop.

"That isn't purple. It isn't even pretty. I made you a Campbell tartan tent to wear."

Lake started to laugh, then worked hard to smother it.

"I couldn't wear it," Betty said. "I'm a McLeod. Not a Campbell."

Kirsty pointed at the dress. "You're not English either."

Betty huffed. "This is in honour of Lake. I think of the Englishman as the son I didn't have."

"And I think of her as the mother I don't want," Lake said.

Then, to Kirsty's disgust, Betty and Lake did a fist bump.

"Can we get on with this?" the vicar said. "I'm usually in bed by nine. I'm so knackered I can hardly stand." He made a big production of looking at his watch. "It's quarter past eleven. You've got forty-five minutes before this Leap Day is over. You can spend it tying the knot, or you can spend it arguing with Betty. I'll be over at the food. Let me know what you decide."

He took a step towards the buffet, and Lake's hand shot out to stop him.

"Vows. Now," was all he said.

The vicar grumped, pushed his bifocals up his nose and took a deep breath.

"Dearly beloved, and Betty. We are gathered here today, in the sight of God, to join together this man and this woman. If anyone has any objections, let's hear them."

Kirsty held her breath and waited, even though she knew no one could possibly object. When Betty made a big production of clearing her throat, Kirsty shot her a glare.

"Okay," Reverend Morrison said, "Lake Benson, do you take Kirsty Campbell to have and to hold from this day forward, until death do you part?"

Lake stared at the minister. "Isn't there more to it? I think you missed a part."

"Son." The old, bulldog of a man stared up at Lake. "It's

late. I'm tired and the snow is making my arthritis act up. If you want the long version, wait 'til the morning. Or spring. Wait 'til spring."

Lake took a deep breath and looked at the ceiling while Kirsty giggled. "Fine." His eyes came back down to fix on Kirsty. "I do."

There was a loud cheer, which made the vicar grumble and demand silence.

"You'd think they were born in a barn." He turned to Kirsty. "Kirsty Campbell, do you take Lake Benson…"

"Benson-McLeod," Betty interrupted. "I'm adopting him."

The vicar glared at her. "Have you done the paperwork? Do you have proof of name change?"

She didn't say anything, but her hand gesture spoke volumes. The vicar narrowed his eyes and took a step towards his nemesis.

"Lake Benson." Lake tugged the neck of Betty's dress to keep her in place. "Just Benson."

"That's an insult, son." Betty got a calculating gleam in her eye. "How about naming the firstborn after me instead?"

"Done," Lake said.

"Lake!" Kirsty smacked him with her bouquet as Betty cackled.

He shrugged. "She's old. She'll be dead by then. She won't know what we call him."

He had a point. Betty kicked Lake in the back of his leg, making him flinch.

"Do you," shouted the vicar, "Kirsty Campbell, take Lake Benson. Only Benson. To have and to hold from this day forward until death do you part?"

"I do," Kirsty said, and there was another whoop.

"Great. I now pronounce you man and wife. You may kiss the bride." The vicar took a step towards the buffet.

"What about rings?" Lake said.

"Have at it," Reverend Morrison called over his shoulder as he kept on walking.

"We need a new vicar," Caroline said.

"Amen to that," shouted the vicar.

Lake took Kirsty's hand in his, glaring at everyone as though daring them to move. Nobody did. In fact, they looked like they were more than happy to keep on enjoying the show.

"Kirsty Benson," Lake said, sending a shiver down her spine. He took her left hand in his and pulled a ring from his pocket. He'd wisely decided not to entrust his best man with the rings. "Kirsty, I give you this ring as a symbol of my love for you. This ring has no end, as my love is never-ending. This ring is made to endure the harsh wear and tear of life, just like my love for you. This ring is made of precious metal, as you are precious to me. Wear this ring as a reminder that everything I am and have is yours. My love is eternal. And only for you."

There was a round of applause and wolf whistles as her blonde warrior put the ring on her finger.

Kirsty felt a tear escape and run down her cheek.

"I think I'm going to puke," Betty declared.

"Here." Lake handed Kirsty his ring. "You don't have to say anything."

She took the gold band and looked up at the man she loved. "No, I want to." She took a deep breath and held his hands tight in hers. "Lake Benson. You came into my life and changed everything. You made me feel beautiful and worthy. You made me feel loved and desired. When I met you, I honestly never thought I'd ever be able to get over my past enough to love someone. You helped me to do exactly that. As well as giving me your love, you've given me the world. A world in which I'm no longer insecure or afraid. For that, I will always love you."

She slid the ring onto his finger.

"I need a whisky," Betty grumbled, and stomped off.

"Time to kiss," Lake whispered.

"Yeah," Kirsty said.

He tipped his head towards hers and his lips stole her senses. His strong arms wrapped around her; his hands were flat and possessive on her back. Vaguely, she thought there was cheering and clapping. She didn't care. She was lost in the man she loved.

And she was married.

On Leap Day.

Their kiss ended far too quickly as one by one their friends and family came to congratulate them. Lake's hot gaze promised they'd pick up where they'd left off later. Kirsty couldn't wait.

"Josh Mark Two is missing," Josh told them miserably, handing them each a glass of champagne at the same time.

Kirsty noted that Caroline looked particularly gleeful at the news.

"I think one of the women ran off with him." Josh eyed the Knit Or Die women, who were laughing raucously as they tried to line-dance in the middle of the room. "I feel sick thinking about what they're going to do with him. It can't be good. I'm going to miss that doll. I used to take him on tour and use him as a paparazzi decoy." He grinned. "There are photos out there of a rubber doll that people think are me."

Kirsty wasn't sure that was a good thing. If you were interchangeable with a rubber doll, then you should be worried. Apparently Josh wasn't.

"I'm sorry about the castle," Kirsty said to Caroline.

"Why? It wasn't your fault." She looked bewildered.

Josh kissed the little worry lines that appeared on Caroline's forehead.

"I don't think I can sleep in my bedroom anymore,

though," Caroline said. "There are bullet holes in my walls and my bathroom was destroyed. What wasn't killed by the gunmen was ruined by the fireworks. There are black burn marks on my ceiling." Her eyes went wide at the thought. "Plus, I can't get the sight of Dimitri tied to my bed out of my head."

"We've got plenty of other rooms," Josh reassured her.

"And holes can be fixed," Kirsty said. "Furniture can be replaced. You'll have the place sorted in no time and all this will just be a bad memory. You love this castle. Heck, you got married just to get your hands on it."

"There is that," Caroline said. "But I'm not sure if I'll ever believe the children will be safe here." She placed a hand on her stomach.

"Yes, you will, because you'll make sure this place has security to rival Buckingham Palace when you're through with it." Kirsty cuddled close to Lake. Although he wasn't showing any outward signs that he was amused, she could feel his body tremble and knew he was doing that silent laughing thing. "I know you, Caroline McInnes. You've been keeping a mental list since the lights went out. As soon as you're able, the castle will be fitted with a generator. There will be independently powered satellite phones. The windows will have discreet metal shutters that appear from nowhere at the touch of a button and there will be at least two snowmobiles in the garage."

Caroline almost smiled. "We don't have a garage."

"There you go, something else to add to the list. You love lists. This will be great. It's been ages since you've had a decent project."

Caroline's shoulders relaxed slightly. "I had a project. I helped plan your wedding." She bit her bottom lip. "I'm really sorry it was a complete disaster."

"It wasn't a complete disaster." Kirsty looked around at

the room filled with people she loved. "It was perfect. I couldn't have planned a better wedding."

Lake leaned down and kissed her softly in agreement.

"Even with the castle in such a mess?" Caroline worried her bottom lip.

"It looks beautiful from where I'm standing," Kirsty said.

"Don't worry, baby," Josh said. "We'll throw some money at the castle and it will all be fine."

Caroline frowned at him. "You and money. It isn't the answer to everything."

Josh's famous blue eyes twinkled as he looked down at his wife. "Name one thing it can't fix?"

"The weather," Caroline said solemnly.

"You win." Josh kissed his wife, making her blush as everyone else laughed. "But for everything else, there's money."

As Josh ushered his clearly exhausted wife over towards the food, Rainne came up alongside the couple. "I'm leaving in the morning. I just wanted you to know that I am really happy for both of you. The wedding was perfect. Even with Betty's dress."

Kirsty frowned in the direction of Betty, who was dancing with four young men Kirsty had never seen before. When she'd asked about them, Betty had said they were her dates, then cackled.

"We'll miss you." Kirsty hugged her sister-in-law. "Are you sure you don't want to stay a couple of days? See Alastair when he gets out of hospital?"

"This is for the best." Rainne's smile was forced. "Besides, I need to get back to work." She gave her brother a hug, kissed his cheek and made excuses about needing some champagne before she rushed off.

"I worry about her," Kirsty said as she rested her cheek on Lake's chest.

"Don't." He kissed the top of her head. "Alastair won't let her go this time. It will be fine. Now, how about a dance for your husband?"

Kirsty beamed up at him as she wrapped her arms around his waist. This was it. Her happy spot. The place she always wanted to be.

As the music played, Kirsty and Lake swayed together on the spot they'd said their vows. Lights twinkled over the snow. Laughter and conversation formed a cocoon around them. With Dougal in charge of the food, everyone was well fed and happy. And Lake and Kirsty danced into the early hours of March the first.

Husband and wife at last.

CHAPTER 32

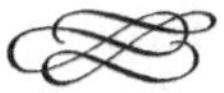

* RAINNE AND ALASTAIR *

Five long days they'd kept Alastair in Fort William hospital. All because of one tiny little infection. He'd begged to be sent home with some antibiotics, but no, that wasn't allowed. Instead he was hooked up to an IV and had to listen to Mitch wax lyrical about his near-death experience. If Alastair heard the word "epiphany" one more time, he was going to lose it and massacre his way out of Scotland just to get away from the American.

By the time he made it back to Invertary, he discovered Lake and Kirsty were married, and Rainne had gone back to Glasgow. He'd figured as much when she'd failed to appear at the hospital. Alastair demanded her address from her brother and packed a bag for his trip south. This time, he wasn't going to skulk off back home when she closed the door on him. This time would be different.

She'd said she loved him.

She'd said she wanted him.

Well, she was bloody well going to get him.

It was raining in Glasgow. Alastair couldn't remember ever visiting the city when it wasn't raining. The further he

247

got from the Highlands, the more the scenery dulled. The green hills around Loch Lomond gave way to grey high-rise housing, red sandstone tenements and concrete-covered ground. Alastair wondered why Rainne would want to live in a place crawling with people. A place where you had to go to a park to see some greenery. It made him feel claustrophobic just driving through the busy streets, with their buildings squeezed together until there was no space left to think.

Alastair sent up a prayer of thanks for GPS as it led him through the narrow streets in Glasgow's West End. It took three turns around the block until he found a place to park his truck. He grabbed his bag from the back seat, pulled up his collar against the relentless rain and ran up the steps to Rainne's tenement building. The old building had been modernised to include a security door with an intercom beside it and a button for each flat. Not that it did any good to keep out strangers. Someone had propped the door open with a brick.

Shaking his head, Alastair climbed the stairs to the fourth floor. Rainne's door was the middle of three. His stomach roiled as his system fought between nerves and anticipation. He'd had a three-hour drive to think about how best to tackle this meeting with Rainbow. After great consideration, taking into account all the things they should discuss, he'd decided the best way forward was to keep his mouth shut and let his actions do the talking.

He lifted his hand to brush his hair off his face and smacked himself with his fluorescent green cast. Great start. He put the cast to good use and thumped the door with it.

"Just a minute," Rainne shouted, and the sound of her voice had the blood rushing through his system at warp speed.

Without checking the peephole, or even asking who was there, she threw the door open. Her eyes went wide and her mouth fell open. Perfect. Alastair threw his bag into the hallway behind her, took two steps into her house, placed a hand on each of her cheeks and took her open mouth with his.

Home. He was home. The anxiety within him fled at the taste of her. He'd missed this. He'd missed her. Not just this past week, but these past three years. He felt her melt against his body. Heard a tiny mewl of need escape from the back of her throat. Her hands clutched at his hips, her fingers clinging to him as Alastair walked her backwards, further into the flat and kicked the door shut behind them.

He pressed her up against the wall, feeling the soft curves of her body flatten against him. He kissed her until they were both panting with need and his lips felt bruised. Keeping their bodies touching, Alastair leaned back to look down at her. Her eyes were heavy-lidded, her cheeks were pink and her lips were red. Need surged through him. It was a living beast that couldn't be tamed. He had to have her. Now.

She was wearing purple leggings and a purple and yellow striped oversized sweatshirt. There was a pair of thick woollen socks on her feet, also yellow, and her hair was up in a high, messy ponytail. He wrapped his left hand in the bottom of her sweatshirt and tugged it up.

"Need help," he said. "Cast." He held up his broken arm.

"Help?" She blinked up at him.

"I want this off." He tugged at the shirt again. "I want you naked. Now."

A low moan escaped her lips. Alastair felt it go straight to his crotch. He took a step back.

"Strip, Rainbow."

"Alastair?" Rainne opened and closed her mouth a couple of times, clearly unable to figure out what to say next. Those little lines appeared between her brows.

Alastair turned and locked the door. Then he toed off his

boots, along with his socks. With his eyes on Rainne, he unzipped his wet leather jacket and let it fall to the floor. Rainne's eyes went wide at each move he made.

"Take off the sweater, Rainbow."

He yanked his own sweater over his head and threw it to the floor. He wasn't wearing anything underneath, and he almost lost the little self-control he had left when she licked her lips at the sight of his bare chest.

"Rainbow." It was a growl.

She didn't move. It was as though she was dazed. Her fingers slowly lifted to touch her lips.

Alastair glanced around. They were in a tiny hallway, painted in a tasteful cream that made him think Rainne hadn't gotten around to decorating yet. On the left was an open doorway into a small living room/kitchen. The lamps were on in the room and he could see an open novel on the sofa. Straight ahead was a closed door—he assumed the bathroom. To the right was another open door, this one to a dark room with a double bed under the window.

Now he had his destination.

His hand went to his belt and he unbuckled it, watching Rainbow's eyes as they followed his every move.

"What are you doing?" she whispered.

"Sorting things out between us." He unbuttoned the top button on his jeans.

"Shouldn't we talk first?"

"Talking doesn't work for us. This is better."

He stalked towards her, pressing her back against the wall, hip to hip. Letting her feel every hard inch of him. Letting her know how much he wanted her. No. Needed her.

He placed his forearms on the wall beside her head and leaned forward to rub his cheek up the side of her throat. Her head fell to the side to give him access. He nibbled on her earlobe, letting her hear his breath, gratified when it made her shudder. She smelled like sherbet. He ran his tongue down the smooth column of her throat to bury his nose in the curve at her shoulder. She tasted like sherbet too.

"Do you want this, Rainne?" He asked the words against her skin, nipping gently at her when he paused. "Do you want me to make love to you?" He honestly thought he might collapse and die on the spot if she said no.

Her fingers hooked into the waistband of his jeans, holding tight.

"Yes," she whispered.

It was all he needed to hear. He grabbed her sweater at the bottom and yanked it up awkwardly.

"Help me," he pleaded.

She released her hold on him long enough to tug the top over her head. She wasn't wearing anything underneath. Alastair groaned as he fell to his knees. Without pausing, he took one of her perfect pink nipples in his mouth and sucked hard.

"Alastair!" It was a plea.

Her fingers wound into his overgrown hair and held him tight against her. He vowed never to get it cut short again. He kissed and licked and bit. Teasing her nipple until her gasps were feverish and her fingers tugged tight at his scalp, making it sting perfectly.

He turned his attention to her other breast and lavished it with the same attention, flicking his tongue rapidly over her nipple until she arched her back and pressed her breast into his mouth. He sucked it deep. Delicious. She was delicious.

Her soft, panting moans were music to his ears. He could listen to them forever. If he had his way, he *would* listen to them forever. He'd spend morning, noon and night making her writhe with pleasure just to hear those sounds.

Using his good hand he tugged her leggings down, taking her underwear with him. He sat back on his heels and his mouth watered at the sight before him. An expanse of soft, milky skin leading to paradise.

"Off." He pulled the leggings and socks.

Swaying, she placed a hand on each of his shoulders to help kick off her clothing. At last she was naked. He felt like a starving man at a banquet. He didn't know where to start first. Slowly, his eyes travelled up her body to find a desire-filled gaze looking back at him.

"Spread your legs," he ordered.

Her gasp made him soar. He helped push her legs apart, and without hesitating he leaned forward to taste her.

"Alastair!" She tilted her hips towards him, making him growl with approval. He wanted all of her. He grasped her backside with his good hand and pulled her tight against his face. Her taste was addictive.

He glanced up her body to find her head flung back against the wall, her lips open and her cheeks flushed. Beautiful. He licked deeper into her, flicking his tongue over that little bundle of nerves until he heard her incoherent begging. Her fingers curled into his hair again. He felt the sharp bite of her nails. It spurred him on. He wanted more. He wanted all of her. He sucked the tiny nub hard and heard her scream his name.

Her body bowed against him as she shuddered, racked by the pleasure he'd given her. Pride surged through him and he pushed to his feet. He took her mouth in his and kissed her with a desperation that bordered on pain. She writhed against him, her soft, naked body a sensuous playground.

With one hand on the small of her back, and his mouth fused to hers, he walked her backwards into her bedroom and pressed her into the bed. The room was dark, lit only by the glow from the hallway. Alastair came down on top of Rainne, bracing his weight on his arms, wishing the damn cast wasn't in his way. Wishing he could have carried her to bed. Another time. There would be another time.

She hooked her leg around his hip, wrapped her arms around his shoulders and pressed up into him.

"Need you," he said into her mouth.

"Your ribs!"

Her worry made him smile. "I'll be careful.

Her answering kiss was out of control. Making it clear she wanted all of him.

Her hands smoothed down his back, around his waistband, until they met the buttons on his jeans. She popped them one at a time in agonisingly slow motion.

"Please." She tried to get his jeans over his hips using her hands and leg.

Alastair pushed up off the bed, keeping his eyes locked with hers. Desire made them heavy and heated. Nothing made him more desperate than watching her want him. He pushed his jeans and underwear down his legs and stepped out of them.

"Gorgeous woman." He needed her to know how he saw her, what she did to him, but the words wouldn't come. "My woman," he said instead, hoping she understood. Hoping she knew it was more than a claim. It was a promise.

Rainne pulled him down on top of her and wrapped both legs around his hips, her heels digging into the backs of his thighs.

"Alastair." Her voice was a low, begging rasp. "Please. I can't wait. Don't tease me."

"I won't, Rainbow." He braced his weight on his good arm and with one move thrust into her.

They groaned together. Rainne's fingers dug into the flexing muscles of his back.

"I have missed you so much," he said.

"I need you," she whispered.

"You've got me." He moved his hips until there were only moans of need. "Love you, Rainbow," Alastair said against her ear. "Love you. Only you. Always you."

She shuddered, calling his name as she clenched around him, taking him with her into the oblivion of pure, glorious pleasure.

CHAPTER 33

* RAINNE AND ALASTAIR *

Rainne woke slowly. She was lying on her stomach and there was a heavy weight pinning her in place.

Alastair.

She smiled into the darkness, taking a moment to enjoy the feeling of his naked body beside hers. His skin against hers. His body heat making her burn, and comforting her at the same time.

His hand caressed from the small of her back to between her shoulder blades, making her press herself into the mattress and moan her pleasure.

"Hey, gorgeous," he said. "Thought you'd never wake up."

She smiled at the husky timbre of his voice as she blinked open her eyes to look at her alarm clock. It was three a.m.

His hand smoothed back down to curve around her behind.

"You have a backside that brings a man to his knees." There was awe in his voice.

Rainne turned her head so she could look at him. The light was still on in her hall and her bedroom door was wide open. He looked good in the soft glow. He looked even better in her bed. Her stomach clenched. He might look edible, but she wasn't sure he should be there.

"Alastair," she started, but he silenced her by leaning forward and kissing her gently.

She sighed as she sank deeper into the bed.

He pulled back slightly to look at her. "So, here's the thing," he said as he ran his thumb over her bottom lip. "I've decided I'm moving in."

Her eyes went wide. "What?"

"I'm moving in. Here. With you."

She blinked. "What?"

He smiled that devastatingly sexy smile that made her mind turn to mush. She couldn't afford a mushy mind. She needed to think straight. She closed her eyes tight against the distraction.

"You can't stay here." Her stomach clenched with panic. She didn't know what to think. He wasn't making sense. What about his business? His future in Invertary? What about not trusting her to stay with him? Was he just going to ignore it all?

"Course I can."

She could hear the smile in his voice. At least she couldn't see it. That helped her resolve.

"We talked about this. You don't trust me. The problems in our past are too big to overcome."

"Well, to be honest, we didn't talk. You talked and then you left. You have got to stop doing that, Rainbow. It makes it hard to have a conversation when you keep leaving."

She opened her mouth to answer that stupidity, but he put a finger to her lips. "Here's what I was going to say before you did my thinking for me. Three years ago I tried to push you into a commitment with me that you weren't ready for. That *we* weren't ready for. I understand that now."

She started to protest, but he tapped her lips. She opened her eyes and frowned at him. If he did that again, she was so going to bite his finger.

"I was immature," he said. "I was trying to tie you to me in order to ease my fears. It wasn't realistic. It made you panic. Then when you left, it made me close up emotionally."

"Close up emotionally?"

"I spent five days stuck in a hospital room with Mitch. When he wasn't talking about the epiphany he had when he almost died, he was analysing me. It was hell."

"And yet here you are, quoting the man." It was amazing how he could make her smile even when they were in the middle of something so heavy.

"I didn't say he was wrong, just that I didn't need to endure all that chitchat, heart-to-heart crap."

"Did you have to go straight out and fish and hunt something to prove you're still a manly man?" She really wanted to giggle.

"No." Alastair's face sobered. "I came straight here."

Oh. Her eyes dropped away from his penetrating stare, but it didn't help. Instead of the emotion in his eyes, she was confronted by ab perfection and temptation of a different kind.

"Anyway," he said. "I sorted out our problems while I was stuck in the hospital."

She looked back up at him. "Do I want to hear this?"

"Aye, you do. Because it means we both get what we want."

"Which is?" Her heart pounded a mile a minute at the thought of getting what she wanted. Of getting him. For real. Forever.

"Each other, Rainbow. Each other." He took a deep breath, and she noticed the waver in it. He was nervous. For some reason, knowing he felt that way too calmed her.

"Here's the plan. I'm going to move in here because this is where you feel you need to be and I'm okay with that."

"You hate the city, Alastair. You said you wanted to live in Invertary forever."

"I do. But I can postpone forever for as long as you need to be here."

Her heart turned to a puddle in her chest.

"As for the rest. According to Mitch, my inner child needs to believe you won't run away again." He rolled his eyes. "I realise it's unreasonable to want you to promise something you can't guarantee. So I've come up with a compromise." He paused, looking quite pleased with himself. "I want you to promise me tomorrow. Just tomorrow. One day. That's all. Promise that you'll be here, with me, tomorrow. Can you do that?"

She noticed a little twitch at the edge of his eye, telling her how anxious he was about her answer.

"Yes," she said. "I will be here, with you, tomorrow."

"Good. Then tomorrow night you can promise me the next day. We'll take it one day at a time. No guarantees on a future neither of us can predict. Just tomorrow." He bent forward and kissed her lips oh so softly. "Then one day, you'll look up and realise you've promised me all of your tomorrows and I'll realise that there was never any chance of you leaving me."

Her heart soared. He was doing it. He was trusting her to stay. Giving her a second chance not to hurt him. It was something she'd never thought he'd be able to do. Brave man. *Her* brave man.

"All of my tomorrows," she whispered against his lips. "Is that what you want, Alastair?"

"Only if you give them to me. I won't force you and I won't judge you if you can't."

She leaned in to kiss him, overwhelmed by his courage and trust. He groaned and kissed her hotly. Deeply. Enclosing her in his embrace. Keeping her safe and secure. Letting her be who she was meant to be. They were both breathing hard when they parted.

Rainne snuggled down into his arms. "I'm still too old for you." She placed her cheek against his chest where she could listen to his heartbeat. It beat for her. She believed that now.

"It's terrible." He trailed his fingers up and down her back. "I can see it now. We're in an old folks' home; you're eighty-six and I'm a mere eighty. And will those other old folks let us forget it? They will not. The amount of teasing you'll have to endure for being married to a toy-boy. It will drive you insane."

Rainne stilled against him. "Married?"

He went tense under her cheek. She heard his heart race and knew he hadn't meant to say that. He was trying so hard not to push her to commit. Trying hard not to make the same mistakes he'd made last time. But she wasn't the same scared girl she'd been three years earlier. She knew what she wanted now. And she'd learned to trust that Alastair knew what he wanted too.

"You expect us to live in sin for the rest of our lives?" he joked, in an attempt to ease them away from the tension.

But Rainne didn't need it. She wanted forever. She wanted to give him all her days. Whether that was one at a time, or in a huge upfront lump sum, it didn't matter to her. They all belonged to him anyway. They always had.

"I want to get married in Invertary. In the summer, so there's no chance of snow. And I don't want to get married at the castle. I think on the side of the loch. That would be pretty. I'll wear a rainbow-coloured dress and you'll wear a dark suit, to match your dark eyes."

Alastair pushed her onto her back and leaned over her. "Rainbow, you don't need to say that. I'm fine with tomorrow."

"I know. And I'll give you tomorrow too. Every day, I'll give you tomorrow. And when we get married, I'll promise you all of my tomorrows. They belong to you anyway. They always have." She bit her lip, stealing Alastair's gaze to her mouth. "I need to stay in Glasgow for the next year or two. Then we can go back to Invertary."

"We don't need to. I'm happy being wherever you are."

Rainne didn't think it was possible to love him more. The man who wanted to sacrifice his dreams for her.

"Two years, maximum, and then we go home. Forever," she promised. "I miss the green hills too. And how will you teach the children to fish if we live here?"

"Children?" The hope in his eyes undid her.

"We'll have two." A tear slid down her cheek. He sucked in a breath. "We'll give them normal names, like George and Susan. None of this Rainbow and Lake nonsense. They'll learn to fish. But no hunting; it's too dangerous."

"Rainbow." He said her name with such reverence it made the tears flow faster. He buried his face in her neck and held her tight enough to make her believe he'd never let her go.

"I want a dog." Her voice was husky with emotion. "We moved around so much growing up, I never got to have a pet."

"You can have whatever you want." He pressed an open-mouthed kiss to her throat.

"I want a house near Lake and Kirsty."

"Done."

"I'd like to start another business and get it right this time."

"It's yours. Whatever you want. It's yours."

"I want to be Rainbow Stewart. I want to be yours."

He looked into her eyes, and the love she saw there over-whelmed her. "You always were, Rainbow. You were always mine."

And then he kissed her, long, slow and hard.

EPILOGUE

Callum McKay looked around his newly assembled team of security professionals. He wasn't impressed.

They'd taken over a building near Victoria train station in London. It was right in the heart of the city. The old offices needed a bit of work, but Julia had told him she had it under control—by email. He'd yet to talk to his assistant in person. Oh, he'd tried, but it never went well and usually ended up with her hiding for the rest of the day. The current meeting was a typical example of their insane working relationship— the rest of his team were sitting around the boardroom table. Not Julia. Her chair was wedged behind a humungous office palm, her back to the wall and a large laptop obscuring most of her face.

And she was the least of his worries. Ryan didn't take anything he said seriously, and Joe seemed to be at a loss without his best friend Grunt. Then there was Rachel. Since Harry's company had merged with Lake's, Rachel now officially worked for Callum in her role as cybersecurity manager. Only it seemed Rachel hadn't gotten the memo about the new hierarchy. She was currently scowling at him as she tapped her professionally manicured blood-red nails on the table in front of her. Her first words to him were: "Really? You're in charge? I don't think so." Callum did not see a relaxed working relationship in their future.

And then there were the last two members of his newly formed team. Dimitri Raast and Megan Donaldson. One was trained but his loyalty was seriously in question. The other had no training at all and far too much enthusiasm to be safe on a job. They glared across the table at each other. The sexual tension between them was palpable. Just what he needed—two operatives who were unstable and more likely to jump each other than deal with the enemy.

"Okay," he said to his team. "Welcome to the first meeting of the London division of Benson Security. We have our first case." As if by magic, a photo appeared on the wall behind him. He glanced at Julia, whose hand was poised over the trackpad on her laptop. Of course she'd set up a PowerPoint presentation. Why hadn't he thought of it? Callum pointed at the man on the wall behind him.

"Rudi Abramovich," he said. "This man has Dimitri's sister and we're going to get her back."

FIRST CHAPTER OF RECKLESS

PRESENT DAY - THE NEW LONDON
OFFICES OF BENSON SECURITY

"Earth to Buffy, come in Buffy."

Dimitri Raast grinned when Megan scowled at him. The blonde beauty was easy to wind up. It had become his main hobby since he'd met her in Scotland two weeks earlier. She sat opposite him at the conference room table in the Regency townhouse that was now the new London office of Benson Security. Her long white-blonde hair was in a high ponytail and the striped T-shirt she wore slid off one creamy shoulder. She could have been a model, instead she'd set her sights on becoming a security specialist. Or as she liked to call it, a gun-for-hire. Yeah, her background in baking and doing hair wouldn't get her far in her new profession. In fact, Dimitri knew for sure that the boss wouldn't have let her anywhere near his business if they didn't need her for this operation.

If *Dimitri* didn't need her.

Her blue eyes narrowed at him. "You do know that calling me Buffy isn't an insult, right? Buffy was a superhero. She saved the world countless times. She had a fantastic wardrobe and got to bonk sexy vampires."

"And she was an airhead." He bit back a laugh. Megan Donaldson was too much. Really.

"Have you even watched the show? Do yourself a favour and look it up on Netflix. Get back to me once you know what you're talking about."

"Would you prefer I call you Blondie?" He folded his arms and watched as her gaze lingered on his biceps. Oh yeah, she felt the burn between them too.

"Blondie was another cutting edge woman. A music pioneer. That isn't an insult either."

"Barbie?"

"Now you're pissing me off."

Dimitri laughed. Which probably wasn't smart, as he'd learned the hard way that Megan was unpredictable when she was pissed off. Unpredictable, wicked and violent, with a penchant for hitting men where it hurt most—and grinning while she did it. He shifted in his seat at the thought, trying to free up more space in his jeans. He wasn't sure if the sudden tightness was due to fear that his crown jewels weren't safe around the woman, or because her being crazy and violent seemed to press all the right buttons for him.

Most of the women Dimitri had gotten hot and heavy with over the years were on the Suzy Homemaker end of the spectrum—naive, pretty, predictable and safe. In other words, reliable wife material. Not that he'd been looking for a wife, but if a man was going to fall into that pit, he'd rather it was with someone he knew would make a good family and home life. Yet, none of those women got him worked up the way crazy Megan Donaldson did. Turns out, at the ripe old age of thirty, he'd discovered his type actually lay more towards the wicked and twisted end of the spectrum. Who knew?

The door to the conference room opened and Joe Barone and Ryan Granger swaggered in. Like Megan, the guys had come down from Benson Security's main office in the High-lands. Unlike Megan, they were both ex-military and knew what they were doing.

"Coffee?" Joe said by way of hello.

Dimitri pointed to the table in the corner of the room where Julia, the office manager, had set up a coffee pot and a plate of Danish pastries. He assumed Joe's grunt of reply was a thank you. The big Italian-American filled his mug, glugged it down and refilled it before taking his place at the table.

"Rough night, old man?" Ryan filled his own mug and snagged a plate of pastries. "Can't keep the pace, eh?"

Joe stared at the younger Englishman. "Unlike you, I was up most of the night working the case."

Ryan shrugged. "Is that supposed to make me feel bad? Yeah, you were working hard, but I'll take a night of hitting London's clubs with a lingerie model over being conscientious any day of the week."

A growl rumbled from Joe's chest. Ryan just laughed. The door slammed open and all heads turned to watch Rachel Ford-Talbot make her entrance. She scanned the room with a look of disgust. Her iPhone was in one perfectly manicured hand, her designer handbag was hanging from the crook of her arm and her equally expensive suit was teamed with her usual red-soled pumps. Dimitri was pretty sure someone who gave a shit about fashion would be able to name each of the designers Rachel wore—he wasn't one of them.

"This," she gestured with a red tipped talon, "is the A-team?"

Ryan pointed a croissant at her. "The A-team is still in Scotland, love. You got saddled with the B-team."

"Kill me now," Rachel muttered as she headed towards the coffee.

"That can be arranged." Megan's tone was pure cat.

Rachel arched an eyebrow at her. "Tell me again why

you're on the team?" She stirred her coffee. "Without your twin to do your thinking for you, and that awful Goth friend of yours to fight your battles, just what use will you be?"

Megan made her own little growl. It was more kitten than monster, which didn't help the menace vibe she was aiming for. "My *Goth friend* should have kicked your scrawny backside harder when you were in Invertary."

Rachel smiled—it made Dimitri shudder. Now *there* was a woman who knew how to do mean. "Thanks for noticing my backside. It's my new Pilates regime. I can recommend a divine personal trainer. She'll help you lose that extra chub you carry in no time at all."

Dimitri thought Megan's head might actually explode. He tensed, ready to jump out of his seat and do some damage control. Or duck. Whatever came first.

Megan faced off against Rachel. "Just because I don't think anorexia is a lifestyle choice doesn't make me fat. You should try eating sometime, it might improve your disposition."

Rachel faked a pout. "Well done. I'm so proud. You used words with more than one syllable."

Megan sprang to her feet as their new boss entered the room. His hand clamped on her shoulder.

"This meeting is about to start." Callum McKay released his hold. "Fight on your own time."

"I'm not sure Rachel can confine being a bitch to her off hours." Megan plopped back into her seat.

"I said enough." Callum's soft Scottish burr rounded out the accents in the room.

"Aye, aye, captain." Rachel smirked at him. "We wouldn't want to undermine your tenuous hold on authority. After all, we know how much a man's ego is tied to his position." Her gaze scanned down his body, lingering on his fly. "It would be *such* a shame to damage your fragile, teeny-tiny ego."

Callum stared Rachel down until the two of them were locked in a contest of wills.

"Should we place bets on who cracks first?" Ryan whispered. "My money's on Callum."

The lights suddenly dimmed and a photo appeared on the wall. Everyone's eyes shot to the picture.

"Sorry," the large potted palm said. "I thought it was time for the slide show."

The lights came back up and the image disappeared.

"Julia?" Megan said, as everyone eyed the plant at the other end of the table from Callum. Sure enough, the office manager was sitting behind it, a laptop balanced on her knees. "Have you been there the whole time?"

There was some shuffling. "Um, yes," Julia said softly.

"I thought we were going to have breakfast together this morning," Megan said. "I waited for you."

Dimitri knew the two women were sharing one of the tiny flats on the top floor of the building. With Megan's extrovert personality and Julia's social phobia, he could only imagine how well that was going.

"Sorry," the plant said. "I had a lot of work to do, so I came in early."

"This is ridiculous," Callum barked. "I refuse to talk to foliage. Get out from behind the plant."

"I can't. I'm plugged in here. The equipment doesn't work out there." Julia's voice was barely a whisper, making them strain to hear her.

"You can make it work out here," Callum snapped. "You're so bloody efficient you're making my head spin. Get to the table."

The plant shook. "I haven't had time to wire up the table area. I will for the next meeting. Right now, if you want a PowerPoint, I have to stay here."

The tremor in Julia's voice was pronounced. Callum was

on fragile ground. Julia had been adopted by half the team. She was practically the office pet.

"Leave her alone," Joe said. "Let her do her job."

"She's hiding behind a plant." Callum pointed at the plant. "How can she do her job from there?"

"Have you had any problems with her work since we arrived in London?" Megan asked, although they all knew the answer. Julia could run the country if she tried. Okay, so she'd do it from inside a closet, but she'd still do a great job. "The answer is no. She's way ahead of schedule with the office renovations. We all have everything we need to work. She's doing her job great. So what if she's a little shy? Leave her alone."

"A little shy?" Rachel barked a laugh. It sounded like nails on a chalkboard. "We've been working together for over a week and I've yet to see her face. That isn't normal. If I was in charge," she directed that comment to Callum, "I'd fire her."

"Aye," Callum told the witch. "But you're not in charge, are you?"

"Yet." Rachel gave him a look designed to make his balls shrivel. "You're not exactly making a great impression as a boss. You can't even get your secretary out from behind a plant."

"Office manager," Joe, Megan and the plant said at the same time.

Ryan laughed until he had to wipe his eyes.

Callum turned his attention back to the potted plant. "Slide show, Julia. And next meeting that damned plant will be gone from the room. Are we clear?"

"Yes, sir," Julia whispered.

"In fact, I want *all* of the plants removed from the building. It's like a bloody jungle in here."

In reply the lights dimmed again. A photo of a man filled the wall.

"This is Rudi Abramovich." Callum pointed at the photo. "This man has Dimitri's sister and we're going to get her back."

Dimitri felt his blood turn to ice. This is why he'd joined Benson Security after the fiasco in Scotland. He needed the team's backing to find his sister. He'd done everything he could on his own, made it as far as he was able, now he needed help.

Dimitri had never felt hate until he'd come across Rudi Abramovich. He hadn't realised the emotion burned like acid. He looked at the man who'd ruined his sister's life. The crime boss could have stepped off the cover of GQ magazine. He was in his early forties and wore it well. His wavy brown hair was professionally styled. His grey suit and open-necked white shirt were tailored to fit his shoulders and make it clear he knew how to use gym equipment. His eyes were contact lens blue, his lips were full like a girl's and his jaw was sharp like a cartoon character.

"Who knew evil came in such a pretty package?" Megan said.

Her approval of the guy's rip-off, George Clooney get-up punched Dimitri in the gut. "There's nothing attractive about him."

Megan blinked before she softened. "Of course not. He's evil. And has obviously had some plastic surgery. Nobody looks that good naturally." She leaned across the table to pat his hand. "He's evil *and* fake."

Dimitri nodded. That was more like it. He lounged back into his chair, twirled a pencil and hoped he hid exactly how much the sight of Rudi affected him.

"As I was saying," Callum gritted out, unhappy at the

chitchat during his meeting. "This guy has Dimitri's sister and our mission is to get her back."

"Don't you mean get her back *if* she's still alive?" Rachel asked the question as though she was enquiring about the weather.

The pencil in Dimitri's grasp snapped in two. So much for keeping his cool. The tension in the room ratcheted up. All eyes were on Dimitri as he carefully placed the two halves of the pencil on the table in front of him. Every muscle in his body felt tight as he fought to control his rage. Slowly, very slowly, he looked up at Rachel.

"What?" Rachel tossed her glossy auburn hair over her shoulder. "I'm not saying anything that everyone isn't already thinking. Your sister has been missing for a year. We haven't heard even a whisper about her whereabouts. She's most likely dead. I know it. You know it. We all know it."

"That's enough," Callum snapped.

Rachel opened her mouth but Callum's palm slapped the table, so she huffed and closed her mouth.

Slowly, Callum turned to Dimitri. "Bring us up to speed. We've all come into this operation at different stages. Start at the beginning so we're on the same page."

As if by magic, the image on the wall changed and his sister appeared. Dimitri felt his chest clench as pain, sharp as a knife, speared through him. She had long black hair, a pretty smile and hazelnut eyes that were identical to his.

"My sister." Dimitri worked to keep his voice devoid of emotion. He cleared his throat and sat up a little straighter. "Katrina Raast. Twenty-five."

"She's only two years older than I am," Megan whispered.

Dimitri totally understood Megan's shock. At twenty-five he'd been on his second tour of Afghanistan. He'd seen a lot of things that had changed him, hardened him. But Katrina had been sheltered. Her world consisted of college classes and fun with her friends. So yeah, she was young. Way too young to be out there on her own, dealing with an evil bastard like Abramovich.

"When she finished her Master's degree at Brown, she decided to take some time out to travel before going back for her PhD. She's smart." He smiled, but the action hurt. "She got a job as an au pair in Germany for six months, to raise money for travel. In February last year her job wound up and she decided to backpack through Europe for the rest of the year."

"Was she alone?" Megan asked.

Dimitri shook his head. "She'd made friends with two other au pairs who were placed by the same programme, both of them American."

Two more images of young women flashed on the wall. Their smiles seemed to mock the people watching.

"Did they go missing too?" Megan said.

"No. They'd split up for a day in Greece. The other two wanted to visit museums, but Katrina wanted to visit the refugee camp." He felt a tiny smile break through his pain. "She majored in development policy and international politics. She wanted to see the problems first hand. She wanted to change the world."

The look in Megan's eyes was the same as the one she'd had in Scotland the first time he'd told Benson Security about his sister. It was the look he'd seen before she held his hand and offered him comfort. A kindness that had almost broken him. Dimitri tore his eyes from her to look back at the image, which had changed to a candid shot of his sister posing in front of the Acropolis in Athens. Her arms were wide and she was grinning.

"She didn't make it back to the hotel as they'd arranged." Dimitri focused his comments on Callum. At least there was no emotion in his boss's eyes to derail him. "The guide she'd hired to take her to the refugee camp disappeared off the face of the planet. When the agency she booked him through was questioned, they had no records of Katrina's booking or the guide."

"Abramovich's organisation was using it to target tourists," Callum said.

"That and several other tourist agencies on the same street. The police found discrepancies in all of them."

"More missing women?" Ryan asked.

Dimitri nodded. "At least eight over the past three years. All tourists. All travelling alone. All women in their twenties."

"And nobody noticed they were missing? Surely family or friends would lodge a complaint." Megan's outrage was a reminder of how sheltered and naive she was. "What about your parents? They must be going nuts."

"They died in a plane crash on a holiday to Alaska six years ago." He kept his tone even and focused on the table in front of him rather than on the sympathy, or pity, he knew he'd see in Megan's eyes.

"People go missing all the time." Joe rescued Dimitri from further questions. "Tourists run out on their bill and leave without checking out. How do you know if someone is really missing or has just moved on to the next stop on their tour? Only five of the women had anyone looking for them. The complaints weren't investigated properly. No one connected the women."

To everyone's surprise, it was Julia who spoke. "I don't understand. How is that possible?"

Dimitri sat up straighter in his seat. "It's more than possible in a country where there's a high turnover of tourists. Where the borders are weak and refugees are flooding in. A country where the economy is a mess and all public sectors are underfunded and run by people who are scraping by. The police are overwhelmed, overworked and lack the resources they need to follow everything up properly. Cases like this fall through the cracks." He looked back at his sister's smiling face. "People fall through the cracks."

"Did they do *anything* to find her?" Megan said.

"They did what they could initially. The time and effort they put in dropped off dramatically after the first couple of months. I realised then that there had to be a private investigation, but I was on assignment and couldn't get away. As soon as I was able I resigned my commission with the US Rangers, headed to Greece and started digging. A couple of months in I noticed one name kept coming up—Rudi Abramovich. I did more digging and discovered he'd built an empire on trafficking women. He targets tourists, homeless and poor women who won't be missed. His speciality is educated, western women. If you want a particular type of woman, he's the man to go to. He kidnaps to order."

His stomach turned at the thought and he was comforted to see the same looks of revulsion on his teammates' faces.

"You're sure he took your sister?" Rachel sounded sceptical.

Dimitri took a moment to gain control of his anger before he answered. The woman didn't seem to realise how her words cut through the people around her. Or she just didn't care. "I found the tour guide who was supposed to take her to the refugee camp."

There was a heavy silence as Dimitri's memory replayed the screams the man had made when he'd beaten the information out of him.

"He was working for Rudi?" Joe said.

He noticed no one asked what happened to the guy.

"He was working for a middleman. I worked my way up the chain until I knew for certain Rudi had her." He turned to Rachel. "So, yeah, I'm sure he's behind my sister's abduction."

"Did you get any idea where she's been taken?" Callum said.

"No." Dimitri ran a hand over his hair which was growing out from its military buzz cut. He suddenly felt exhausted. No, not exhausted, worn out. "That's where I ran aground. Then I heard about the job Reynard Durand was putting together and manoeuvred to get on his team. Word was the guy had a straight line to Rudi and I wanted to get on that line."

"Instead you ended up in Scotland." Megan glared at him. "Trying to kidnap *my* sister."

Yeah, that had been the job.

"Hey." He held up his hands, hoping the gesture would make him appear non-threatening. Megan didn't seem to buy it. "Don't blame me for the plan to kidnap your sister. That was all Rudi and the idiot he hired."

"The idiot who then went on to hire you," she pointed out.

The woman would not let this issue go. Every time he turned around she was needling him about it. "I. Was. Under. Cover."

"Which brings us to the second aim of this mission." Callum glared at Dimitri and Megan, making it clear their argument was over. "Rudi wants Claire Donaldson."

"Claire Dayton," Megan interrupted. "She married that freaky man mountain. I don't know why, but then Claire has always had a thing for lunatics."

Callum raised his voice, "As I was saying, Rudi wants Claire and will go to any length to get her. That means this mission has two aims. We need to retrieve Katrina and eliminate the threat to Claire."

"And by eliminate you mean—" Megan made a slicing motion at her throat.

Everyone stared at her.

"Why is she here?" Rachel pointed at Megan. "She knows nothing about security. She has no training, or experience. She's a liability." She turned to Callum. "Does your boss know she's here?"

Callum looked like he'd had his fill of Rachel. "Lake isn't my boss. Benson Security is owned by three partners now—Lake Benson, myself and Harry Boyle. Who, if you care to remember, *is* your direct boss."

The woman rolled her eyes. "Harry is more like my younger brother than a boss."

"And now Harry, Lake and I own Benson Security and you work for us." Callum leaned forward. "If you don't like the new situation, I'd be happy to accept your resignation."

"Like that's going to happen." She tossed her expensive haircut. "Someone needs to stick around to pick up the pieces once you screw up." Her eyes narrowed. "And when you do, I'll be waiting in the wings to take charge."

"Or, I could fire you," Callum said softly.

"You can try." Rachel tapped her talons on the table in front of her before turning to Joe. "Why on earth does this Rudi person want Claire Donaldson?"

"Dayton," Megan said again and was ignored.

"Claire is married to Grunt," Joe said. "Grunt and I helped Rudi's wife escape him and get back to America. We think Rudi wants to take Grunt's wife from him as payback."

Rachel held up a hand to stop Joe. "What on earth kind of name is Grunt? Is that one of those Highland things? You'll have to forgive me if I'm not up to date on the goings on in Invertary. Unlike some people, I actually like to spend my time in civilisation."

Dimitri was pretty sure he could actually hear Callum grinding his teeth.

"What?" The woman smirked at Callum. "Am I disrupting this extremely professional briefing?"

"Professional or not, after the meeting I want you in my office, Rachel."

"Of course, *boss*." Rachel's tone made it clear she'd do exactly what she felt like after the meeting.

A threatening rumble sounded from Callum just as loud music blared throughout the room. It took Dimitri a few seconds to realise it was Bette Midler singing *Wind Beneath My Wings*. He fought a grin as he watched Megan cover her mouth with her hand to stifle her laughter, at the same time as Ryan turned his into a cough.

"Julia!" Callum roared.

The music stopped dead.

"Sorry," Julia said. "I told you there were gremlins in the system. I will make a note of each one and personally ensure they're dealt with. There are more pastries in the kitchen, if anyone is interested. Along with another pot of coffee."

"I'll get them." Ryan's chair scraped the floor as he rushed to get at the food.

"I'll help." Joe followed their teammate. "If we let you get them they'll be gone before you get back."

"I can't help it if I have a better metabolism than you." Ryan grinned. "It's age. I bet you could eat what you liked when you were my age." Joe swatted the back of Ryan's head.

"Bring me a Diet Coke," Megan called after the men.

"Honestly." Rachel's voice had all the subtlety of a PA announcement. "It's like being back in kindergarten. There is nothing professional about this new business. Harry should never have joined forces with Benson Security. It will damage his reputation."

Callum growled again, but this time Julia was smart enough to keep her finger off the media controls. The guy stared at the ceiling. Dimitri bet he was praying for help. He recognised the action because he'd used the same one quite a bit since he'd met Megan.

Megan clasped her hands and leaned onto the table. "Tell me," she said to Rachel. "Are you even aware just how bitchy you are?"

Rachel gasped, her hand flew to her chest. "I'm bitchy?"

"I'll take that as a yes. You really don't give a crap, do you?"

"Darling." Rachel smirked. "I care about things that *matter.*"

Before Megan could waste any more breath on the woman, the guys came back with supplies. Joe carried a coffee pot and two cans of Diet Coke. He put the pot onto the counter, tossed a can at Megan then headed for the huge plant. He crouched down in front of it and smiled as he offered Julia a drink.

"I like your conflict management style, babe," he told her.

A timid hand appeared and took the offered drink. Joe sat back in his chair, his legs stretched out in front of him. He reminded Dimitri of a leopard he'd seen on a stint in Africa. He looked relaxed but he could pounce without a hint of warning if the need arose.

"As I was saying, before you and Callum got into a pissing contest," Joe said to both of them, earning almost identical death glares which made him grin. "Grunt is a nickname because the monosyllabic bastard barely talks. His wife calls him Samuel. She's the only one who does. Well, she's the only one who's been allowed to live after calling him Samuel. Anyway, Grunt and I were in the marines together. When we got out, we partnered up to work private security. One of our first jobs was to escort a woman back to the States from Romania. Her father wanted to help her escape her abusive husband. He told us she was married to a business man, someone who owned a chain of coffee shops. We didn't do more than a surface check and the information was solid. Speaking of coffee…"

Joe waved his empty mug at Ryan who was over at the snack table, working his way through a platter of pastries. With a sigh, Ryan lifted the coffee pot and sauntered over to Joe.

"What did your last slave die of?"

"Heart attack," Joe said solemnly. "Too many baked goods."

Ryan gave him a one fingered salute before he headed back to the pastries. Joe's amusement faded as he looked back at them.

"We thought the job was a straight bodyguard deal—protect the woman while she got the hell out of there. We were wrong. When we met with her, all hell broke loose. She was being followed by a whole load of Rudi's men. I grabbed the wife while Grunt stayed behind to deal with the assholes that jumped us. That's probably how they got Grunt's ugly mug on camera. Knowing Rudi's rep, he'll think it's quid pro quo to take Grunt's wife away from him. Poetic payback, so to speak—a wife for a wife."

"Did you get Rudi's wife to safety?" Ryan sat back down beside Joe—with a plate piled high with snacks.

Joe nodded. "But it was a total cluster f—"

Julia cleared her throat loudly, cutting him off. Joe grinned at the plant.

Clearly, Callum's patience had reached its limits. The guy stood, folded his arms over one of the many Henleys he owned and wore like a uniform. He was six foot of honed instincts and sharp muscle. If you didn't know the guy was walking around on two prosthetic legs, you would never have guessed.

"We all up to date now?" It was clear his question was purely an exercise in sarcasm so there were no replies. "Great, then maybe we can get down to business. As Dimitri said, with Durand out of the picture his investigation's hit a brick wall. That's where we come in. Lake is working his London contacts to see what info he can dig up as to Rudi's whereabouts. Abramovich moves around a lot. For Dimitri to set up a meet with him, we need to pin down a location fast."

"The plan," Dimitri said, "is to get a personal meeting with Rudi, disable him and access his files for Katrina's location."

"Disable him in a way that will make sure he keeps away from Claire," Megan added.

"But no killing." Callum stared her down. "We're security professionals, not hitmen."

She waved the words away with a flick of her hand, making Dimitri worry about exactly what was going on in her fluffy little head. He made a mental note to grill her about it later. It was important that the whole team were on the same page when it came to Rudi. They couldn't afford anyone to go off plan—especially not when his sister's life was at risk.

"Even if Abramovich is in one place long enough to arrange a meeting with," Rachel waved her phone in Dimitri's direction, "what makes you think you can get close enough to him to access his records? He doesn't know you from Adam."

He swallowed his irritation at her condescending tone. "Because, I have something he wants. Rudi Abramovich wants Grunt's wife, Claire. He's desperate to get her. And Claire is an identical twin. So…"

All eyes turned to Megan who gave them a royal wave.

Rachel's glee was almost palpable. "You're going to give him Megan and pass her off as Claire." Her grin was face-splittingly wide. "This is so much better than I could have imagined it would be. Well done, Megan. You do have a purpose on the team. One totally befitting your station in life —you're bait."

ABOUT THE AUTHOR

I'm a Scot, living in New Zealand and married to a Dutch man. I write contemporary romance with a humorous bent – this is mainly due to the fact I have an odd sense of humour and can't keep it out of anything I do! If I wasn't a writer, I'd like to be Buffy the Vampire Slayer, or Indiana Jones. Unfortunately, both these roles have already been filled. Which may be a good thing as I have no fighting skills, wouldn't know a precious relic if it hit me in the face and have an aversion to blood. When I'm not living in my head, I'm a mother to two kids, several pet sheep, one dog, four cats, three alpacas, two miniature horses, eight guinea pigs and an escape artist chicken.